THE PHYSICS OF RELATIONSHIPS

GUERNICA WORLD EDITIONS 70

CHAS HALPERN

THE PHYSICS OF RELATIONSHIPS

A Fictional Memoir

TORONTO—CHICAGO—BUFFALO—LANCASTER (U.K.)

2023

Guernica Editions Founder: Antonio D'Alfonso

Michael Mirolla, general editor
Kaiya Smith Blackburn, editor
Cover and interior design: Errol F. Richardson

Guernica Editions Inc.
287 Templemead Drive, Hamilton (ON), Canada L8W 2W4
2250 Military Road, Tonawanda, N.Y. 14150-6000 U.S.A.
www.guernicaeditions.com

Distributors:
Independent Publishers Group (IPG)
600 North Pulaski Road, Chicago IL 60624
University of Toronto Press Distribution (UTP)
5201 Dufferin Street, Toronto (ON), Canada M3H 5T8

First edition.
Printed in Canada.

Legal Deposit—Third Quarter
Library of Congress Catalog Card Number: 2023936023
Library and Archives Canada Cataloguing in Publication
Title: The physics of relationships : a fictional memoir / Chas Halpern.
Names: Halpern, Chas, author.
Series: Guernica world editions (Series) ; 70.
Description: First edition. | Series statement: Guernica world editions ; 70
Identifiers: Canadiana (print) 20230220282 | Canadiana (ebook) 20230220290 | ISBN
9781771838498 (softcover) | ISBN 9781771838504 (EPUB)
Classification: LCC PS3608.A48 P59 2023 | DDC 813/.6—dc23

For Pouké

1

Disruption

"MOM, DO YOU REMEMBER Danielle?"

Tasha always expected me to remember every friend and acquaintance she had met over her thirty-two years, even ones I had never actually met in person. And I always felt that I disappointed her if I couldn't remember, as if I had failed to perform my motherly duty.

"Danielle ... you mean ... the Danielle ... from school?" I was faking it. Buying time.

"Yeah, we used to hang out in high school. She's the one whose father died in that weird accident."

That detail jogged my memory. "Right, right. That was so sad."

"Yeah. So, anyway, she's been living in New York making jewelry. Now she's back in town."

"Wonderful. Are you going to see her?"

"I did. She's moving back here. She broke up with her boyfriend. And that was the only thing keeping her in New York. She's looking for a place to stay ... temporarily ... until she can find something affordable."

The warning sirens were blaring. First of all, there was nothing affordable in the Bay Area. And second, I knew what was coming next.

"Could she stay with you ... just for a while?"

There was a long silence while I contemplated my answer. I was hardly looking for a roommate at the age of sixty-three. And I knew that "a while" could mean a long time. On the other hand, I didn't want to appear to be mean and uncaring. Sensing my hesitation, Tasha added, "She'll pay rent. She just can't afford that much. And she's a good cook ... vegan mostly."

Raising the topic of food preparation only increased my anxiety. How would we handle meals? Would we each buy food separately and make separate meals? I didn't want the complication. One of the few pleasures of growing old is that life becomes less complicated. That little pleasure would be stolen from me.

I didn't even know this young woman. How cooperative would she be? Was she messy? Did she like to listen to loud music? Would she want to have boyfriends over and stay up late?

"Please, Mom. She really needs some help. She's kind of depressed."

My daughter—this powerful, generous woman whom I love—was asking for a favor. It was hard to refuse. And, since my husband's death some months ago, I was living alone in a three-bedroom house with plenty of room for a "temporary" guest. I had no excuse. So, I did what I often do in situations like this. I offered a cowardly compromise.

"Okay, Danielle can stay here for a week. But after that she'll need to find someplace else. I'm serious." By adding "I'm serious" as an addendum, I was clearly trying to convince myself more than Tasha.

A troubling memory came back to me. As a young girl, ten or eleven years old, Tasha had the habit of bringing home kittens. We let her keep the first one, a black cat whom she cleverly named Purrsia. We forbade her from bringing home any more kittens. She brought home two more. We kept them. What else could we do? They were so cute, and they needed a home. I feared that Danielle would be the new kitten.

2

Danielle

DANIELLE WALKED INTO THE house rolling a medium-sized suitcase and carrying a small backpack. I wondered if this was really all she had. Was it possible that a thirty-one-year-old woman could single-handedly carry her entire belongings with her? On the one hand, it made me feel sorry for her, as if she were a kind of refugee, which, in a sense, she was. On the other hand, I envied her lightness, her freedom from accumulated things.

"Is that all you have?"

"Yeah, pretty much. I left most of my stuff at Austin's place. And I sent my jewelry-making stuff to my mom's place."

I was left to fill in the blanks. Who was Austin? Where was her mother's place? But I was used to this kind of youthful assumption that, as a mother figure, I would have an omniscient knowledge of her life. After all, her life was of such central importance that she probably assumed Tasha had already told me everything about her.

"Austin is your ex?"

"Yeah, when we broke up, I just wanted to get out. So I wasn't going to haggle about who owned what … you know what I mean?"

"And your mom lives nearby?"

"No, she lives in Arizona."

"I'm just curious … you didn't want to stay with her?"

"Ugh! Arizona," she said, as if I would understand her disgust, which I did, sort of. When I thought of Arizona, I imagined a hot desert where everyone survived in climate-controlled enclosures, a bit like a Mars colony. That, I'm sure, was a gross exaggeration. But, still, I had a hard time understanding why anyone would voluntarily move to Arizona. Danielle had an answer.

"She married a guy and moved there. I hardly know him. He's kind of a gun nut. And he drives around the desert in some kind of all-terrain vehicle. I guess she was lonely and willing to compromise."

"Your mother ..."

"Right, sorry."

I had decided that Danielle would sleep in Tasha's old bedroom. I had cleaned out most of her young adult stuff, and I was using her bedroom mostly as a place to store office supplies and other accumulated items, like an old fax machine, along with some soap-making supplies Tasha had asked me to store for her. The closet held bulky, winter coats and a large box of Tasha's childhood things. I'm pretty sure there was her favorite doll (stripped naked) and a blue teddy bear (won at a fair) in the pile, along with some old school yearbooks. I had contemplated clearing out the closet to make room for Danielle. Then I decided against it. I didn't want to make it too comfortable for her. Tasha's old bed and hand-painted, blue nightstand were still there. And I changed the bedding. That was enough.

"Oh, wow! This is Tasha's old room," Danielle exclaimed.

"Yes. I thought you'd be comfortable here." Damn! Why did I mention comfort?

"Absolutely! Thank you so much! It's like ... like I'm your new daughter ... or something."

Danielle gave me a hug as she said this. I could feel my hardened heart melting, as I wrapped my arms around Danielle's boney, little body. At the same time, I told myself, *No! You are NOT going to adopt another stray. Stay strong!*

I gave Danielle an extra key. And later that afternoon she left without telling me where she was going. I was a little troubled by this. Where was she going? When would she be back? I knew these concerns were a little silly. I wasn't responsible for her. She was an independent adult who could do what she wanted, as long as it didn't intrude on my life. But it still seemed odd. We were starting a little life together, however short-lived it might be. And shouldn't my "new daughter" have at least told me—her "new mom"—what her plan was? I realized that I didn't even have her phone number. What if I needed to reach her?

I sat down in the living room to contemplate how to handle the Danielle question. First realization: no matter how relaxed I wanted to be about this new situation, having a roommate was inherently complicated. Second realization: I would need to work out certain things. I would let her know what my daily routine was—mealtimes, reading time, TV time, bed time. And I would tell Danielle that she would need to accommodate my life, not the other way around.

At least, that was my intention. In reality, I dreaded having that conversation. I was not a natural dictator.

When I came back from grocery shopping that evening, there was an unusual odor wafting through the house. I followed my nose into the kitchen to find Danielle busy at the stove, wearing one of my aprons. I was annoyed. This was exactly what I didn't want. I was hungry. And here she was taking over the kitchen. My annoyance must have shown on my face.

"How was your day?" Danielle asked sympathetically.

"It was fine," I replied tersely.

"I'm making some veggie burgers for you."

"Well, I have groceries. And I need to put them away."

"Sure, I'll stay out of your way. Let me just flip these burgers."

Danielle turned back toward the stove. I noticed that she was wearing flannel pajama bottoms with little red hearts on them. It was 6:40 pm. It seemed a little odd to be wearing pajama bottoms. But I supposed that was her usual home wear, which meant that she was making herself comfortable. I was fine with that, as far as it goes. I didn't want her to feel awkward or uncomfortable. But a little reticence on her part would have been appreciated. Enough reticence, for example, to have talked to me in advance about my meal plans.

On the other hand, the pajamas were kind of cute and a little child-like. That pricked at my heart. Here was a young woman who had been dumped by her boyfriend, who had moved back across the country to her childhood home, but who didn't actually have a home there anymore. She was an only child. And she was semi-estranged from her mother, who had moved to the planet Arizona to live with an alien. Her father was dead. And she was attempting to make dinner for me. I could hardly scold her. As I put away the groceries, I thanked her for making dinner.

"That was so nice of you to think of that," I said, and I meant it. But I was still a little angry. The situation threw me back into mother-of-a-teen mode. That is when you have to be careful about every word you utter, lest you instigate either rage or a crying fit. Those, apparently, are the two emotions teen girls experience, at least when dealing with their mothers. Danielle, however, was not a teen. And it irked me that I felt compelled to spare her feelings.

We sat down at the table with our veggie burgers. Danielle had carefully stuffed them with the usual condiments—mayonnaise, ketchup, lettuce, and pickles—all items she pilfered from my refrigerator. I felt petty for thinking that. Sadly, however, that is how our minds work. We have selfish thoughts. And the only difference between evil people and the rest of us is that evil people act on those thoughts.

Danielle watched expectantly as I took a bite of her burger. The veggie patty tasted like ground straw. How far was my forbearance supposed to reach? Was I required to tell her it was delicious? Instead, I opted (as I often do) for the coward's way out.

"Hmm," I said, with a neutral inflection. "What exactly is this made of?"

"It's seed based. Mostly ground flax seeds. Some sunflower seeds. Some lentils for bulk, but not too much or it'll get soggy."

A little more moisture would've helped, I thought. And maybe some flavor—onions, garlic, salt, and pepper. I kept those thoughts to myself, however, and changed the subject.

"So … here you are back in town. What are your plans?"

"Well, I guess I need to find a job," she replied, as if it were a sad, but necessary, duty.

"How about your jewelry-making?"

"Oh, that's going to take a while. First, I need to find a space to set up my workshop."

Aha! I thought. That will give her an incentive to find a new place. My moment of relief was quickly followed by a terrifying realization. There was plenty of space in my near-empty, three-bedroom house for a jewelry workshop. Was that her plan … to ply me with veggie burgers and worm her way into my heart so she could set up shop here?

"Have you started looking for a jewelry space?" I asked, hoping she would get the hint.

"No, first I need to find a job, so I can make some money. Everything is so expensive here. I think it's actually worse than New York."

"Any prospects yet?"

"No, not really. I applied for a job at an art store, but I never heard back from them."

"Maybe I can help you look for a job."

"Uh, no, that's okay. I don't want to trouble you. I've already signed up for three online job listings."

"There's a vegan café not far from here. Have you tried them?"

"You mean, just walk in and ask?" She seemed taken aback by this bold concept.

"Yes, that's what I mean. I've gotten jobs that way before."

"Really? I don't think that would work now."

She seemed to be implying that things might have worked that way in a previous century, but that quaint approach was no longer an option today.

"You'd be surprised. There's nothing like making a personal contact."

Danielle laughed a little, presumably at my naiveté. "That's okay. I'm good. I posted that I'm looking for work on Facebook. Somebody might come up with a contact."

This conversation was not going well. I was avoiding the central issue.

"Tasha told me you would only be staying here for a week … or two … (why did I add that?) … just until you find another place to live."

"Well, that's the plan."

"You know that you can't stay here indefinitely, right?"

"Oh, of course. I mean, that would be a whole different deal. I would need to pay rent and everything."

"But I'm not offering that kind of deal. I'm just trying to help you out until you find a place."

"Right, I know."

Danielle's face flushed momentarily, and there was a hint of panic in her eyes. My resolve was weakening. How do you look a stray kitten in the eyes and not take care of it?

"Well … let's see how it goes. In the meantime, we need to talk a little about the house rules."

I immediately regretted using the word "rules." I was starting to sound like some crochety, Victorian boarding house mistress. I think I was overcompensating for my lack of resolve.

"What I mean is … we need to kind of coordinate in terms of meals and … well, just accommodating each other's needs."

"Oh, of course."

"Good."

I suddenly realized that I hadn't actually thought through what the "rules" should be. And other than the food and meals (which required some thought), I wasn't really sure there needed to be any other rules. Simply being respectful would probably be enough.

"Why don't we think about how to plan the meals. I mean, I appreciate your choice to be vegan, but I'm not vegan. So, we probably won't be sharing meals that much."

"Okay." Danielle nodded, as if she understood.

"And I usually eat dinner around seven."

"Yeah, me too."

"So … we could obviously eat together, but we might need to prepare our meals separately. We'll need to figure out how that would work."

"I could prepare my meals in advance and just use the microwave."

Was I going to relegate Danielle to the microwave? This whole thing was turning Dickensian. And I was the scrooge.

"Well, I'm sure we can work something out where you don't need to rely on the microwave."

My last bit of resolve was melting away.

I had a hard time going to sleep that night, fretting over the situation. I kept telling myself just to relax and let things run their course. But my brain wasn't buying it. I kept imagining different scenarios. *She'll get a job soon and that will be that. No, she won't. Even if she gets a job, she won't be making enough to rent a place of her own. I'll have to get tough with her.* I tried to imagine the words I would use to kick Danielle out of the house. But I knew I couldn't.

Maybe I could contact her mother. No, that would be weird. And what was her mother supposed to do anyway? She doesn't have any money. And on it went for several hours until I fell asleep out of exhaustion.

The next day, I called Tasha and explained the situation. "She can't make money with her jewelry because she doesn't have the space to set up her jewelry stuff. So, she needs to get a job. But she doesn't have any prospects. And she's looking for jobs like a store clerk. You can't earn enough to rent a place with space for a jewelry studio on that kind of money. This is just … it's a big problem."

"You're freaking out before you even need to freak out. She'll figure it out. And if she doesn't, you'll just kick her out."

"Easier said than done."

Tasha just laughed. Was she remembering the stray cats she used to bring home?

"Calm down. I'll talk to her," she said.

Was that a promise to do the dirty work? Probably not. Calming down was not a strong point of mine. But what choice did I have? I would need to live with the situation for a while. I would need to take it a day at a time, or a moment at a time, as my former Zen instructor would advise. Good luck with that, I thought.

3

Withdrawal

WHEN TASHA CALLED ABOUT her friend, Danielle, I was living alone. You could say it was my fault. I had married a man who was sixteen years older than I was. You do that when you think you're in love and you're desperate for a lifeline.

It was a second marriage. I was twenty-eight when I married for the first time. Nine years later, I was divorced. Tasha (née Natasha) was six and my son, Brandon, was two. After Tasha was born, my first husband, Greg, didn't want another child. He was focused on building his accounting practice. And he was having a hard time with the idea of being a father. He loved the kids in his own way. But being a father felt like a burden to him. It was a burden, of course. It meant spending time and mental energy. It meant thinking about another whole human being other than himself. Adding yet another whole human being to his life was more than Greg could handle.

Then there was the affair. Vicki was a young actress who was starting to make good money doing commercials and appearing in small parts on TV series. A client of Greg's, a producer, had referred Vicki to him. Greg started meeting her for lunch to go over her finances. Vicki became a fantasy for Greg, an escape from obligation, responsibility, age … the usual.

For Vicki, I assume it was the flattery. As a young actress, her fragile sense of self was crushed every time she failed to win an audition. That happened on a daily basis. And there was the excitement of playing the bad woman, the temptress. It was a meatier role than anything she had been offered up to that point.

Out of jealousy (or spite) I searched out TV shows in which Vicki had appeared. It took some in-depth research. Her "filmography" consisted of several small parts with few or no lines—roles like the tipsy young woman in a bar who flirts with one of the main characters, the purpose of which is to assert the protagonist's integrity by allowing him to gently spurn her advances and thereby stay true to the woman he loves.

In another TV show, she was the third of three girlfriends surrounding the principal character. If I recall, she had one line: "Well, I think he's cute." I must admit that being cast in these tiny, frivolous roles would be frustrating for a talented actress. I doubt, however, that Vicki was particularly talented. I liked to think she was getting the parts she deserved.

Playing the part of an illicit lover gave Vicki a role she could really sink her teeth into. (I imagine them as vampire teeth.) But the role inevitably lost some of its initial excitement. After a few months, Vicki moved on to another role, another acting partner, so to speak.

Greg was devastated and regretful. He told me many times that he was sorry. I believed him. But it felt more like self-pity than true contrition ... or true love. I never got the feeling that he would have left Vicki if she hadn't left him first. And, while he made a half-hearted attempt to spend more time with the kids, his commitment waned over time. I felt as if I were married to a stranger, someone I couldn't trust on a deep level.

We grew increasingly apart. Greg spent long hours at the office. When we met at home, our conversations became perfunctory. We would discuss obligations we needed to carry out. *Can you take the kids to school today? Do you mind picking up a quart of milk on the way home? Do you remember if Tasha had a tetanus shot? Can you call the cable company and find out why our bill increased by fifteen dollars this month?* We were leading separate lives. After a while, it felt as if Greg were a boarder who only came home to eat and sleep.

We tried couple's counseling for a while. Greg was uncomfortable in the sessions. He seemed to be shocked when I described our relationship as two people orbiting around each other without actually interacting on any deep level. He insisted that he had a deep commitment to me and the family. But when the therapist asked how he demonstrated that commitment, all Greg could manage in his defense was to say that he worked hard to support us, showed up every day and fulfilled his obligations as a husband and father.

When the therapist asked if he thought that was sufficient, Greg was confused. After three sessions, Greg complained that the therapist was taking my side. He started making excuses, cancelling our appointments due to "business." Eventually, the forces that kept us in orbit (obligation, sympathy, a residue of affection, guilt) weakened.

A few months after the divorce, I met Lawrence. He was in his fifties, virile with his bald head and close-shaved, graying beard. As a manager at a well-established insurance company, his professional life was settled. He just wanted to enjoy life. And he wanted me to enjoy it with him, which I was so ready to do. The capper was that he and the kids got along well. And he loved the idea of being a father.

When I married Lawrence, despite our age difference, I never imagined him getting old, much less sick and feeble. But that's what happens when you're well into your eighties. So, I was alone in a house that reminded me every day of Lawrence. His clothes were still in the closet. His desk was still intact with his manly blotter, his pencils and pens, a powerful electric pencil sharpener (which he had requested as a birthday present), an old dictionary that he had kept, even though he hadn't opened it in years.

Everywhere I looked there were reminders—chairs he sat in while watching TV or eating dinner, the floor he walked on daily for twenty-five years, a family picture taken some fifty years ago with his mother and father. In the photo, he still had a carpet of dark hair on his head. He was handsome and smiling. And he had his arms around his parents. It made me wish I had married him first. I still don't know why he waited so long to marry. He was evasive when I asked him that question. I guess it took him a long time to sense the void that can only be filled with a steady, strong relationship. Now that was gone for me.

When I told my friend Amy that the house still smelled like Lawrence, she advised me to move out and sell. She assumed that somehow you could wipe away the pain by moving away from it. But grief has a funny way of following you wherever you go. So, I decided to stay. It was partly for practical reasons. The house was paid for. Other than taxes and maintenance, I was living there for free. If I sold it, I'd be forced to live in an apartment at the mercy of a landlord. I wasn't used to that.

I liked my neighborhood. My house was on a street lined with trees and intellectuals. There was a PhD in literature across the street who specialized in helping people struggling with writer's block. Next to her house, there was a zither-playing librarian. Up the street from him, lived a Jungian psychotherapist who made extra money selling psychedelic paraphernalia from the sixties. On my side of the street, a few houses up, there was a Berkeley anthropology professor, an expert on Michel Foucault. These were my neighbors.

Their gardens were full of weeds, but their minds were fertile and well-cultivated. I could talk to these people. They were my tribe. So, I stayed in the house that refused to let me forget the past. Was I bravely confronting my grief? Hardly. After Lawrence died, I fell into a sloth-like existence, punctuated by half-hearted meals that marked the day. Often, I would eat a sandwich for lunch and dinner. I didn't have the will to make myself an actual meal.

Getting up in the morning was the hardest part. I had little reason to do so. My career as a freelance copywriter was dwindling quickly. At sixty-three, I was not exactly a hot commodity. It was probably a good thing that few people wanted to hire me. I started to resent the work, and it showed in my writing. Living in the Bay Area, most of my jobs were for large tech companies. Each job meant stuffing unwanted information into my head.

I always had the vague feeling that I was back in school cramming for an exam, forced to ingest a new vocabulary, arcane acronyms like IoT, AI, SaaS, BaaS, and HaaS. I'm not complaining, really. It wasn't difficult for me. But the effort seemed meaningless. What was all this technology bringing us? Somehow it felt as if the only point of the whole endeavor was to make obscenely rich people even richer.

When I wasn't forced to get up for a job, I would lie in bed letting my mind wander. I would review scenes from the BBC series I was binge-watching at the time, something about a former queen with marital problems. (It seems men have always had trouble playing second fiddle to a more powerful woman.) Or I would remember moments I spent with Lawrence and the kids. Days on the beach at Tomales Bay. The kids building forts in the sand, dipping their toes in the cold water, screaming. Lawrence swooping Brandon up and carrying him into the water. Brandon screaming with faux terror. Tasha coming to my side to dry off and snuggle. The memories were comforting and painful.

Eventually my thoughts would return to my current obligations. Did I have anything that I had to do that day? The answer was often "no." When you have no obligations, there is a void in your life that begs some unpleasant questions. Who am I? My children no longer need me. I am no longer a wife. My clients are abandoning me. What exactly is the point of getting up? To feed and groom this person, this purposeless body? To simply continue for the sake of continuing?

I remained in a state of numb stasis for many months.

At one point, almost a year after Lawrence died, Tasha staged an intervention of sorts. It started with a phone call.

"Mom! My studio is tiny, and you have a whole house!"

Tasha had called to ask me (or I should say "demand") to store her soap-making supplies, along with some books and skeins of yarn she had collected from her knitting days. It was true that I had a "whole house." But that house was stuffed with things Lawrence and I had collected over the years. Every closet, every shed, even the attic was full of stuff: clothes we hadn't worn in years, old financial records, Tasha's and Brandon's childhood mementos, and god knows what else. This was the law of entropy at work, the second law of thermodynamics that states that any isolated system naturally evolves toward disorder. And, while I was fighting a personal battle with entropy, I had no energy left to extend that battle to my whole house.

When I explained this to Tasha, she decided she was going to "grab the cock" and help me get rid of things.

"You're going to only keep the things that bring you joy," she said.

I acquiesced, although I wanted to tell her that, generally speaking, things didn't bring me joy. In fact, there was not much of anything that was bringing me joy. At the time, I was hardly working. But once a week I would tutor a twelve-year-old young man who showed promise, and that brought me a kind of joy. What else brought me joy? Breakfast? My afternoon tea? Those were little pleasures, not joy.

An occasional visit with my friend, Amy? Yes, that friendship gave me joy. And having a visit with my daughter would certainly bring me joy, or so I thought.

Tasha and I were, recently, on good terms. I think age was softening her judgment of me. She was beginning to see me as a whole person, with an interior life beyond my role as parent. Although she certainly had her insecurities, one of the words I have used to describe Tasha is "powerful." As a teenager, she once slammed a door so hard that it cracked. And I remember the first time she called me a bitch. I was shocked and angry. I forbade her from using that word. But that just gave the word more power. And Tasha understood power. So, she used the word as a weapon.

Of course, "bitch" meant something different to her than to me. I'm not talking about the literal meaning of the word. I'm talking about the cultural context. To Tasha's generation, the word might simply mean "young woman"—in the context of a hip hop song, for instance. I recall a song called "Boss Ass Bitch." In that case, the word "bitch" became part of a feminist declaration. In other contexts, it might almost mean "friend," as in, "You bitches want to party tonight?" In any case, it carried very little weight. It was culturally declawed, so to speak. It took me a while to understand that. And when I did, I no longer expended energy or emotion when Tasha used the word.

Conserving my energy was imperative in raising Tasha. As powerful as Tasha was, she would have exhausted me on a daily basis had I chosen to fight her on all fronts. Instead, Lawrence and I carefully chose our battles. Curfews, dinner with the family, and study time were some of the few battle lines we drew. As a consequence, Tasha got away with a lot. I don't remember her ever having to do chores on a regular basis. We rationalized this by telling ourselves that we were prioritizing her school work. But, really, we were too exhausted to enforce the concept of chores.

When she was young, Tasha took extraordinary measures to assert her independence. She began by piercing her ears when she was sixteen, without our permission. Other piercings followed—her septum and a recent nipple piercing. As soon as she could afford it, she began adding tattoos to her beautiful body. I say "beautiful" because, as a mother who has cradled the perfect body of an infant in her arms, the idea of transforming that body seemed like a violation. Nevertheless, I have accepted those choices, as I have accepted her other choices.

Tasha has taken to calling herself Sage. She explained that the herb has many healing properties. I assume she is aware of the other connotation—wise. She hasn't legally changed her name. But she takes the name change seriously. Therefore, she expects me to take it seriously. I am required to make an effort to call her Sage rather than the name I have given her and used most of her life.

There are other adjustments I've had to make to honor Tasha's asserted identity. She uses the pronouns "they" and "their." The need to use these pronouns rarely comes up in normal, one-on-one conversation with her because "you" and "your" suffice. And "you" and "your" are gender-neutral. If you have spent thirty years referring to your daughter as "she" and "her," it's hard to change. If I slip up, Sage will reprimand me immediately. Clearly, she doesn't understand how a sixty-three-year-old brain works.

As much as I suspected that I had failed by being too lenient a parent, that feeling was assuaged by the fact that Tasha had become a wonderful adult. It took some time, though. After high school, she spent several years bouncing from one entry-level job to another. Her best job was as an assistant at the SPCA, which involved more cleaning of cat litter than helping people adopt pets.

Eventually, Tasha had enough of making poverty-level wages and sharing run-down apartments with immature, unreliable roommates in dubious parts of town. On her own, she applied for financial aid at a local four-year college. A few years later, she graduated with honors.

Tasha had become an independent person with many talents. She was a fiercely loyal and compassionate friend. And, happily, that loyalty and compassion extended to me. Our relationship wasn't perfect, however. Tasha held some ancient grudges. She felt that I had been unnecessarily judgmental in a way that damaged her psyche. When she was twelve, and gaining weight, I started restricting her food intake. She never forgave me. In her mind, it was a sign that I had stopped loving her unconditionally, as a mother should. I regretted it. I was willing to admit that I had made other mistakes along the way. There must have been times when I was overly critical. I thought I was being helpful. Tasha remembered those times as traumatic moments in her childhood.

Since then, I taught myself to be a better listener, and to let Tasha make her own mistakes. I still wanted to give her advice that would help her avoid those mistakes. Instead, I would nod my head and try to look sympathetic. Sometimes, I wondered if Tasha would get impatient with my silence. I wondered if she wanted to know what I was thinking. But she never asked. And our relationship grew closer because of it.

Now, Tasha was coming to help me excise my past, the material possessions that were weighing me down with lingering grief. I dreaded the task of going through Lawrence's things, although I welcomed her support. As it turned out, Tasha needed some support herself. When she arrived at the house, she collapsed on the couch, looking despondent. Her girlfriend had gone on a business trip and had stopped communicating. Up to that point, they had kept in close touch, talking daily by phone and texting throughout the day. The sudden silence was disturbing, to say the least. Tasha was bewildered and crushed. She assumed that her girlfriend had met someone else on their trip. And, although I thought that was the most likely explanation, I tried to comfort her.

"Maybe their cell phone has no service," I said.

"No, they're just being a dick," she replied.

Tasha revealed that her friend was starting to take male hormones. She conjectured that the hormones were making them act weird.

"They're acting like a man. Egh!" Tasha said.

I understood. So many young, straight men had broken my dear daughter's heart.

Perhaps those old wounds had made Tasha more resilient. She soon picked herself up from the couch and announced, "Okay, let's get started." I followed her throughout the house as she inspected all the closets and storage spaces.

"There's a bunch of crap you've got to get rid of," she declared.

I knew she was right, but I resisted. "Can't we just wait until I die? Then you can hire some people and just clear out the house."

Tasha was indignant. "Mom! I'm doing this for you, so you can get on with your life. Stop talking about dying. Ugh!" Then she looked me in the eye with a sympathetic, but stern look. "You've got to let go of Larry's shit. It's important."

Was she right about that? I had no idea. But I knew one thing. I didn't have the courage to go through Lawrence's things. I slumped into a chair. Tasha studied me for a moment, as if to decide whether I could bear the pain.

"It's been like a year. It's time. We're going to make it into a healing ritual," she announced.

I closed my eyes and nodded. Tasha began pulling Lawrence's clothes out of the closet and dropping them on the bed. I glimpsed at the disheveled pile of clothes. That's my life, I thought, a jumbled pile of memories, of use to no one.

"We're going to bring all this stuff to Goodwill and give it a new life," Tasha said. Her offer was meant to make me feel better, but the "new life" had nothing to do with my life, which was hollowed out and lonely. I tried to smile at Tasha to show my appreciation for her sentiment. But my generosity of spirit was curtailed by self-pity.

When all of Lawrence's clothes were bundled up in garbage bags and out of sight, Tasha brought out a sage smudge.

"We're going to do a healing ritual," she declared. "Just sit there and relax."

I was in no condition to resist. And, although the idea that sage smoke could heal anything seemed ludicrous to me, I was happy to try anything that could help lessen the pain in my battered heart.

Tasha lit the end of the sage bundle, held it in front of me and looked me in the eyes. An acrid, pungent, minty odor filled my nostrils. Tasha waved the smoke toward my heart. Tears filled my eyes. It felt like a release. I had no idea if it was the effect of the sage or simply the acknowledgment of my pain by a caring person. Tasha continued to wave the smoke around my body, across my chest, down each arm, down my legs, finally ending at my feet. As Tasha knelt before me, I took her head in my hands and kissed her forehead. She smiled up at me.

"This is a cleansing, Mom. It's a renewal. Say good-bye to your old self. It's time for a new journey to begin."

I was so grateful and so proud of my daughter. She had done this for me, even while her own heart was breaking. Now it was my turn to carry on for her.

And I did. As the months went by, the numbing grief I felt became a smaller and smaller part of my life. I was able to assess my situation with more objectivity. I was a financially comfortable, relatively healthy widow with many years of life ahead of me. The question was: how was I going to spend those years?

I didn't have an answer to that question. But I knew one thing: becoming a mother figure to a stray young woman was not part of the plan. My dear, generous, powerful daughter had asked me to do just that, however. And I had acquiesced. For the foreseeable future, I would be playing host to Danielle, a lovelorn young woman in need of "temporary" shelter.

4

Attachment

AFTER SEVERAL WEEKS OF living with Danielle, we fell into a routine of sorts. The upheaval in my life never happened. True to her word, Danielle would often prepare her vegan meals in advance and warm them up in the microwave. I was free to make my own meals as usual. Sometimes, out of pity or curiosity, I would suggest that we prepare a vegan meal together. Her recipes tended to be monastic, bland dishes relying heavily on tofu, nuts, seeds, and noodles. I would push her to add lusty spicing and sauces. The results were often delicious and quite satisfying.

"Why are you a vegan?" I asked one day.

"Animals have emotions."

I was oddly stunned by this brief answer that pierced my heart. Of course, I knew that animals had emotions. I had been the mistress of three lovable, loving cats. How else could you explain their habit of curling up on the bed near me and asking, in their nonchalant way, to be petted? I had read that cats never meow when among their own kind. They only meow in an attempt to communicate with their human co-inhabitants. And contrary to conventional wisdom, cats (like dogs) recognize their name. Unlike dogs, however, they most often choose to ignore it.

So, yes, I knew animals had emotions. And I was willing to participate in their slaughter in order to enjoy, say, a nice roast chicken. Just the thought of roast chicken made me salivate. I could only conclude that I was an animal, with animal needs. Did this make Danielle less of an animal? Was she a better person? She was certainly a better person to other animal species. I was still wondering, however, if she was a better person to her own species.

Danielle's mornings were spent in a leisurely fashion. She would emerge from her room around 9 a.m., make her breakfast and stare at her phone. Later in the morning, she would dutifully sit down at my computer, search job listing and send out resumes. After lunch, she would leave for the afternoon. Was she meeting with friends? Going for job interviews? Hanging out at the public library? Turning tricks? I had no idea. I only knew that she didn't have a car, and she would move about primarily on public transportation.

At mealtimes, our conversation tended to remain superficial. How was your day? was the habitual starter question. The answers were often cursory. Sometimes we would share little stories. I would complain about the "asshole" who stole my parking space. Or she would describe the woman on the bus who was shouting obscenities at non-existent passengers. Our exchanges often involved these odd little incidents that marked the day. Of course, I would occasionally ask her about her work prospects. And she would tell me that she was hoping to hear back from a couple of people.

Despite these conversations, I never truly understood what Danielle did with her time. Nor did I understand what was truly going on in her mind and heart. One evening, I decided to dig a little further.

"Tell me what happened with Austin."

Danielle stopped her fork midway to her mouth, set it down and stared at her plate.

"That's okay. You don't have to tell me."

"No, I don't mind." She took a deep breath, as if summoning up the courage to re-enter that dark space.

"It was weird. I still don't really understand what happened. We were each doing our thing. And we were … happy, I thought. I was making my jewelry. Austin was working as a barista, and he was in this band. I thought it was just a fun hobby for him, but he took it seriously. He really wanted to make it … get a record deal and everything. Stupid Genius—that was the band name, kind of ironic. Everything they did was kind of ironic and gag-y."

I'm a word person. And the name, Stupid Genius, was so compelling, I had to interrupt her. "Stupid Genius? Where did that come from?"

"I don't know. It was something about how only stupid people think they're geniuses and geniuses think they're stupid? Something like that. Austin said it was in a psychological study."

I had read about that study, the Dunning-Kruger experiment. Dunning and Kruger, two well-respected psychologists, discovered that incompetent people have a built-in bias that makes them unable to recognize their own incompetence. And they tend to grossly over-estimate their intelligence. I was interested in the Dunning-Kruger effect because it seemed to explain a lot about how badly things were going in the world.

"So what happened with the band?"

"Not much. They used to put stuff up on YouTube, but they never really got a following. They would get like ten thousand hits which doesn't get a you a record deal. It doesn't even help you get gigs that much. Anyway, I don't think he was very happy. He was bored with his job, and Stupid Genius wasn't exactly killing it. So … "

Danielle's eyes became red, as if preparing to spill her emotions into tears.

I said, "That can happen, when one partner is unhappy, they can take it out on the other, as if it were somehow their fault."

"It didn't seem like that though. Austin never got angry with me or anything. And I always tried to encourage him. I'd tell him to hang in there with the band and everything. Things would get better. I told him to quit his job if he wasn't happy. So, I don't know, I thought we had a really good relationship."

"What do you think happened?"

"Tasha didn't tell you? He started seeing this woman on the side. She was like a pole dancer or something. One of my friends saw him with her. She was pretty and everything, but, what the fuck! A pole dancer? Ugh!" Danielle shook her head, as if she were still in disbelief, still in shock.

I put my hand on hers to comfort her. "My first husband had an affair with an actress. She was pretty too, but heartless."

"Really? What happened?"

"She left him after a while. Greg, my husband, said he was sorry, but it was never the same after that. Eventually I divorced him."

"It wasn't like that for me. Austin left me. He said he was sorry, but … he didn't ask to come back. His only excuse was that he said it was exciting, this relationship he had with her. Exciting … I mean, how lame is that? He told me that she was going to sing in their band … like that was some kind of excuse or something."

This was the first time I saw Danielle express anger. It was righteous anger, and I was glad to see her express it. It was an acknowledgment that the human species also has emotions.

"You know, after I divorced Greg, I was grateful. I was grateful that I discovered who he was early enough so that I could find someone else, someone more worthy of my love."

"I haven't discovered that person," she said, with a sigh, as if she no longer believed in true love.

"You will. You'll find that person. You're still young. I was older than you when I got divorced. And I had two young kids. It'll happen."

"Thanks," was all she said.

Danielle was thanking me for being kind, for attempting to soothe her pain. She wasn't necessarily thanking me because she believed my prediction that she would find her true love.

Nevertheless, I felt good about our conversation. I had shared my experience, my accumulated wisdom, and it seemed to have helped Danielle. This was highly unusual. Neither of my own children, nor any other young person in my life, for that matter (unless you counted the young man I was tutoring), was open to my advice. They assumed that whatever experience I had was no longer valid. Things had changed too much for me to understand the complexities of their lives. But this was not the case with Danielle. I had acted as a kind of surrogate mother to her, and the fact that I was not her actual mother had probably elevated the interaction in her mind. It afforded me a veneer of objectivity. I was the wise nurturer. And I was valued for it.

This thought troubled me. Obviously, I enjoyed the feeling of being valued … perhaps too much. But I had not signed up to be Danielle's surrogate mother. And Danielle had been living with me for over three weeks. How long was this going to continue?

The next day, Danielle didn't come home for dinner. We hadn't planned to eat together. And our understanding was such that we didn't need to report to each other about our whereabouts. I dutifully prepared my meal—fresh peas, rice, and sautéed tilapia. As I was shelling the peas, I realized that my eating habits had changed since Danielle started living with me. In the past, I often wouldn't cook anything for dinner. I would settle for bread and cheese and maybe an apple.

Danielle made me more conscious of the food I was eating. And the fact that I had someone to eat with (although we often ate different food) made it seem worth preparing an actual meal. This evening, however, I was alone. It suddenly felt ridiculous to be shelling fresh peas. Why make the effort? I had thought that I would be sharing the peas with Danielle. I thought she would be delighted.

I finished preparing my dinner and ate it in front of the TV watching the "shit show," as Tasha called the news. They were discussing the President's intention to ease regulations so that oil companies could drill in the Arctic National Wildlife Refuge. I hardly tasted my food.

The next day, I called Tasha. I told her that Danielle was a nice young woman. I liked her, and I felt bad about her situation. It was sad that she felt estranged from her mother, who could have comforted her at this time in her life. I told Tasha that we were living peacefully together, accommodating each other's needs, and it was becoming a routine. I left out the part about enjoying being in the company of a young woman who was willing to receive my maternal wisdom. Nevertheless, I sensed a slight bit of jealousy on Tasha's part.

"Are you like … letting her live there for free?"

"Well … yes, she doesn't have a job yet."

"That's wrong. That's just totally wrong. She needs to start paying you rent or something. She can't just freeload."

"She helps sometimes clean up around the house."

"Sometimes? She should be like, at least, cleaning the bathroom and shit like that. And she should be paying you whatever she can afford. Don't tell me she has no money at all. We went out to lunch last week, and she paid for both of us."

Of course, she did, I thought. *She's desperate for your friendship. She scraped together her last few dollars to treat you to lunch.* Nevertheless, Tasha had a point. Danielle could do more around the house, contribute more. I didn't want to treat Danielle like Cinderella. *Clean the floors! Scrub the toilet!* On the other hand, she was an adult. And she wasn't my child. The current situation couldn't go on indefinitely.

I was being soft-hearted. I was also being a coward. I was secretly hoping that this sweet little vegan would voluntarily bring up the subject herself. Maybe if I waited another week or so ... Ha! How likely was that? She had a sweet deal and no incentive to change anything. Tasha was right. I needed to say something.

5

Confrontation

I RUMMAGED THROUGH THE refrigerator, looking for something simple to make for dinner. I was tired, hungry, lazy, and alone. An odd thought crossed my mind. There must be thousands, perhaps millions, of other women in the United States who were just like me, alone and searching desperately through their refrigerators for something quick to eat, something that would assuage their hunger, but not their soul. Strangely, that thought didn't make me sad. It made me feel less alone. I was part of a group—albeit a group of desperate, older women—but a group nonetheless.

Then I had another crazy thought. Maybe I should connect with those women, perhaps start a hashtag on Twitter: #desperatehungryoldwomen. As I contemplated that hashtag, my professional training kicked in. I shouldn't say "desperate." Too negative. Just #hungryoldwomen would do. Of course, "old" also has a negative connotation. "Senior"? Would that work? #hungryseniorwomen? Awkward. Maybe it should just be #hungrywomen. Uh oh! Great name for a "hook up" dating site. Oh well, I wasn't even on Twitter anyway. And did I really want to spend my time moaning with other women about how sad our lives were? No, my imagined sisterhood was enough to sustain me.

I looked in the cheese compartment, figuring I'd just go for my usual bread-and-cheese meal. But I hadn't shopped in over a week, and the only thing I found in the cheese box was a moldy piece of Gouda. When I cut off the mold, all that remained was a dry inedible crust, a fitting metaphor for my situation. I reached for a jar of peanut butter and a stale slice of bread. Prison rations.

Just then Danielle walked in the door carrying a cloth shopping bag. When I turned to look, I had the peanut butter jar in one hand and the stale bread in the other. Danielle stopped and sized up the situation.

"I bought some tofu nuggets and bok choy. I have too much. Want some?"

I could have kissed her, this well-meaning, young vegan who was invading my house. How was I going to confront her about her overlong stay?

"Yes!" I said, too enthusiastically. "Yes, I would love some ... if it's not too much trouble."

"No, it's super easy."

After my last phone conversation with Tasha, I had resolved to get firm with Danielle. She would either need to move out or start paying rent. Her generosity in sharing her tofu nuggets, however, was making that hard. I told myself that I didn't need to feel guilty. After all, I had used my peanut butter to make a peanut sauce, without which the nuggets would have been practically inedible. And then there was the fact that this was my house. And she using my gas and electricity. As soon as I had those thoughts, I felt small and selfish.

While it compromised some of my individual freedom, I enjoyed her company. I would be lonely without her. I decided to bring up the subject in as gentle a way as possible.

"So ... how is your job hunting going?"

Danielle looked uncomfortable. "It's hard. I mean, there are so many people looking for work. Everybody's looking for people with experience, even for crappy little jobs in restaurants or selling in stores and stuff. Like you need five years of experience to be a waitress!"

"So ... what are you going to do? What's your plan?"

"I don't know. Keep looking I guess."

"You know I'm okay with you living here. I want to help you get on your feet. But it ... it can't go on indefinitely."

Danielle's eyes teared up. "I know. But I don't really have any place else to go."

"I'm not trying to kick you out. But you would need to start sharing some of the expenses. That's only fair. Don't you think?"

"But … I can't really afford it."

"What about your parents? Can't they help?" As soon as said that, I kicked myself. I knew her father had died long ago.

"No, not really. My father died when I was in high school. And my mom … she's on Social Security. She'd have to ask Burt for money. And he wouldn't give her money to support me. He doesn't even really know me."

"Anyone else who can help you? Siblings? Relatives?"

"No. I don't have any brothers or sisters. And there's nobody else I can really ask for money. It's not like that in my family."

I was trying to repress a growing sense of anger. I like to think of myself as a generous person, but I didn't choose this form of generosity. I didn't choose to contribute to the Danielle Charity. It was foisted on me under false pretenses. I let out a frustrated sigh. And my face must have grown stern because Danielle reacted strongly.

"Are you going to kick me out just because I can't pay you right now? That would be really fucked up!"

"Excuse me?"

Danielle's face distorted in an anger I didn't think she was capable of.

"You've got this whole fucking house! It's not costing you anything for me to live here! And I … I don't have any place to go! *And you know that!*"

I sat there, stunned. I was accused of being a selfish witch, knowingly casting out a poor wretch. I didn't know how to respond. Danielle averted her eyes, probably preparing for an equally angry response on my part. But my silence must have confused her. She finally looked up at me and started sobbing.

"I'm sorry," she whispered between sobs.

I came around the table, knelt down beside her, and put my arm around her. "Okay, shhh. I'm not putting you out on the street. We'll figure this out. Let's talk it through."

After Danielle's sobs died down, I invited her to sit in the living room with me so we could talk calmly.

"When you were making jewelry, were you making a living from that?"

"Yes. I had stores in New York that were carrying my stuff, and I was selling some stuff on eBay. It was working. I was really starting to make some money … get some recognition. That's what's so fucked up … that I had to stop."

"So if you could make jewelry again, would you be able to earn some money?"

"Yes, absolutely. I've been getting emails from a couple of the boutiques in New York asking me when I can send them more stuff. It's so frustrating."

We concluded the conversation with what seemed the only obvious solution. Within a week, Danielle had set up her jewelry studio in the spare bedroom, the room where Lawrence had his home office. The invasion was complete. What had I done?

I was hesitant to talk to Tasha about the new arrangement. I knew she would scold me. But I figured she would soon find out about it anyway, so there was no avoiding that conversation.

"She's what?!"

"Making jewelry in the spare bedroom."

"Mom! That is fucking insane! You can't let her do that!"

"It's the only way she can make money. The only way I can get her to pay rent."

"Mom, she's scamming you."

"No, I was the one who suggested it."

"Oh my god! She's never going to leave. You know that. Right?"

"Whatever. She knows it's not permanent. We'll see how it goes. When she starts to make some money, I'll ask her to leave."

"You better get it in writing. I'm telling you, she's going to keep fucking taking advantage of you if you don't."

I hung up the phone with Tasha knowing that, on some level, she was right. I was being taken advantage of. But I was doing so willingly. I was being kind. I was being generous. I was being useful to at least one person on earth. I was being the person I wanted to be.

6

Meditation

DESPITE MY RESOLVE TO help Danielle, I found myself in a state of confusion. Was I doing the right thing? What would be the effect on my relationship with my daughter? What exactly was I doing with my life, anyway? I was supposed to be finding new meaning in my remaining years. Instead, I had a sense that I was drifting, simply acquiescing to circumstance.

When I was young, in my early twenties, I was also in a state of confusion. It was a young person's confusion. Who was I? What should I become? With whom should I become it? Hoping to find some kind of enlightenment, I had signed up to take classes in Zen meditation. I was taught to focus on my breath and my posture.

Whenever troubling thoughts arrived, I was instructed to come back to my breathing. It was a simple, yet powerful, form of meditation. A few times I achieved a state of deep relaxation. I would be free of internal worries and present in the moment. I was good at meditation, but hormones and a young man in my meditation class ruined it all.

We found that spending time together and having frequent sex was much more stimulating than meditation. Sex, however, was not a path to enlightenment. It was, at least in this case, a path to pain and disillusionment. This beautiful young man with his long blond hair, soft beard, slender, athletic body, and deep soulful eyes seemed like a god to me. He also seemed like a god to many other young women.

I never returned to my meditation practice. Perhaps I associated it with the painful breakup. Or perhaps life just got in the way. Now, at my advanced age, neither hormones nor life stood in my way.

The Still Water Zen Center was near my home. How many people can say they have a Zen center in their neighborhood? But this was Berkeley. We could choose from a menu of places to practice meditation.

I arrived at the beginner's meditation practice at 7 pm. Normally I would be eating dinner at that time. So, I arrived already a little annoyed by the disruption to my schedule. The leader was Oshō David Blau. David was a slender, studious-looking young man who appeared to be in his late twenties. I learned later that the honorific "Oshō" designated a sort of trainee Zen master.

While David provided brief instructions in a soft voice that was difficult to hear, my eyes wondered around the room. I counted eleven people, including myself. There was a range of ages, from what looked like college students to men and women my own age. None of these people were particularly attractive, at least by traditional standards of beauty, nor did they seem to take any particular pains to present themselves to any advantage.

The women tended to wear their hair long, pulled back into a simple ponytail. They were dressed in loose, cotton or linen blouses and pants. One woman, perhaps in her mid-thirties, wore a wide ankle-length skirt with what looked like a hand dyed Guatemalan print on it. None wore any discernible make-up. The men sported various types of facial hair. T-shirts and sweatpants seemed to be the agreed upon male uniform. This was all to be expected. Doing nothing to enhance your self-presentation was a Berkeley tradition.

As I scanned the group, I had a sense that I was surrounded by deeply troubled people who had not been able to find a successful way to navigate life. This was a vaguely disturbing thought because it begged the question: Was I one of those people?

I did my best to push those thoughts out of my mind. I was here to practice Zen, and making judgments was not part of that practice. We settled into whatever crossed-legged position we could manage with the help of zazen pillows tucked under our butts.

Because it was a beginner's class, we were asked to meditate for "only" twenty minutes. Throughout the session, people fidgeted. There were heavy sighs. One person actually moaned. It was such a deep, mournful sound that I couldn't tell whether it was emanating from a man or a woman. Another would-be Zen disciple rolled over on his side to stretch out a cramped leg. Occasionally, Oshō Blau would whisper encouragement and attempt to draw us back to our zazen practice.

I found myself pondering the Danielle question. As I considered my contradictory feelings, from warmth to resentment, I noticed my jaws tensing and the small muscles around my eyes contracting. As instructed, I would return to my breathing. Then I would become aware of my back starting to ache. The backache would be followed by an awareness that my left foot was going numb. Then Tasha's disapproving face would appear. I would suddenly become aware that I was holding my breath.

The meditation went on like that, alternating between my mundane worries and an awareness of my aches and pains. For a brief moment, I allowed my consciousness to take stock and become a simple observer. I became aware that my mind was thinking thoughts. My body was hurting. But I was not my thoughts. I was not my pain. I was simply awareness. That moment of meta-consciousness lasted for a matter of seconds … until my attention was drawn back to my numb foot. I thought, *I'm going to lose that foot if I don't release it.* With a heavy sense of failure, I extricated my leg and rubbed the blood back into it. A minute later, Blau sounded the gong, ending our session.

I wondered how many of the aspiring acolytes who had come to this session would return for another round of mental and physical torture. I wondered if I would. After the meditation, Blau gave a dharma talk. The topic was "Doing Nothing." *How appropriate!* For a moment, I thought this was a sign, a message sent just to me. Then I remembered that I didn't believe in signs or messages from unseen powers.

The dharma talk turned out to be a rambling, improvised speech that never quite arrived at a conclusion. It started with a story about Blau's difficulty getting to the center on time. He usually rode his bicycle, but his bicycle had a flat tire. He considered walking, but that would mean arriving late. He called a friend who had a car, but the friend was unavailable. Blau stopped at this point in the story and paused for a long time, as if he were collecting his thoughts or letting the acolytes absorb the dilemma.

A young woman, who clearly didn't understand the true nature of Zen, broke the silence with a question: "So how did you get here on time?"

"Yes," Oshō Blau responded, nodding his head knowingly.

I involuntarily rolled my eyes. Although Oshō Blau intended this to be a teaching moment, I couldn't help thinking he was imitating a technique one of his teachers had used. Later, as we were leaving the session, a woman about my age whispered to me that she saw Blau arrive in a hired Lyft car.

At the end of the dharma talk, I didn't remember the young Oshō ever having mentioned the ostensible topic of doing nothing. Instead, he talked about the multi-generational fabric of Zen transmission and confessed that he was imperfect and not in any way prepared to receive that transmission. One could assume, perhaps, that he needed to get better at doing nothing, but that point was not clearly articulated.

I thought about how I had taught the young student I tutored to organize his thoughts, to state a clear thesis and then support it with examples and arguments. Apparently, that was not allowed in a dharma talk. It required too much thinking, and thinking was not the point. In Zen, words were used to annihilate themselves. That was the purpose of a "koan," a paradoxical statement that could only be understood by setting aside the thinking, conceptualizing mind. I have to hand it to Blau. His dharma talk had successfully interfered with my ability to think critically. It was a twenty-minute koan.

After the talk, people were allowed to ask questions. A young woman asked, "I'm having a really hard time focusing on my studies. I keep getting distracted with stuff. When I'm on my phone, time just goes by for, like, hours. But when I try to read my assignment, fifteen minutes seems like forever. I feel like, sometimes, I should just let go, like I'm too attached to this idea of being a college graduate."

The Oshō replied, "It sounds like you're too attached to your phone."

The young woman blushed and let out a forced little laugh. After an uncomfortable moment of silence, Blau said, "Right livelihood is one of the principles of the Buddha's Noble Eightfold Path. Working is part of life. No work, no eat. Have you chosen a path that is compatible with your spiritual practice? Will it cause harm? Will it do good? Consider your path."

After that answer, which was not exactly advice, I gained a new respect for young David. It would have been easier simply to say, "Maybe you've chosen the wrong major. Find something that you're passionate about. Find something that will lead you to doing some good in the world." But the Oshō had made his point, circuitous though it may have been. I wondered what he would say to someone like me who was no longer seeking "livelihood."

A man, perhaps in his mid-fifties, said, "I'm struggling with this idea of letting go. My wife left me, and … " The man choked up for a moment. "And I still have feelings of anger and sadness. I'm trying to accept what is, but … it's hard."

Blau took a deep breath. I wondered what experience he had of heartbreak in his young life.

"Yes … this is a sad moment for you." Blau took a moment to contemplate. "What did you do this morning after you got up?"

The man looked startled. "I … I don't know, I peed … " A little chuckle rippled through the room.

Blau nodded his head wisely. "And then?"

"I ate breakfast."

"Then what?"

"I cleaned up the dishes."

Blau nodded again. "This is your life … now. The past is gone. The future is not here."

The man smiled and nodded his head as if he understood. I thought that the answer was sound from a sort of clinical, Zen point of view. But I knew in my heart that the man would continue to suffer. What he needed was a sympathetic friend who would comfort him and reassure him that he was a worthwhile person, and that time would help heal his trauma. It would have also been helpful for him to see a therapist who could have helped him understand what went wrong in his relationship.

But, of course, that was not Zen advice. The object of Zen practice was to overcome suffering by being in the moment and letting go of attachments that create pain. Suffering is part of life. We lose loved ones. We get old. We have health problems. We die. That kind of suffering is unavoidable. Pining over a divorce, on the other hand, is avoidable. Fearing a lonely old age is avoidable. Driving oneself crazy over what to do with one's life … avoidable. Or is it?

I tried for some time after the class to continue my meditation practice on my own. I told myself that I would sit zazen before breakfast. After several days of regular meditation, hunger overcame my commitment. I told myself that I would meditate after breakfast.

And I did … for several more days. Over time, that commitment also waned. I was disappointed with myself, of course. But disappointment was not an approved Zen emotion. As my yoga instructor once said (quoting her guru), "If you have no appointments, you have no disappointments." I asked myself what exactly I hoped to gain through meditation. Enlightenment? I had read enough Buddhist literature to know that seeking anything, including enlightenment, would only lead to attachment. I would not find definitive answers to my quest for meaning. "Answers" were not the goal of Zen practice.

So, what exactly was the goal? No goal? I could accomplish that without Zen practice. In fact, I had already achieved a perfect state of "no goal." At that moment, I received my "enlightenment." I needed to do nothing more than to eat my toast and jam, to drink my tea … and to carry on. I soon discovered, however, that simply carrying on with no ostensible goal was not a recipe for avoiding problems.

7

Dissension

"I think Tasha hates me," Danielle announced during dinner.

"Why do you say that?"

"I tried to talk to her, but she won't even answer my texts. And she unfriended me."

"She wasn't happy that I let you stay here. I think she was a little jealous."

"She was the one who told me to stay with you."

"I know, but she thought it was just a temporary thing. She didn't think you'd move in."

"What difference does it make to her?"

"People are complicated. Let's say, for example, that you went to your mother and asked for some financial help. She refused. Then she turned around and gave money to a friend of yours, someone in need."

"That's not the same. Tasha doesn't need your help. She has a job and a place to stay and everything."

"Right. That's not a perfect analogy. It's just … I'm offering something to you that I never offered to Tasha. I never suggested, after my husband died, that she move back in with me. I don't think she would have, but I guess on some level she thinks you're taking her place, even though it doesn't make any sense logically."

"Yeah … I wish I could talk to her. I think she thinks I'm taking advantage of you. But I'm not. I'm going to pay you back."

Danielle looked down at her food, as if she were surprised that she was eating. Her head and shoulders drooped. "I thought we were friends," she said to her plate.

I wanted Danielle and Tasha to be friends. Friends are precious.

Danielle needed a friend. And I wanted Tasha to have good friends. Why did this unfounded resentment need to come between them?

I remembered an old Zen story I had read many years ago, something about a monk who adopted a child. I looked it up and found it online. The story is about a young, unmarried woman who becomes pregnant. Her parents are upset and demand to know who the father is. The daughter accuses the monk, a celibate man with a sterling reputation. When the child is born, the parents bring the child to the monk.

"Here. This child is yours. Take him," they say. The monk accepts the child without objection and raises it as his own. The accusation that he is the father, however, ruins his reputation. Some years later, the young woman confesses that the father of the child was actually a young man in the neighborhood. Upon hearing this, her parents return to the monk and take the child back. The monk gives up the child with the same equanimity he had displayed when he had accepted the child.

I had accepted a child, and it was ruining my reputation as a mother. Unlike the monk, however, I didn't have perfect Zen equanimity. I wanted to have the child and have my reputation remain intact.

I had learned over the years that the best place to have a serious talk with Tasha was in a restaurant. She couldn't easily cut off the conversation, and she was constrained in her response by the presence of onlookers. So, I invited her to have dinner with me at one of her favorite sushi restaurants. She ordered the Dragon Roll, a combination of shrimp tempura, avocado and cooked eel, a dish that was way too complicated for my taste.

I confess that I was very calculated in my approach. I decided to avoid any topic that might upset her, nothing about work or romantic relationships. I asked her instead what she was watching for entertainment these days. She talked about a dark fantasy series she was streaming and a well-known office sitcom. I smiled appreciatively as she extolled their virtues, although I knew I would never watch either of those shows. Then I waited strategically for her to finish her first dish and encouraged her to order another one.

Finally, I casually slipped in what I thought sounded like an innocuous question.

"So, what's going on with you and Danielle?"

"I knew that's what this was about."

"What?"

"This dinner."

"No, really, I just thought it would be nice. I haven't seen you in a while."

"Okay, then if you want it to be 'nice,' let's not talk about Danielle."

"Danielle told me that she thinks you hate her."

"I don't hate her. I just don't want to associate."

"Why?"

Tasha glanced away as if she were looking for an escape route, then turned back to me and said, "You want me to pay?"

"No, of course not. This ... this situation is hard for me. I made the decision to help Danielle. And I don't have any regrets. But I don't want it to cause any dissension between us. You're my daughter. I love you."

"Whatever ... you're making a big deal out of it. Danielle is just annoying."

"How is she annoying?"

"She's just ... she was never like a close friend or anything. I mean, I would comment on her Instagram once in a while. Then we'd maybe text a little. But now she's here. She moves in with you, and, like, takes over ... and all of a sudden she wants to be my best friend."

"She's lonely."

Tasha let out a little snort. "She just wants to make sure you don't kick her out."

"Really? You think she's pretending to be your friend, so I don't kick her out? Do you really believe that?"

"Yes, she's playing you. But I won't let her play me."

"You know how you get upset if I seem not to respect your judgment? Well, I'd like you to respect mine. I think Danielle is in a difficult situation, and she needs help ... our help. She needs a friend."

"I hope she finds one," Tasha replied, coldly.

I tried, and I failed. My reputation as a mother was tarnished. Danielle was still friendless. The situation would only get worse as time went on. I thought of the Zen monk. With his reputation in tatters, he spent years raising a child who had been imposed on him. Then the child was summarily taken away. He must have grown attached to the child. But he accepted his fate without complaint and did his best to be a compassionate person. Could I do any less?

8

The Gift

Ever since Danielle started living with me, when I got up in the morning I would go straight to the bathroom and try to make myself presentable. By "presentable" I mean that I would check my face in the mirror, make sure I didn't have any dry spittle around the edges of my mouth, splash a little water on my eyes to wash away the sleep, and straighten up my hair. I would also make sure I didn't have any embarrassing stains on my nightgown or bathrobe. These are things I used to do when Lawrence was alive.

This morning, however, I didn't bother. Was it because my relationship with Danielle was so comfortable that I felt I didn't need to bother? Or was it a subtle, passive-aggressive statement, a kind of protest I couldn't verbalize?

Whatever the emotion, it all dissolved when I walked into the kitchen. There, on the table, was a check for two hundred and twenty-five dollars. Danielle had left it for me the night before. I was touched by this gesture. Danielle was making good on her promise to pay me back. But I didn't want the money. It seemed to spoil my act of generosity and compassion.

When Danielle finally emerged, I thanked her for the check and handed it back to her. "You keep this. You need the money to save up for your own place."

Danielle looked hurt. "No, really … I'm making some money now. I don't want to be like a freeloader or something."

"You're not. Not at all. I'm happy to have you here. I'm happy to help you."

I didn't mention the dissension it caused with Tasha.

"But you want me to leave."

"No, I didn't say that."

"You said you want me to save up for my own place."

"Right, eventually, when you're ready."

"That could take a while. It's so expensive here."

"Yes, I understand."

I had the distinct impression that Danielle was reluctant to leave. Over the weeks we had grown used to each other's company. I felt motherly toward her. And she seemed to need that. But it was not a normal life for a young woman, especially one who was very much at an age when she should be looking for a permanent partner. I was puzzled that she had never had a friend over to the house, not to mention a potential partner. Was she trying to be as inconspicuous and accommodating as possible? Was she afraid I might be annoyed and ask her to leave?

"Since you're going to be here for a while, I want you to know that it's perfectly fine for you to have people over. I just would like to know in advance."

Danielle started to tear up. Was it out of gratitude? Or did she not have any friends or lovers to invite?

"Thanks," was all she said. Then her eyes sparkled for a moment. "I want to give you something."

She took me into her jewelry studio and pointed to a necklace lying on her workbench. It was a simple metal band with a series of small metal pieces in silver and bronze attached to it, forming a slightly asymmetrical pattern. It wasn't something I would have chosen for myself. I hardly wore jewelry of any kind. But it was lovely and delicate. Danielle picked it up and handed it to me.

"I want you to have this."

I couldn't refuse a gift from the heart. "Wow! It's beautiful. Thank you so much!"

I gave her a kiss on the cheek.

"Put it on."

I slipped it around my neck. Danielle held up a hand mirror for me to see. I had to admit, it looked good.

"I love it!"

"I knew it would look good on you."

I did love the necklace. But I wondered whether it would draw attention to my increasingly aging neck. Or would it distract from my neck? *Stop thinking so much!* I told myself. *Who cares? You like the necklace. That's what counts. And it was given with gratitude. Now wear it with gratitude.*

9

Amy

SHORTLY AFTER LAWRENCE DIED (but before the arrival of Danielle) my friend, Amy, asked me over for dinner with her husband, Phil. It was a gesture of kindness. Amy wanted me to feel as if I were still a family friend, that life would go on as usual. Without Lawrence, however, it didn't feel the same.

I liked Phil, but we struggled to find topics of common interest. When Lawrence was alive, our meals together with Phil and Amy were fluid. As clichéd as it sounds, the men would talk about investments or politics, and Amy and I would drift into a separate conversation about books we had read or movies we had seen or personal issues we were having at work.

Phil and Amy met during a summer trip Amy took when she was a freshman in college. Amy's mother had a cousin who lived on a farm in Minnesota. He had invited her to visit; and Amy thought it would be fun. Her idea of a farm was a storybook place with friendly pigs, clucking chickens, and loyal, tail-wagging dogs. In her mind, it was a happy, healthy place, grounded in the rhythms of nature.

Much to her dismay, however, it turned out to be a huge, mechanized operation. Instead of friendly pigs, there were acres of corn and soybeans. Instead of the family gathering around a cozy kitchen table at the end of a day to share a satisfying meal that was gathered from the fruits of their labor, they often would eat frozen meals in front of a giant TV.

Bored and disenchanted, Amy started hanging out in the local town. That's where she met Phil. He was the son of the only lawyer in town, a respected, genteel position in this rural community. Phil had a quick smile and a combustible energy, fueled by unformed ambitions that could not be fulfilled in a rural, Minnesota town.

Most summer romances dissolve quickly. There might be a promise to write and stay in touch. But after a few letters and the distraction of a co-ed college full of datable young people, even the most ardent intentions waned. Amy and Phil's relationship stuck. They stayed in contact throughout Amy's college years.

Phil was a handsome, confident young man. After waiting several years for Amy to finish her master's degree, he decided it was time to move from Minnesota to California in order to be with her. He was twenty-three. With an associate degree from a community college and a thousand dollars in his bank account, Phil was certain he would find a job and succeed. A few months after Phil arrived, he and Amy got married. And a few months after that, Amy was pregnant with their first child. Some twenty years and two children later, Phil had become the vice-president of sales for a large manufacturing company.

Now at the table, after a brief but uncomfortable moment of silence, Amy asked me, "So, how are things?"

This apparently innocuous conversation-starter threw me into a minor state of turmoil. If Amy and I had been alone together, I would have told her how things were. I would have told her that it was hard, that I was almost too dazed to be lonely, but that loneliness haunted me like an uninvited guest popping up at awkward moments, just when I thought I had achieved a moment of repose.

I would have told Amy that I knew I should find things to do, but that doing anything felt impossible. I was unable to make any decisions. I would have half-seriously told her that I wanted her to stay with me, sleep in my bed, and comfort me, even though I knew that was impossible.

But I was not alone with Amy. So instead, I said something idiotic like, "Okay, hanging in there." Phil smiled and nodded, as if it were comforting to know that I was doing what he would have done— boldly face the situation and move on. Amy knew it was an evasion. She put her hand gently on my shoulder and looked at me, not with compassion, but with a conspiratorial smirk that implied "Who are you kidding?"

After that, the discussion turned to our children, an easy, fallback topic. Phil and Amy had two daughters. They were both married, had good careers and well-behaved children of their own. With such contented lives, there was not a lot of meat for interesting discussion. The topic soon turned to their grandchildren. I was forced to listen to the grandkids' cute little exploits and accomplishments. I smiled and nodded in appreciation, although I didn't really know them. And I had nothing to add.

My children had no children. And the only interesting things to say about them were concerning areas that I considered private, like their romantic lives. I assumed that my son, Brandon, met young women and probably had sex with them. But he never talked about it. I wasn't even certain of his gender identity. My daughter, Tasha, was currently dating a lesbian, but I considered her gender identity to be her own business. I didn't feel it was my place to discuss it.

Before dessert, we had run out of things to talk about. I was sorely tempted to say something controversial, like, "I read recently that the top one percent of households own more wealth than the bottom ninety percent combined. Don't you think it's time we limit the amount of money people can accumulate?" Phil, who aspired to be in the top one percent (and was possibly close to being in that category) would have argued vigorously with me. His was an individualistic view of the world.

After all, he told himself that he came to California with nothing but determination. And he had succeeded on his own. In his mind, he deserved whatever wealth he had accumulated. If poor people were poor, it was because they didn't have the drive to do better. My counterarguments about gender, class, and racial privilege would not have dented his iron-clad opinions. So, I kept quiet. And another uncomfortable silence fell over the table.

Amy, always perceptive, asked me to help prepare the dessert. Once in the kitchen, she squeezed my arm and whispered, "We'll talk later." I couldn't help wondering why she had invited me to dinner, when what we clearly needed was time alone together. But, of course, I knew the reason. She was attempting to simulate some sense of normalcy. She wanted to signal that things would go on as before. I could still come to her house as a guest and enjoy their company as a friend, not only of hers, but of the family. It was a sweet attempt.

Eventually, we did meet separately. Amy had invited me for teatime at a local café that had delicious, Eastern European desserts. She knew that the one time of day I cherished most was teatime. At four-thirty, I would stop everything and have a cup of tea with a cookie or two. Sometimes I would check my Facebook feed and see what my friends and acquaintances were doing. It was mostly unenlightening—meals they had enjoyed, pictures of kids or pets, humorous videos they wanted to share, trips they were taking, and occasionally an outraged plea to stop the destruction of the planet.

Otherwise, I would flip on the TV and watch the news. None of this fed my soul, quite the opposite. But it was a distraction, a few moments to forget about myself and indulge in the self-puffery of Facebook or the human comedy of greed, corruption, and inexplicable violence displayed daily on cable news.

Teatime with Amy, on the other hand, was not a distraction. The point was to talk about myself. To my surprise, however, Amy began by talking about Phil. In his early sixties, Phil was still completely mired in his work. Amy wanted to retire soon. She was a part-time lecturer in French literature at the university. A lecturer was the lowest ranking teaching position at the university. It was poorly paid, and lecturers were given the least desirable teaching jobs.

Amy taught freshmen who needed to meet their language requirement. It was something the students just wanted to get out of the way in order to pursue their real studies. Amy was tired of it. And she and Phil didn't need the money. She wanted them both to retire together.

Amy had conjured up a fantasy retirement. She would have time to pursue her interest in painting. She and Phil would take frequent trips together. They would visit Phil's family in New York more frequently and springboard from the East Coast to romantic getaways in Italy or Spain. They would spend days taking care of the grandchildren and creating lasting memories. They would cook extraordinary meals that she and Phil would enjoy with friends and family. The two of them would spend peaceful time together just reading or watching movies. It would be all pleasure, all the time.

But, as Amy explained, when she broached the subject of retirement with Phil, he got nervous. Or as Amy described it, he had the look of a raccoon trapped by a dog (an analogy she must have picked up on the farm in Minnesota). Phil would tell Amy that he couldn't leave his job yet. He was still looking for a worthy successor. He found that each of the younger men around him lacked some important quality—vision, drive, street smarts.

This seemed like an excuse to Amy. What exactly was Phil afraid of? That's what she wanted to figure out. To me, it was obvious. He was afraid of the same thing Amy was afraid of—time alone together. Amy had no more in common with Phil than I did. She loved going to art exhibits. She read poetry for pleasure. Occasionally, she would treat herself to an expensive opera ticket and cry silently when Violetta died in Alfredo's arms or when Butterfly relinquished her son to Pinkerton and his new wife.

Phil politely refused to accompany Amy to the opera, or to art exhibits, for that matter. His main interest was sports—football mostly, basketball, and more recently golf. He had tried, but failed, to get Amy interested in watching any of those sports.

What would life be like when they were both padding around the house together or taking long trips where they would be forced to spend hours with no one else to talk to and no work to distract them?

Amy and I were close friends. We had shared many confidences in the past. But when it came to Phil, I didn't feel that I could bluntly say what I was thinking. After all, they had been married for thirty-nine years. And it was a marriage that, from the outside, seemed perfect. So, when Amy asked me what I thought Phil was afraid of, I simply replied, "What are you afraid of?"

Amy looked back at me, seemingly stunned by my question. "What do you mean?" she asked, in what appeared to be an attempt to stall for time.

"I mean, is there anything that you're afraid of? It might be the same thing Phil is afraid of," I answered.

Amy's face went pale for a moment. Then her eyes started to tear up. I was sorry that I had been so blunt. But I should've trusted Amy more. After a moment of reflection, she looked up at me and said, "I'm afraid that my little picture of retirement bliss may be a bit unrealistic. To be brutally honest, I think Phil would have a hard time adjusting. I can see him sitting for hours watching sports on TV, eating crap, getting bored and dissatisfied. He'd be frustrated and angry. He would be … " She trailed off.

"He would be what?"

"He would be … lonely."

Amy's eyes teared up again. She was getting close to admitting that her company would not be enough for Phil. And she understood that his company would not be enough for her. There were other issues, too. The same qualities that had helped Phil succeed in the business world, made him difficult to live with. His confidence made him stubborn. He was the type of man who knew what was right, and was not open to nuanced discussion. His metal-plated opinions caused dissension in their relationship in the past, especially when it came to questions of childrearing.

Amy understood all this as she contemplated a life in retirement with Phil. It was hard for me to watch my dear friend's retirement dream begin to melt. I tried to comfort her.

"Of course, there would be adjustments. Phil would need to find new interests and meet new people. And just because you're both retired doesn't mean you can't still live independent lives."

I was skirting the issue. We both knew it. But Amy nodded and simply said, "Of course."

Anxious to change the subject, she turned the conversation back to me.

"What about you? Are you thinking of retiring any time soon?"

I told her that I was thinking of retiring. To some extent, I was being retired without my choosing because clients were dropping away. I wasn't panicking. I had no debt, and Lawrence had left me a comfortable income from his retirement fund. If I maintained my modest lifestyle, I wouldn't need to work.

"Then you should retire!" Amy said. "We could retire together! Then you could be my retirement companion. Wouldn't that be amazing?"

Amy gave me a hug. I agreed that it would be lovely. We imagined all the things we could do together, everything Amy had imagined doing with Phil.

Now it was my turn to tear up. Lawrence's death had not only left a void in my present life. It had left a void in my future life. And our future life—the plans we cherished—when stolen from us, cause us a special kind of grief. Amy's idea of our retiring together made me feel a surge of pain, the pain I had been holding inside as I contemplated old age alone, my current life stretching out day after day, year after year, all while getting more feeble and more helpless. I had watched Lawrence die. I knew what it was like. Lawrence had me by his side. Who would I have?

I expressed these thoughts to Amy. She gave me another hug and said, "I'll never leave you. Besides, who said you'll never have another relationship ... pretty and together as you are?"

Starting a new relationship was the last thing on my mind. It seemed inconceivable when the essence of Lawrence still filled my heart and mind. But I smiled and said, "You never know." I said that as a concession to Amy. I wanted to reassure her that I was being positive and beginning to recover from my grief. But I didn't feel positive. I doubted that I would ever have another close, loving relationship with a man. In any case, the effort seemed overwhelming. How would you even begin to bring two fully lived lives together?

How do you blend a lifetime of habits, relationships, ways of relating to the world together into a new relationship? Age may bring with it a certain wisdom (the wisdom of acceptance, for instance), but it does not increase your ability to adapt.

Amy and I joked about the fifteen-year rule. That's the rule that says that older men look for women who are at least fifteen years younger than they are. That would make my potential new partner close to eighty years old. We laughed and imagined what type of eighty-year-old man would court me. He would be a horny old man who lived a self-absorbed, dissolute life ... someone with a highly inflated image of himself. It would have to be someone like that because all the good men die young or stay in a relationship until they die. I didn't know how close to the truth this prediction would be.

10

French Lessons

AMY WAS A FRANCOPHILE. She loved the food, the wine, the cheese, and the general joie de vivre that French culture represented. This love stemmed from a crystalized memory of a year abroad spent with a French family in Bordeaux. Amy had been shocked by the care and attention given to meals. She learned that the French valued vacation time. And Sundays were spent with the family. All businesses were closed. Amy was exposed to a culture where the enjoyment of life took precedence over work and the accumulation of wealth.

Some months after Lawrence's death, Amy convinced me to go on a trip with her to Paris. She had been to France a half a dozen times. I, on the other hand, had only been out of the country once—on a family road trip where we dipped our toes over the border into Vancouver, Canada. Amy offered to be my guide. She tried hard to convince me that it would be good for me.

I didn't require much convincing. There was nothing holding me back—no attachments, no work assignments. I didn't have the money, but Amy (who did have money) offered to pay for our hotel room if we shared it.

I studied French in school. What was the use of learning a language if not to exercise it in the land of its origin? I told myself that I would be derelict in my duty to myself if I didn't go. Granted, the notion of a "duty to myself" seemed a hastily constructed pretense to indulge a whim. But there was something deeper at work. I desperately needed something to pull me out of my dull, emotionally battered life. And I felt a strong urge to bathe myself in the sublime. What better place to do that than in Paris? Land of art! Culture! Cuisine! Romance! Cafés!

The café part especially intrigued me. I imagined that the cafés of Paris were filled with people engaged in intense conversations about politics, philosophy, or the quandaries of romantic entanglements. In my mind, these café-going Parisians were all Jean-Paul Sartre and Simone de Beauvoir.

On the trip, I learned that things have changed in France since Amy's student sojourn. The French joie de vivre is tarnished with issues like terrorism and a growing nationalist movement, not to mention the introduction of fast food and giant super-markets (known as hypermarkets). And the cafés were more often than not filled with people staring at their laptops or phones, rather than engaging in intellectual discourse. But the French still seemed to respect the arts and the life of the mind. They have prime time talk shows where the guest is just as likely to be a philosopher as a movie star.

After arriving in Paris, the first item on my must-see list was the Musée du Louvre, the one-time royal palace that held a wondrous trove of art, from ancient Egypt through the Renaissance and beyond. When I mentioned the Louvre, Amy almost imperceptibly rolled her eyes.

"Okay, let's get that over with," she said, and promptly called the concierge to buy us tickets.

I began to understand Amy's reaction when we arrived at the Louvre. The first thing we saw was a line of tourist buses parked outside, disgorging hundreds of sightseers. My guide book mentioned that there were almost nine million visits to the museum every year. Apparently, a good portion of that nine million decided to arrive this particular day. Amy took my hand and led me through the throngs.

There before us was the Louvre, a sprawling palace that had once been the Paris residence of a series of French kings. Having grown up in California, I had always thought of history as taking place in some mythical past to be discovered only in books. But here was history, the culture of a nation, in physical form.

I must have been standing with my mouth agape because Amy felt the need to nudge me toward the entrance. And what an entrance! It consisted of a glass pyramid, planted right in the middle of this ancient courtyard. How bold the French were to have installed this twentieth-century addition right in front of an iconic, historical structure. Weren't they afraid they would ruin it with something so incongruous?

As usual, Amy had a theory. "The French see art and culture as a kind of continuum. They weren't ruining a cultural icon. They were adding a new icon. It's all part of a living, evolving process."

Art as something alive. Culture as part of a living, breathing present. It was inspiring.

The Louvre turned out to be overwhelming. Every place you looked there were awe-inspiring masterpieces. And the place was huge. Consequently, hordes of tourists (on a limited sight-seeing schedule) were literally trotting from one well-known masterpiece to another.

There must have been fifty people surrounding the Mona Lisa. But simply to be in the presence of a revered art object restored something in my soul that had been withering. Yes, the Mona Lisa was a brand of sorts. People came to gawk more often than to absorb its beauty and mystery. But the very fact that a painting could be so cherished throughout the centuries meant that humanity understood the value of the sublime. This is what I had come for, my quest to bathe myself in beauty. And I promised myself that, somehow, I would incorporate that beauty into my life. Perhaps, I would even find a way to contribute to the "continuum," as Amy put it.

That evening, back at the hotel, I slipped into bed next to Amy. It was a strange feeling to lie down next to a woman. Yet this act of sleeping with another body next to mine was so familiar. It was something I had done my entire adult life.

Amy reached over to her nightstand and picked up a small box.

"Here," she said. "I snore."

There were two earplugs in the box.

"I'm sure I won't need these."

"Yes, you will. Sometimes I snore so loudly that Phil has to sleep in the guest room. I don't know what happens. We get old and something starts flapping around in there," she explained, gesturing toward her throat.

"That's pretty much true of your whole body, the flapping part," I said.

Amy laughed through her nose, then took my hand and said, "You don't look so flappy to me."

The touch of her hand almost made me cry. It was, of course, a simple gesture of affection. But being touched like that, especially at night in bed, made me ache for the warmth of a caress. It had been so long, and the prospects for having that in my life again were almost non-existent. I held on to Amy's hand for a long moment.

Then I flipped on my side to face her. "Amy?"

"Yes, dear?"

"Remember the taxi driver who said *putain de merde*?"

"Yes?"

"What do you think about him using 'whore' as an expletive?"

"Well, that's the French." That was not really an answer.

"How would you say that French men are different from American men?"

"They're not different, really. They all want the same thing, but French men are willing to play the dance of seduction. And they dress better. They don't wear shorts."

"Have you ever made love to a Frenchman?"

"What?! No, of course not. I met Phil when I was a student."

"So how do you know about how Frenchmen 'play the dance of seduction?'"

"Are you questioning my knowledge of French culture?" Amy laughed, but she still seemed slightly offended. "I've had friends who had French boyfriends, and I watch French movies and I read."

This was a sufficient response to establish Amy's authority, and I had to admit that in our brief stay I had not seen a single Frenchman wearing shorts, only American tourists. I was, however, disappointed that Amy had never had an affair with a Frenchman. I was hoping for some interesting details.

Amy and I chatted in bed for what must have been several hours. Sometime early in the morning we finally got sleepy. Amy rolled over and gave me a quick kiss on the lips.

"G'night," she said, before rolling back to her spot and closing her eyes. The kiss left me a bit stunned. Was Amy so sleepy that she forgot that I wasn't her husband? Was it simply out of habit? Or did it have some other significance? The kiss wasn't unpleasant, but it left me puzzled. I slipped in the earplugs Amy had given me, but I had a hard time going to sleep.

The next morning, Amy insisted that we visit the Musée Carnavalet, dedicated to the history of Paris. The museum was just a short distance from our hotel. It featured re-creations of Parisian rooms dating back to the 1600's. It was Paris history told through interior design. I loved it. But there was one attraction that Amy was especially excited to re-visit—the re-creation of Marcel Proust's bedroom. The distinctive feature of Proust's bedroom was the walls, which were lined with cork tiles. The tiles acted as sound insulation. Proust was rather sickly and craved quiet.

Amy was a huge fan of Proust. It was a thrill for her just to see the room where the author wrote his novels. I remember having read (or having tried to read) *Swann's Way*, the first volume of Proust's masterwork, *Remembrance of Things Past*. We were assigned *Swann's Way* in a comparative literature class. It contained a series of dreamy memories of places and people Proust had met early in his privileged life. But not much actually happened.

Many consider Proust to be one of the greatest writers of the twentieth century. I remember having been bored by his writing. Of course, I was nineteen years old. A lot of things were boring at the that age which I would later find absorbing. Amy's enthusiasm made me determined to re-read *Swann's Way*. I promised myself that it would be the first book I read when I returned home.

After the museum, we did what Parisians do when they need a break from the bustle of city life. We stopped at a café for a drink. After sharing our delight at having visited the Musée Carnavelet, I decided to broach the topic of the kiss.

"Remember last night when we went to sleep?"

"Yes?"

"You kissed me."

"Yes."

"On the lips."

"Did that bother you?"

"No."

"Alors, tout va bien. N'est-ce pas, ma cherie?"

With that, Amy took my hand and kissed it ceremoniously, as a Frenchman might have in the time of Proust. Was this a tease? A genuine gesture of affection? Or something more? Honestly, I didn't care. I was in Paris, the land of romance, with a reputation for tolerance of the louche tendencies of human nature, especially when it came to love. And I had come to Paris seeking passion, in whatever form it took.

On that trip to Paris, I was looking for some kind of inspiration. And I had found it. An ancient desire to write began to burn again inside me. In my college days, I wrote several short stories. I tried once or twice to send them off to magazines, but they were promptly rejected. In my youthful ignorance, I thought that the rejections meant that I was not talented enough to be a writer. I too easily discarded the importance of persistence and hated the notion of self-promotion, two essential characteristics of writing success. Was it too late to try now, with the perspective of age? Persistence and self-promotion. Was I ready for that?

I let those questions simmer. But after the trip to Paris, France continued to inspire me. I cooked French meals. I read French classics. I fell in love with Flaubert. His flawless writing both intimidated me and taunted me to write a novel of my own.

Despite my enthusiasm for France, I could only carry on the most rudimentary conversation in French. During our trip, other than a "merci Madame" or a "un café, s'il vous plait," I let Amy do all the talking. It was shameful.

So, on my return, I decided to take a French class at the local Alliance Française. The class was held in a converted house. There were seven students; a young woman who was planning a student year abroad; a man in this late twenties planning a business trip to France; two middle-aged women who, like me, had vague plans to visit Paris; a man in his fifties who acted as if the class were beneath him because he had lived in France some years ago when he worked for a large, global corporation; an older man who looked to be about eighty years old; and myself.

The teacher was an energetic French woman in her late thirties, who had married an American. She spent a lot of time encouraging our pathetic attempts at French conversation. In the great French pedagogical tradition, she used both praise and denigration.

"Non, non, non! C'est *la* France … *le* français," she would insist, impatiently, as if it were obvious that a country would be female, while a language would be male.

At one point, the young man was perplexed by receiving a direction that included meters. "Vous tourner à droite et c'est à peu près à cent metres." (Turn right and it's about a hundred meters from there.)

"What's a hundred meters? Don't they have blocks in France?" he said.

"Oh, là, là! A city in France is not divided like a … a cookie cutter, as you say, into little squares. If you go to France, you must stop your American way of thinking!" our instructor replied, thereby squelching any further attempt at American cultural imperialism.

After the first class, the eighty-year-old man, Gordon, followed me out the door.

"Let's grab a coffee," he said.

"It's 9:30. I don't drink coffee this late at night."

"Really? When do you go to bed?"

I found this question oddly impertinent. But Gordon had a little twinkle in his eye and a slight, loopy grin on his face.

I answered, "When do you go to bed?"

"Hmmm. 2 a.m.? Around there."

I surmised that Gordon was quite good-looking in his youth. He had fine features and a fairly tall, still-slender body, marred only by a round paunch that sat on his belly like a mixing bowl implanted in his stomach. He had white hair that he kept long around the edges, with a wisp of hair on top that he proudly combed into a little wave.

A slight breeze momentarily blew the wave into a kind of halo. He seemed harmless. And I appreciated the fact that he was taking a French conversation class at his advanced age. It indicated a certain tenacious joie de vivre. And, after all, I had taken the class to recapture a bit of joie de vivre. So, I relented and went to have a decaf coffee with him at a local café.

It turned out that Gordon had also studied comparative literature at university, but eventually went into business with his father-in-law selling some kind of specialized machine parts.

According to Gordon, he was an abysmal failure at the job due to an utter lack of interest. Eventually, he inherited some rental property from his father and was able to survive off the income it afforded.

I asked Gordon what he usually did between 9:30 p.m. and bedtime at 2 a.m. This was not a question I would normally ask a stranger, but Gordon had a self-deprecating honesty about him that encouraged this kind of prodding.

"I smoke weed … watch MSNBC … or a Great Course DVD. I'm watching a course on Eastern Europe. Yugoslavia was fucked over by NATO and the U.S."

It turned out that Gordon was a pothead, a leftist, and a student of history. He suggested that I come to his place and smoke some of his cannabis. I was hesitant at first. Gordon was a stranger, after all. Could I trust him enough to go to his house?

Despite these misgivings, I found myself strangely tempted. After all, I had been using toast with jam to dull the edges of my grief. Marijuana would certainly do a more effective job. And, in my current state, what-the-hell seemed like an appropriate response.

Gordon lived in a large house that looked as if it had been furnished in the 1940's. We sat on a velvet couch that, like Gordon, had seen better days. The cushion was lumpy, as if it were stuffed with horsehair. The bong Gordon offered me, however, was quite modern, the only modern object in the house, it appeared.

Unpracticed as I was in the ways of marijuana, I got high quite quickly. Before I knew what was happening, I realized that Gordon was cradling my breast. This realization somehow woke up my sober side. I had what seemed like a rather long internal conversation between two parts of my brain, the high part that was mostly absorbed by sensations and the rational part that was sending warning signals.

Finally, the rational part won out. I removed Gordon's hand. And, by summoning an unusual amount of will power, I was able to stand up. I said goodnight to Gordon.

Gordon looked up at me and made a sad face. "Sorry, did I offend you?"

I looked down at Gordon. His eyes seemed alert, sober. And he was able to construct a coherent sentence. Clearly, he had developed a certain tolerance to the marijuana he smoked on a daily basis. I, on the other hand, was too high to carry on a normal conversation. Instead, my eyes drifted to the wispy little wave on top of his head. It made me laugh out loud.

Gordon smiled. "Ha! Good! You're not mad at me. You hungry?"

Gordon stood up. For some reason, this scared me. I took a step back and managed a tentative, "No." I took a step toward the door. "Thank you," I said on my way out. During the ride home, I had to consciously focus my attention away from the glowing, red lights emanating from the brake lights of the cars ahead of me. Together, they seemed to create a beautiful, slow-moving light show. Somehow, I made it home safely.

The next day, rather than being disturbed by my misadventure, it brought a perverse little smile to my lips. It may have been a misadventure, but at least it was an adventure of sorts. I promised myself that I would never be seduced by Gordon again. But I might buy a bit of his weed.

11

Blind Date

AFTER MY "DATE" WITH Gordon, I naturally called Amy and recounted all the crazy details: his invitation to drink coffee late at night, the perplexing comment about Yugoslavia being a victim of U.S. imperialism, my rash decision to go to his place, the getting high and the getting felt up.

"Geez, really? I haven't had anyone try to feel me up since I was in high school," Amy commented, a bit wistfully.

"Would you have let him?" I asked.

"If I were you? Of course not. He'd have to do more than buy me a coffee."

We both had a good laugh.

After hearing my adventure with Gordon, Amy (being Amy), decided she would take it upon herself to set me up with a more suitable date. A few weeks later, she did. As it turned out, her cousin Jimmy was coming to town, and Amy decided that we needed to meet. Jimmy was an eligible bachelor, who had been living as a bachelor since his divorce twenty-one years ago. He was sixty-five, a successful tax attorney, and a bon vivant who rode a motorcycle for fun on the weekend. He had an adult son from his first marriage who had been in and out of rehab throughout his troubled life.

Amy contacted him and proposed a date with me when he was in town.

"He said he'd be willing to meet you," Amy announced with a hint of excitement in her voice.

The phrase "willing to meet" had a hint of coercion in it, implying that Amy had to do some arm twisting to convince him. I had to ponder whether I was willing to meet him under those circumstances. I didn't want to disappoint Amy. Clearly, she had gone to some trouble to arrange the meeting and expected me to be grateful.

But the description of Jimmy I was able to coax out of Amy didn't sound particularly auspicious. Let's start with the fact that he had been single for twenty-one years. I had been divorced myself, so I understood how one can fall into a relationship that turns into an unfortunate mistake. But to give up on the idea of a committed relationship altogether seemed to me a bad omen. As a man with a successful career, Jimmy certainly could have easily found another woman with whom to begin anew. Men have an advantage in that respect. He was forty-four when he divorced. That is considered a relatively youthful and attractive age for a man. And Amy assured me that Jimmy was very nice-looking. The fact that he never remarried must have been a conscious choice.

I was willing to accept that his son's drug addiction was not his fault. We now understand that drug addiction is a disease that is very difficult to treat. But Jimmy's motorcycle hobby gave me pause. For some women, it might conjure up an image of an adventurous "bad boy." For me, however, it conjured up an image of a foolish, self-centered man with aspirations of Hell's Angel machismo.

Then there was his profession. I couldn't help associating tax attorney with my cheating first husband's occupation—accountant. The association led me to imagine unflattering scenarios: Jimmy having affairs with vulnerable female clients who relied on his expertise to save them from the prying eyes of the IRS, or helping wealthy women establish tax havens in offshore accounts in return for sexual favors. None of these imaginings were justified, of course.

The main issue I had, however, was doubt about the viability of a relationship with a man like Jimmy. How would a sixty-five-year-old bachelor of twenty-one years accommodate himself to a life together? He had his own life, his own habits, his own way of thinking. As we aged, would he be loyal to the end? Would he be resentful if I became infirm? Would I be resentful if he became infirm before I did? I had spent half a life with Lawrence. He was kind and loving to me. He was generous with my children. Toward the end, I nursed him with an unambiguous heart full of gratitude. It could never be the same with a late-life partnership. There were simply not enough years left to create that kind of bond.

Why was I even thinking about creating a bond? I knew I could never replace Lawrence. And I had convinced myself that romance at my age was more of an undesirable disturbance than a blessing. Paradoxically, this attitude freed me to agree to the "date" with Jimmy. I had nothing to lose. It would be an experience. That's all. And I was right. It was an experience.

When Tasha heard that I was going out on a "date," she decided to come over and do my make-up. My idea of make-up was a touch of eyeliner or unobtrusive lipstick. Tasha went for the full "glam" treatment—foundation, concealer, cheek contouring, brow pencil, eye-shadow, mascara, lip-liner, and gloss. That was her look when she presented herself in public. It reminded me of my mother, who would describe her morning make-up ritual as "putting my face on."

Nevertheless, I accepted Tasha's proposal. It was an act of kindness that I could not refuse. And I enjoyed being pampered.

When it was over, I looked at myself in the mirror. I had to admit that the make-up had transformed my face. I looked younger and more vibrant. I had eyebrows! My gray-green eyes were more prominent, as were my normally non-existent cheek bones. I was almost pretty ... from a distance. I thanked Tasha sincerely and praised her for her skill. But I knew that when she left, I would immediately remove the make-up. It felt like a mask, a vain attempt to cover my aging face and my feelings of insecurity. Neither was necessary.

Jimmy suggested we meet at a local restaurant of my choosing. I selected a moderately priced French bistro near my home. When I arrived, Jimmy was nowhere to be seen. The place was busy, so I decided to take a table. I was already annoyed at Jimmy for being late. I hated people who were late. It showed a lack of respect for others. After ten minutes, I ordered a glass of wine and an appetizer. I could have waited, of course. But I was determined to take revenge on Jimmy for his inconsiderate lateness.

After a sip of wine and a bite of my toast with tapenade, I saw a man walk through the door of the restaurant and scan the tables. He was stocky with a full head of gray, wiry, close-cropped hair. He had a pleasant face, even features, and strong eyes. There was something forceful, almost bull-like, about his presence. Surprisingly, he bore very little resemblance to Amy. It was his features—the nose, the mouth, the eyes—and their arrangement on his face that finally convinced me that he could be Amy's cousin. I waved to catch his attention.

Jimmy arrived at my table and promptly extended his hand. I stood up to greet him and was surprised to see that he was approximately my height. He had given the impression of being taller from a distance.

"Nice to meet you," he said, taking a seat across from me. "Sorry I'm late. There was some road construction, and the traffic was backed up for half a mile. Crazy."

"That's okay," I said. "Sorry, I started without you."

As soon as I said "sorry," I regretted it. Why was I apologizing? Jimmy's excuse was weak. He was in a new town. He should have left early enough to deal with a minor setback.

"That looks good," he said, eyeing my toast. "Mind if I ... ?" Without waiting, he took a piece of my toast and eagerly spread the tapenade on it.

"So friggin' hungry. I had an early lunch. Wanted to get out to Point Reyes in time for a hike."

Point Reyes was a national preserve along the coast north of San Francisco. It encompassed beautiful, wild beaches and inland forests of redwood and bay trees. I was beginning to warm up to Jimmy. He had energy, and I assumed that anyone who could appreciate the natural beauty of the northern California coast couldn't be too evil or depraved.

"What brought you up to San Francisco?" I asked. I expected him to answer that he was here to visit his beloved cousin.

"Metallica concert! Best fucking band ever!" he replied. "You might be able to still get tickets, but only from a scalper. It'll cost you a boat load."

So Jimmy was a motorcycle-driving, heavy metal fan. This was not auspicious.

"That's okay" I replied. "I'm not that into heavy metal."

"Really? What are you into?"

I had to stop and think about my answer. In truth, I wasn't really "into" any particular kind of music. I enjoyed classical music from time to time. I had a nostalgic attachment to the music of my youth—the Beatles, Dylan, Al Green. But I would never have used the term "best fucking band ever." I just was not that kind of fan. And I had to admit that that lack of passion was characteristic of my general approach to life. I rarely chose favorites. If someone asked what my favorite ice cream flavor was, I would respond, "I like a lot of flavors." Faced with Jimmy's unabashed passion for his favorite band, I felt somehow lacking. What held me back from choosing a favorite band, from choosing a favorite anything? I couldn't help wondering if, spending time with Jimmy, his zest for life would rub off on me.

I was being a little unfair with myself, of course. I had a passion in life. But it was a quiet passion. I had loved my husband fully and loyally. I loved my children. I loved my dear friend, Amy, who had fixed me up with Jimmy. But enduring love was not the same as passion. Was passion the antidote to my dulled emotions? Or was I just being a mature adult, learning to honestly accept what life offered and lowering my expectations accordingly? I had a suspicion that passion was a kind of trap. Like an addiction, it promised a high that was not sustainable. It led only to disappointment and despair.

Yet, I couldn't help feeling the pull that Jimmy's enthusiasm exerted on me.

"I think I would have to nominate the Beatles as the best band ever," I replied to Jimmy's question.

"Okay, safe choice. Probably the most popular band ever."

His comment annoyed me. Was he implying that I simply went with popular opinion? That I lacked the character to make a bold choice of my own? I decided to disregard his comment. Why did I care what he thought?

"In fifty years, which band will be remembered?" I asked pointedly.

I was being unduly defensive, combative for no reason. I honestly didn't care which band would be remembered fifty years from now. I didn't care because I lacked a fan's enthusiasm. I lacked commitment. I lacked ... yes, passion.

Jimmy just laughed at my response. "I guess we won't know, will we? We won't be around. I'm hungry. Let's order. What's good here?"

Ignoring my recommendation, Jimmy ordered the steak frites,

which he seemed to devour in about three gulps. After finishing his meal, he asked for the dessert menu.

"Hmm. Crème brulée … " He patted his rounded stomach. "I shouldn't, but what the hell. You?"

"Do you want to share the crème brulée?" I asked, thinking I was doing him a favor by mitigating his intake of high-calorie, artery-clogging food.

"Share? That little thing they serve it in?" He formed the shape of a ramekin with his fingers to emphasize how small it was. "Please, indulge. Get your own dessert, whatever you want."

I was tempted to say, "I like them all, but I don't love any of them. I lack your passion." But, instead, I just said, "That's okay. I don't think I really have room for dessert."

"There's always room for dessert. It goes down a different hole."

"Really? Where does that hole lead to, if not your digestive tract?"

"Your foot," was his prompt answer.

This was a lopsided battle. Nothing I said even slightly disturbed Jimmy. I found his indifference oddly attractive.

I decided not to have dessert. It was a lame attempt at taking a bold stand. And I wanted to punish Jimmy, to force him to compare my abstinence with his gluttony. It was a childish reaction. And I found myself eyeing his dessert, wishing he would share a spoonful or two with me.

When the bill came, Jimmy swooped it up. "Let me get this," he announced. I resisted. I didn't want him to think I was for sale. But he insisted.

"Look, it's nice to have some company when you're out of town. You took time out to meet me. You chose the restaurant. And, honestly, I'm not hurting for money. So let me repay you."

I relented, but I was curious (and a little concerned) about what would come next.

"You know, Amy spoke very highly of you. And I can see why she likes you," Jimmy announced, after paying the bill. "You're kind of fun. How old are you?"

"That is not something you ask a woman of a certain age," I said.

"Ha! Who gives a shit at our age? Really … I was just curious. I'm sixty-five."

"I know. Amy told me."

"Yeah? What else did she tell you?"

"Not much," I said, lying.

"Okay. Well, you know, it's been very nice meeting you. Maybe next time I'm up here, you and me and Amy can all get together. I might bring my girlfriend, rent a place up in the Point Reyes area."

"What does your girlfriend do?" I asked.

"She's a florist. Has her own shop. Pretty good business. Does a lot of weddings and events, stuff like that."

"That sounds like a lot of hard work. Is she thinking of retiring soon?"

"Retiring? No. She's a long way from retirement."

So, Jimmy had a younger girlfriend, probably practicing the fifteen-year rule. He wasn't such an eligible bachelor after all. And it was obvious he found me too old to be a potential romantic interest. You don't ask a woman her age unless you think of her more like another man, a potential buddy.

I left the restaurant with mixed feelings. On the one hand, I was humiliated by the encounter. I had reluctantly agreed to the meeting, mostly to assuage Amy. And I had come with my prejudices firmly in place. Instead, I found myself almost embarrassingly attracted to Jimmy, or at least attracted to his enthusiastic spirit.

On the other hand, it turned out to be exactly the "experience" I was hoping for. Jimmy had stirred up something in me. I wasn't quite sure what it was, or even if it was healthy. But disturbing as it was, it was something rather than nothing.

On my way home, I struggled with my unsettled feelings. I had to accept who I was. I was not a fan. My passions would never spill over into impulsive trips, for instance, to see my favorite band perform. How could they? I didn't have a favorite band. I didn't have a favorite anything. But I did have passion, a slow-burning, long-lasting passion. I wondered how I could take my kind of passion and translate it into something worthwhile. It occurred to me, once again, that writing required just such a tenacious passion.

Later, when I talked to Amy about the "date," she asked me how it went. I was reluctant to be too critical. She obviously liked her cousin, Jimmy, or she wouldn't have set us up.

"It was pleasant," I said. "Jimmy's an energetic guy."

"So, what do you think? Did you like him?"

"Amy, he has a young girlfriend. He wasn't interested in me romantically."

"Really? He didn't tell me that. I'm sorry. I thought … "

"I know … and I love you for it."

"I can't believe he didn't tell me. It's like he was willing to check you out … see if he could have a little fling on the side. What an ass!"

"Never mind. It was interesting. I kind of enjoyed it … a little break in the routine. And it kind of stirred up some feelings."

"What feelings?"

"Stirrings about … taking your passions and translating them into action."

"What passions?"

"Creative passions."

"Jimmy did that? That's kind of surprising because he doesn't really have any creative passions, as far as I know."

"No, but … you know why he came up here?"

"I thought he was just sight-seeing."

"No. He came to see a Metallica concert."

"They're still playing?"

"Apparently. It's his favorite band. I don't have any favorite bands. I don't have any favorite anything. But his enthusiasm rubbed off on me."

Amy shrugged. "Okay, then I guess you got something out of the experience. He's still an ass for doing that."

"Doing what?"

"Not being honest about his girlfriend and everything."

"Oh well, maybe he just misinterpreted your suggestion."

"You're being too charitable."

"I'm just curious. Did you talk to him after? Did he say anything about me?"

"Not much. He said you were feisty. I think he meant it in a positive way."

"Feisty" was hardly a compliment, if that's the best you can say about someone. I imagined he thought of me as an ornery older woman who had resisted his charms. And for men, that is an unforgiveable crime. I decided at that moment to assume the mantle of feisty older woman. If a man were to charm me, he would have to earn it. My moment of righteous resolve didn't last long, however. I began to doubt that I would have an opportunity to exercise my newfound feisty attitude. That would require a man to actually try to charm me.

12

Separation

AMY BROKE A PIECE of her scone off and nervously squashed it into a pile of crumbs. She had asked me to meet her at our usual tea place to "talk." It was an unusually urgent request.

Amy looked up from her crumbled scone.

"Where did you get that necklace? I love it."

"Danielle gave it to me."

"Oh, that's nice," Amy said, a bit unenthusiastically.

Amy and I had discussed the situation with Danielle. She knew that it was causing dissension with Tasha. And she had encouraged me to do whatever I could to encourage Danielle to leave. That was, of course, the logical response. What I was not able to fully convey to her, however, was how much I had become attached to Danielle. And how satisfying it was to be helping someone. I didn't tell her, I suppose, because I thought it would sound a little delusional. I didn't want to be accused of being taken advantage of.

"So, you wanted to talk."

"Yes," Amy said, crushing another piece off her scone. Amy didn't look good. Her eyes were puffy, small, and tight, and her face was pale.

Amy sighed. "Phil and I are having problems."

This was the first time that Amy had ever admitted to me that she was having "problems" with Phil. She had complained, of course, over the years about things that couples complain about. Once Phil had gone off to a sports bar to watch a basketball game with his buddies, forgetting that they had a dinner date with a colleague of Amy's. She was angry, but not enough to threaten their relationship. She had just vented and finally laughed about it, threatening to throw away the television (Phil's main source for sports viewing). This time, however, it seemed different.

"Tell me."

"You know that Phil didn't want to keep my mother in the house, right?"

"Yes, you told me."

"He claimed that we couldn't take care of her properly. But I wasn't about to put her in a facility. It would've killed me. And I think it would've killed Mom."

Tears were forming in Amy's eyes. I took her hands in mine. "You did the right thing."

Amy wiped away a tear. "So after she died … he … " She hesitated, her mouth twisting with bitterness. "Phil told me that we should have put her someplace with medical facilities. He blamed me for keeping her at home. This was just days after her funeral. I couldn't believe it." She wiped away another tear. "So cruel."

"That was wrong. I'm sure he regretted it, though."

"Regretted it? You don't know Phil. He'd never admit to regretting anything. He's always right."

"He never apologized?"

"No. And now I feel like … I don't know … I'm seeing him differently now. Our lives are just different. We're different. And I don't feel like I want to put up with it anymore. I'm over it. What's the point?"

"The point is that you have had a good and long relationship. You don't throw that away over one disagreement, even if it is deeply hurtful."

"No … you're right. It's been a long relationship. But I'm not sure it was ever good. I'm looking back on it now and seeing it differently. I feel like I'm finally being honest with myself. We're a bad match. We always have been. And now I'm retired, and I have a chance to … . I don't know. It sounds so stupid to say, 'Spread my wings.' But something like that. I just feel like he's pulling me down. And this is my last chance."

"Nobody's perfect. There is no perfect match. You just need some time."

"Maybe. But right now I don't want to even be in the same house with him. I don't want to go through the motions, pretend like everything is fine, kiss him good-bye on his way out, wait for him to come home late for dinner … lie in the same bed with him." These last words were said with disgust.

"Then don't. Go on strike for a while. Let him know how hurt you are."

"What? You think that he'll come begging for forgiveness?" Amy scoffed, almost spitting in the process. "He'll just get angry … angrier and angrier."

Amy knew Phil better than I. And I had run out of advice. "I'm so sorry you have to go through this. Is there anything I can do to help?"

Amy took a gulp of her tea, spilling a little on the table. She wiped it up brusquely with her crumpled napkin. "Could I come and stay with you?"

I must have shown a bit of shock on my face because Amy quickly followed up with, "At least for a while. I don't want to be in the same house with him. I can't."

"Well, of course, you can stay over tonight. But you know that Danielle is staying in Tasha's old bedroom, and she's taken over the other bedroom for her jewelry studio. There's not much room left."

"It's okay. I can sleep with you," Amy said, a little too quickly. "Remember Paris? It was nice sharing a bed, wasn't it?"

I had fond memories of our time together in Paris. Other than the snoring, which I was probably guilty of myself, it was easy and fun in a kind of teenage sleepover way. But as a permanent situation, that was entirely different. And I remembered the kiss goodnight on the lips. It seemed innocent. But I couldn't help wondering about Amy's intentions. I pushed those thoughts out of my mind. This was my dear friend, my best friend, and she needed the solace I could provide.

"Yes, it was nice. And, of course, you can stay with me. We'll make it work."

"Thank you, dear. This is so important for me. I need some space to process my feelings."

And that was that. On the way back from our tea, I thought, Amy, little Amy, is a force to be reckoned with. How had I let her convince me to move in and share my bed? What was happening? A few months ago, I was learning to live alone. And now I would be living in a house full of women. I was in a minor state of shock, but I wasn't entirely unhappy.

13

Adjustment

"Cool," Danielle said when I announced that Amy would be moving in with us. But I suspected that it wouldn't be entirely "cool," and she knew it.

Amy arrived with two suitcases full of clothes. I was taken off-guard. Clearly, she was prepared for more than an overnight stay.

"Maybe I can make some room in the closet for you. I can put some of my things in the studio closet."

"Oh, that would be great. Thank you."

Unexpectedly, Amy walked up to my closet and started inspecting it. She pulled out a wool coat.

"Maybe we could move some of your winter things."

I had expected Amy to arrive tearful and distraught. Instead, she seemed quite chipper and quite ready to rearrange my life to accommodate hers.

We carried some clothes into what used to be a bedroom, but had become Danielle's jewelry studio. The room was transformed into a kind of miniature blacksmith shop. A sturdy wooden workbench was covered with small hammers, files, pliers of different shapes and a miniature anvil. Besides the hand tools, Danielle had more sophisticated equipment, something she called her "spot welder" and a newly acquired engraving machine.

"Wow! Look at this. You've got a regular factory going on here," Amy said.

"Yes, Danielle is serious about her business. It's not a hobby."

When I opened the closet door, I was surprised to see it filled with shipping supplies: boxes of different sizes, bubble wrap, padded envelopes, tape. I had seen Danielle walk out the door carrying boxes and envelopes, but I never stopped to think where she stored these things.

"Well, we're just going to have to clear out some of this stuff," Amy said with surprising authority.

"Wait. We can't just start moving things around. We have to talk to Danielle first."

"It's your house, my dear. She's not even paying rent."

"She's not paying rent because I told her not to."

Amy shot me a look of disdain. How had I let that information slip out? It was none of Amy's business what my arrangement with Danielle was.

"You mean she offered, and you said no?"

"Right. If she's ever going to move out, she needs to save her money."

"Okay," Amy said, unconvinced. "But there's plenty of room over against that wall. We can pile some of the boxes there."

Amy picked up an armful of boxes and started to move them.

My authority was being ignored. But it's hard to resist that kind of assertiveness. And Amy had made me feel slightly ashamed of my generosity toward Danielle. I resented that feeling. *Is the whole world calling me foolish for being kind? Then the world can go to hell.*

Despite these thoughts, I joined Amy in moving the boxes.

"Okay, that's enough," I declared. "We just need a little room for my coats."

I imagined Danielle walking into her studio and finding things displaced. I told myself that I'd explain to her that the disruption was just temporary. Of course, I was beginning to doubt the whole notion of "temporary" stays.

That afternoon, Amy told me she had to run out and do an errand. Later, she came back carrying a grocery bag.

"What's this?"

"I'm going to make you a nice dinner à la Française."

"Wow! That's so nice."

Amy set the bag down on the kitchen table and started to unpack the food she bought.

"Can I help?" I asked.

"No, go away. It's a surprise."

"Go away? Where?"

"Just go and relax. Read a book or watch TV or whatever."

The idea of lounging around while someone else made dinner went against my instincts, or I should say it went against my training as a traditional wife and mother. Of course, Amy was also a traditional wife and mother. She was just doing what came naturally to her. So, I accepted her offer.

I wandered into the living room and picked up a book I was reading, a memoir by a woman who was a Beat Generation writer. She knew Allen Ginsberg, was close with Jack Kerouac, and friends with LeRoi Jones. The parts I liked, however, weren't the gossipy sections about well-known writers, but her internal struggle as a young artist. I could relate to the frustration of yearning to express one's creative soul to an uncaring world. It was like an unrequited love affair. The artist wants to shout: *Listen to me! Hear my voice! Recognize who I really am!* I had felt that as a young woman. But I had pushed that voice into a storage closet. Despite my best effort, however, I still heard muffled cries emanating from that closet. "*Let me out!*" the voice cried.

I put the book down and contemplated my situation. If I were experiencing a creative frustration, I had no one to blame but myself. One cannot be a frustrated artist until one commits to *being* an artist in the first place. I had not yet made that commitment.

In the meantime, my current life was not conducive to creating art of any kind. Instead, it was becoming unexpectedly crowded … and perhaps too comfortable. I was now living with two women. Both made meals for me. Both were grateful. I felt a glow of warmth and protection. This was nice. This was a pleasant way to live for a sixty- three-year-old widow. Men, at this point, would just constitute a demanding disturbance. Perhaps all women of a certain age should abandon their male spouses and lovers and congregate together.

Perhaps that was the natural way of things. Perhaps I was wrong. But, for the moment, I was smelling delicious odors coming from the kitchen, and all was good in the world … except for that muffled voice in the closet.

Then Danielle walked in the door. She stopped and sniffed the air. "Oh, you're cooking dinner."

"Well, actually, my friend, Amy, is cooking dinner."

"Oh, okay. I was going to make something for us. But I guess I'll wait."

Danielle started to walk toward her room.

"Wait. I want to introduce you to Amy. And maybe you can join us for dinner ... although there's probably some meat involved. She's making something French."

I walked Danielle into the kitchen. Amy, who was busy at the stove, heard us walk in. Without turning around, she said, "No! Stay out!"

"Amy, I wanted you to meet Danielle."

Amy turned around and wiped her hands on her apron. "Oh, so this is the famous Danielle." She shook Danielle's hand. "Enchantée, mademoiselle."

"Nice to meet you," Danielle replied. "I don't speak French. I studied Spanish in high school."

"Well, no one's perfect," Amy said with a laugh.

Danielle didn't laugh. We all stood there awkwardly for a moment.

"You're going to join us for dinner, right? Since you guys are already here snooping ... I might as well confess, I'm making a coq au vin. It's actually a simple recipe. But ooh là là, c'est bon!"

Danielle just looked back at Amy, blankly.

Observing Danielle's non-reaction, Amy continued, "It's a traditional French chicken dish. I was saying it's good ... *c'est bon*."

"Yes, I understood. But I don't eat meat, so ... "

"Oh, well, there are some green beans, and we're having a cheese course. I got an amazing Gaperon."

This time we both looked at Amy, puzzled. "It's a cheese, a little like camembert."

"I don't eat dairy. I'm a vegan."

"Oh ... then this might be a little ... "

"That's okay. I'll just wait till you're done. Nice meeting you."

With that, Danielle headed for her studio. I rushed to intercept her, but it was too late. I found Danielle staring at the pile of shipping boxes in the corner.

"I'm sorry. I needed to make some room in my closet for Amy, so we moved some of your shipping materials. I hope it's not too … "

"Okay," Danielle said, looking a bit like a cornered animal. She was cornered, in a way. She was powerless in the situation. Her space had been invaded, but she wasn't in a position to complain.

Having relied on my generosity, she had no financial leverage. And she had no chance to win a contest of loyalty with Amy. Amy was my oldest and best friend. Danielle was at my mercy. And I had shown her very little in this incident. I regretted it.

"It's only temporary. I hope it doesn't prevent you from doing your work."

"No, I'll be fine."

My heart ached for poor Danielle, as I left her alone in her marauded jewelry studio. Nevertheless, I sat down with Amy to enjoy her "dinner à la Française." Amy was in great spirits. She kept plying me with her "amazing, eight-dollar Côtes du Rhone." I tried my best to enjoy the meal. It was delicious, of course. But I kept thinking about Danielle. We were preventing her from eating her meager little vegan meal, while we gorged ourselves on French delicacies. I was feeling like Marie Antoinette, feasting while the peasants starved.

I ate quickly so that we could clear the kitchen for Danielle. But, apparently, Amy had no such compunction. She kept rattling on about movies and books. She was particularly enamored with an Italian author whose trilogy combined literary merit with an engrossing plot that portrayed the intimate lives of ordinary women. I nodded approvingly and told her I would certainly read the books. I hoped that by agreeing without comment, it would cut the conversation short. But Amy was a teacher by instinct and training.

She had to elaborate on her critical praise with supporting examples. And, for my benefit, she argued against the critics who had disparaged the work for being thin, without any profound ideas or stylistic innovation. This was, according to Amy, a typical male response to a woman's attempt to capture the real lives of women. Of course, this judgment led to a discourse about sexism in the world of criticism, a discourse which was clearly being fueled by the quickly diminishing bottle of Côtes du Rhone. Meanwhile, my attempt to bring the conversation to a close by agreeing without comment to everything Amy said only served to encourage her.

That evening, by way of compensation, I offered to let Danielle use the bathroom first, but she declined. She was in the middle of a jewelry project that was going to keep her up late. When I offered Amy the chance to go first, she insisted that I go ahead of her.

I slipped into bed and waited for Amy to join me. When she walked in, she stopped for a moment and said, "Oh."

"What?"

"Nothing. It's stupid. I usually sleep on that side of the bed," Amy said, pointing to my side.

"You want me to move?" I said, assuming that Amy would politely defer to me. This was, after all, my bed. And I had taken the left side of the bed ever since I married Lawrence. It was my "droit du seigneur."

"Well, no ... that's okay. I'll get used to this side. No biggie."

She was implying that she would be here long enough to get used to something. How long was that? A few days? A month? Forever? There was something disturbing about Amy's behavior. She seemed so happy at a time when she should have been despondent, grappling with the potential dissolution of a forty-year marriage.

What was the source of her ebullience? Was it some kind of forced levity aimed at avoiding the pain of her internal struggle? Or was she simply delighted to be here with me, to have escaped a dismal marriage, to be starting a new life?

"So ... Amy ... "

"Yes, my dear?"

"Have you had a chance to think about your situation? What you're going to do?"

"No, not too much. I decided to put aside notions of duty or obligation and just see how I feel."

"And how do you feel?"

"I feel ... light."

"Light like ... ?"

"Like I've let go of a weight, something that was dragging me down."

"Something like Phil?"

"I wouldn't put it that way. In a way, yes. But it's more all the expectations that go along with Phil, all the ways being with him forced me to compromise. I know that sounds selfish. We always have to make compromises for the ones we love. But those are compromises having to do with ... I don't know ... your time, your effort. I'm talking about compromises of your self, who you really are. Does that make sense?"

"Yes, it does. It makes total sense."

We both lay on our backs for a moment, each processing the situation in our own way.

Finally, I said, "Thank you so much for the dinner. That was such a nice gesture. I loved it."

"You are so welcome, my dear. I owe so much to you."

With that, Amy rolled over toward me and gave me a warm hug. Our bodies touched as she pressed against me. It had been a long time since I had had a warm body pressed against mine. It felt good, comforting. But as Amy held on a few seconds longer than was necessary, I started to feel uncomfortable.

I shrugged off this feeling and said goodnight. Before I could find sleep, however, I thought about Danielle. Was she feeling displaced in my affection? Abandoned once again? Vulnerable? How could I reassure her? I finally drifted off with these questions unresolved.

14

Accommodation

It started with clearing a shelf in the bathroom for Amy's toiletries. Then, after several days, I was obliged to empty a drawer in my dresser for her socks and underwear. In the kitchen, I made space for the food and beverage items Amy brought home. These included a variety of white and red French wines, fresh breads (which she referred to as "pain de campagne"), and very ripe, soft cheeses, with a faint ammonia smell. She explained that Phil hated ripe cheese and forbade her from buying it. So, it was particularly thrilling for her to freely eat cheese the way the French do, in its "full, delicious ripeness." When she said this, Amy made an expansive gesture that seemed to include her body as part of the "full, delicious ripeness."

Clearly, Amy was moving in and enjoying it. I had mixed feelings. Her exuberance was contagious. But how long was this giddy phase going to last? Was her reaction something akin to a kid going off to college for the first time, free of parental (or, in this case, spousal) supervision? And just as college freshmen often over-indulge in drinking and sex, before realizing that they have to face reality (classwork, grades); I was wondering if Amy was, likewise, over-indulging and heading for a crash with reality, the reality of a lifetime partnership possibly coming to an end.

This begged the question of how long she was planning to stay. I felt it was too soon to broach that topic. She needed time, as she herself had said, to process her emotions. So far, however, the only emotion she seemed to express was glee.

Amy was determined to enjoy the pleasures of life, starting with eating à la française. I was determined not to exclude Danielle again.

So, I proposed to Amy that we all make a vegan meal together. Amy understood my desire to include Danielle. She wasn't cruel by nature. In fact, she was quite generous. But she resisted my proposal.

"We're humans, my dear. We're omnivores, just like our primate ancestors. We don't survive well on a diet meant for birds."

"I've shared vegan meals with Danielle. They're delicious and quite satisfying."

"Satisfying? Have you looked at Danielle? She's shrunken, physically and emotionally. She's like a wraith, flitting about the house."

"That has nothing to do with her diet."

"What does it have to do with?"

"She was dumped by her boyfriend. She's lonely. And ... she's just skinny and shy by nature."

"Then she needs to change her nature. She needs some wine, some good cheese ... and some sex."

"Uh ... it would be great if we could all just follow your wine-cheese-sex diet and solve all our problems, but it's a little more complex than that."

"Is it? Or would we just like to make it more complex? Maybe we've just become slaves to our over-active brains."

"What are you saying? That thinking is bad? That we should just go around satisfying our bodily impulses?"

Amy laughed and seemed, for a moment, to contemplate a life of pure bodily impulse. It left an involuntary smile on her lips. Returning from her momentary flight of fantasy, she said,

"We started thinking in order to survive. It helped us outwit our enemies and our prey. Then our brains sort of took over and started outwitting us. We have to give our bodies, our pleasures, equal time."

"And that will solve all our problems?"

"Many of them. Life becomes simpler. More joyous."

Amy's eyes brightened as she said this, as if it had come as some sort of divine revelation. Her face had the gleam of a recent convert, undoubtedly unleashed by her recent liberation from spousal duty. I wondered how long it would last. But I didn't argue with her. After all, I agreed that too much thinking can cause pain. That was the basic tenet of Zen Buddhism. Hedonistic self-indulgence, however, was not recommended by the Buddha, as far as I knew.

I decided to bring this philosophical discussion back to the question at hand.

"There's some truth to what you're saying. But the fact is that Danielle is a vegan. And we all live together. And I don't want her to feel left out of all our joyous meals. It's just too cruel."

Amy looked at me, clearly conflicted. Her convert's passion was being challenged by my appeal to human compassion.

"Okay. I'll make a deal," she replied, slyly. "I'll eat a vegan meal with Danielle. But she has to eat a meal that I make. Ideally, she would have sex afterward, but we'll have to work on that later."

"I don't think she's going to go for it. She's a committed vegan. She told me that animals have emotions, and it's true. They do."

"I'll get pasture-raised meat. I'm all for humane husbandry." Given the situation, I had to laugh at Amy's choice of words.

"What's so funny?"

"Husbandry. 'Humane husbandry.' Is that a Freudian slip? Are you expressing a desire to eat Phil?"

"Ha, ha," she replied dryly.

"Sorry. That was stupid. I'll propose a meal trade with Danielle. But don't hold your breath."

To my surprise, Danielle accepted the proposal. I think she was desperate to avoid exclusion. And she knew instinctively that Amy was a threat to her. My ties to Amy were built on a long-standing friendship. My ties to Danielle were built on flimsier ground—compassion. For her, getting along with Amy was a question of survival.

Danielle wanted to go all out for our Vegan Reconciliation Dinner (which is what I had dubbed the meal in my own mind). Was she hoping to convert Amy to veganism? Perhaps. Or perhaps she thought, more realistically, that she could make a vegan meal that was good enough that Amy would agree to share a vegan meal on a weekly basis. Here was her menu:

- *Poblano peppers, stuffed with sweet potatoes, beans, and corn, covered with a creamed avocado sauce*
- *A mixed green salad with vinaigrette dressing*

- *Roasted fingerling potatoes*
- *Tartelette shells (made with oil instead of butter), filled with a creamy cashew, coconut, and lemon custard*

Amy ate it all with gusto. She complimented Danielle, going so far as to call the meal "great." But when I asked her about it later, Amy wasn't as laudatory. Instead, she shrugged her shoulders and made a face that was meant to convey a so-so judgment.

"I mean, don't get me wrong. For a vegan meal, it was pretty darn good. I was surprised. But I still don't understand the idea of restricting your pleasures when you have access to delicious things like butter and cream and meat. Why? Are we punishing ourselves for being human?"

"No, I don't think it's about self-flagellation. I think it's about being kind to animals … and maybe helping to mitigate climate change."

"I appreciate the sentiment. But … "

"But what?"

"Life is hard enough without purposely making it harder. We're old, Lexi. Can't we just be left in peace to enjoy a few pleasures while we still can?"

Amy's response resonated with me. I did want to be able to enjoy a few remaining pleasures before my aging body stole those pleasures away. But Danielle's veganism also resonated with me. It was up to her generation to try to save the world from the reckless cruelty and avarice that was leading us toward disaster.

And it was up to our generation to support that effort, for the sake of our children and their children. I knew that Amy would have laughed at this notion of saving the world through veganism. She would have seen it as naïve. And I would have agreed with her. It would certainly take more than changing our diet to save the world. It would help, of course. But even if millions of people became vegans, there would be billions who would remain adamant omnivores.

I found myself in the strange, uncomfortable position of agreeing with two opposing worldviews. And those two worldviews were embodied by two women who were living in my house. I decided that I would either have to choose sides or live with the uneasy tension of not choosing sides. Softhearted coward that I am, I decided to choose the latter. I knew, however, that this wishy-washy stance would not prevent the situation from coming to a head.

15

Playmates

AMY WAS DETERMINED TO live out her fantasy of retirement life. At her instigation, we were on our way to see an exhibit of early paintings by Peter Paul Rubens at the San Francisco Legion of Honor museum. As usual, the traffic on the bridge was horrendous, and we had plenty of time to talk.

It had been over a week since Amy started hiding out in my house. And during that time, I had not seen or heard her communicate with Phil. My urge to find out what was going on between them overcame my reticence to interfere.

"So ... have you spoken to Phil?" I asked as nonchalantly as I could.

"A couple of times," Amy replied tersely.

"And? How'd that go?"

"Fine. We were just dealing with some personal business we had to take care of."

"How did Phil sound?"

"Like he usually does ... like he doesn't need any advice because he knows the answer already."

Amy was skirting the issue. I could have acceded to her desire for privacy. But she was using my place as a marital hide-out, and we were best friends. I had a right to know what the hell was going on.

"Okay, what's the deal between you two? Has Phil made any apologies? Asked for forgiveness?"

"Phil?" Amy scoffed. "He doesn't do apologies."

"So, neither of you is budging. You're both being stubborn."

"No, Phil is being stubborn. I'm having a ball."

"So you're punishing him, and ... and just waiting for him to crack.

Is that the plan?"

Amy shrugged her shoulders and was pensive for a moment. Finally, she said, "I'm not sure I'm waiting for anything. I don't want Phil to suffer. But I'm not sure that, even if he were suffering, even if he apologized, that I would go back to him."

I was left speechless for a moment. What was her plan? To divorce Phil? To stay with me forever?

"Amy, you can't say that. You don't just give up on a forty-year marriage, a marriage to a man who has been a good father, who has been faithful, and who … who is a decent person … you don't just give that up on a whim."

"A whim? How can you say that? You think this is easy for me?"

"I don't know. It shouldn't be … but sometimes you act like it."

"It's not … not easy at all. I'm just trying to be honest. And being honest is painful … for both of us. But it's better than lying."

Amy's eyes were tearing up. And I figured I'd done enough damage.

"Okay … I'm sorry. I trust you. I know you're trying to do what's best. Let's just enjoy ourselves."

"Yes, let's."

The Legion of Honor has to have the most beautiful setting of any museum in the world. It's on a forested hill overlooking the Golden Gate Bridge. If you look across the bridge to the other side, you can see the beginning of a wild coastal area preserved by the National Park Service.

The museum itself is stunning. You enter through a spacious, neo-classical courtyard, surrounded by columns. In the center is a bronze cast of Rodin's *Thinker*. The museum appears to be a relatively small, single story building, like the courtyard of a Roman nobleman's house. But when you enter, you realize that it extends back from the façade, and the exhibit area is below the main floor.

After buying our tickets, we went down the stairs, turned and were confronted with a twelve-foot-long spectacle of a painting. It depicted a boar hunt, frozen in time just at the moment when the ferocious boar was about to receive the coup de grâce from a pack of dogs and two semi-clad, spear-wielding, well-muscled men. The poor boar didn't stand a chance. Meanwhile, noblemen dressed in fine attire and riding on horseback pretended to be hunting the boar alongside the dogs and servants, who were doing the actual killing.

"Look how the servants are doing the dangerous, dirty work," I said. "They're the brave ones. And he's put them right in the center of the action. Do you think Rubens was making a statement about class?"

"Are you kidding? Those noblemen, the guys on horseback, were his patrons."

"Yeah, but maybe Rubens was being sneaky."

"Sneaky? Like sending a secret message to the servant class? That would assume that peasants could freely walk into a nobleman's castle to gaze at this painting. Not very likely. They would never have even had a chance to see it."

"Maybe it was a message to the noblemen: Appreciate your loyal and brave servants."

"Nice idea. But I think Rubens featured the servants because they make for a more dramatic, dynamic centerpiece. I really don't think he had any Marxist tendencies. He was enjoying his prestige too much, and the life that went with it. He was known as 'the prince of painters and the painter of princes.'"

"Yeah, I suppose you're right. But he certainly demonstrated an appreciation for the humanity of the servants. He portrayed them with strength, bravery—a certain nobility of their own."

Amy sniffed at my analysis. "He liked their flesh," she said, succinctly undercutting my argument.

I looked around the room at the grand, brightly colored paintings. They were all based on religious or mythical themes, subjects that, I assume, were considered acceptable at the time. But they were anything but solemn. "The Raising of the Cross," for instance, was a huge, dynamic painting with fleshy bodies everywhere—Jesus being lifted on the cross by six muscular men, angels floating in the upper corner, women and babies crying below, and soldiers in the distance dragging another poor soul to be crucified. It was a crazy depiction of violence and despair.

"Rubens was all about entertainment. He was a showman," Amy commented.

"Yes, I can see that. In a world without movies or TV, this must've been as close as they got to something like today's special effects extravaganzas."

We moved on to another large-scale painting of David surrounded by lions. A short, distinguished-looking, older man with a carefully trimmed white goatee walked up next to us to admire the painting.

"Look at the figure of David, that flesh ... you could touch it," he said with a faint European accent.

I wondered if he wanted to touch David's flesh. He was wearing a suit, which is highly unusual. In the Bay Area, dressing up for a man meant wearing a nice pair of jeans and a pressed shirt. Who would wear a suit to a museum on a weekday afternoon?

"Yes, it's superbly rendered," Amy said, moving a little closer to the mysterious gentleman.

"You can see the technique he developed ... the technique he used later for the female figures he is famous for."

"Right ... those rubenesque women."

"Yes, those lovely, rubenesque women," he said with a wistful sigh. "I like that in a woman."

I noticed that he glanced down at Amy's full-figured torso.

Apparently, the mysterious gentleman was more interested in touching a voluptuous woman than touching David. Amy blushed a little, which was extremely rare.

"It's so nice to meet a man who appreciates a full figure," Amy said, smiling.

"Not all men want ... what do you call it? A bean pole?"

It turned out the dapper gentleman was named Andrea, which in Italy (I learned later) is actually a common name for a man. He worked in the food import/export business. As we moved through the exhibit, he tagged along with us, commenting on the color and sensuality of the paintings. Amy encouraged him with nods of appreciation. I felt she was dumbing down her usual perceptive, historically based criticism. I felt left out of the conversation.

Before we left, Andrea handed Amy his card and said, "I hope we can see each other again."

Amy smiled and said, "Forse," which is Italian for "perhaps." I expected her to laugh and toss the card in the trash on our way out.

Instead, she dropped the card into her purse. I don't consider myself to be a prude. But I have to admit, I didn't approve of Amy's behavior. After my first husband, Greg, betrayed my trust, I put great value on faithfulness and loyalty. And Amy was, after all, still married to Phil.

On the drive home, against my better judgment, I was compelled to stick my nose in Amy's business.

"You're not going to contact that little peacock of a man, are you?"

I immediately regretted my choice of words. I was letting my disapproval show, and perhaps a bit of jealousy.

"Andrea? I don't know. We'll see."

"I get that it's fun to flirt. But really ... you're not seriously considering ... "

"What?"

" Having an affair?"

Amy sighed. I couldn't tell if it was a sigh of disapproval (disapproval of my prudish meddling) or a sigh of disappointment (the disappointment of someone who realizes that she is not in a position to carry out her little fantasy).

After a moment of reflection, Amy said, "Maybe I'm being selfish. I don't know. But I've never been selfish in my life before, and maybe I want to try it out, see what it feels like."

I involuntarily pursed my lips in disapproval.

Amy continued, "How many men have flirted with you in the last twenty years?"

"None, but that's because I'm not sending out the flirty vibe. And ... because men don't flirt with older women."

"Well, apparently, European men do. They have a different attitude toward age. Une femme d'un certain age can still be appealing, sexy, experienced."

I was getting impatient with Amy. Where was her usual piercing intelligence? Where was her caustic cynicism? Where was her perspective?

"Fine," I said. "Keep the card. You can decide to contact Andrea after you've sorted things out with Phil."

"Yes, mother, I'll be a good girl."

Amy was mocking me, but I suspected that she had accepted my advice.

We rode in silence for a while. Then she said, "Phil … Andrea … which name is more attractive? Which name in a novel would portend love and adventure?"

"Phil," I said to spite her.

16

Tension

I WAS DOING A little dusting around the living room when I saw it. On the side table, next to the armchair where Amy habitually sat to talk on the phone, was the business card Andrea had slipped her. I remembered walking into the living room the night before and catching Amy on the phone, laughing with someone. As soon as she saw me enter, she got up and gestured magnanimously toward the chair, as if she were offering me the seat. But her departure was so abrupt, it was clear that what she really wanted was privacy.

One could reasonably assume that she was talking to Andrea, the Italian Lothario. It felt like a betrayal. Hadn't she promised to be "a good girl" and not contact Andrea? And why was she sneaking around like a teenager trying to hide that fact from me? One great foundation of our relationship was our utter honesty with each other. So, in a sense, it was a double betrayal—a broken promise on one hand, and dishonest subterfuge on the other.

Had I somehow brought on this betrayal? Admittedly, I had been indignant and moralistic, like a disapproving mother. Was it any wonder that Amy was reacting like a teenager?

I could have left Andrea's business card on the table and pretended that I hadn't seen it. That would be a way to avoid the whole discussion. Instead, I picked it up and marched into the kitchen where Amy was typing on her laptop.

"Here," I said, handing her the card. "You left this in the living room last night."

Amy looked up at me and studied my face. I tried to maintain a look of perfect non-judgment, but I suspect I might have been trying too hard. I could feel my jaw clenching, and my lips narrowing in disapproval.

Amy took the card and coolly said, "Thanks."

She placed the card, face up, next to her on the table, as if to demonstrate how unconcerned she was about my discovery. As I turned to leave, she called me back.

"Lexi?"

"Yes?"

"I won't be having dinner here tonight."

"Okay."

"I'm going out."

I nodded and left the room. My suspicions were confirmed. She plotted this dinner behind my back. She could've at least made a full confession. She could have said, "I'm going out to dinner with Andrea. I know you don't approve, but … " and followed that with an honest defense of her action. Instead, she chose to remain silent. Was it her way of punishing me for my disapproval? Was she claiming her independence, like some rebellious adolescent? Or was she simply intimidated by the strength of my disapproval? In any case, the whole thing was ridiculous and avoidable. After all, we both knew what was going on, and we both knew that the other knew.

That evening, around dinner time, Amy walked through the kitchen wearing a drop-waist dress that flattered her full figure. Around her neck, she wore a yellow scarf with an astrological pattern on it. Very French. Lipstick and a touch of eyeliner completed the look. I had to admit that she looked good. Normally, I would have complimented her. Instead, I said, "Have fun!"

Why that came out of my mouth, I don't know. I suppose it was a passive aggressive way of saying, "You're acting like a teenager, so I'm going to act like your mom." It was doubtful that Amy got the message. Or she pretended not to.

She simply replied, "I intend to." With that, she left on her date, or whatever it was. I moped around the house, picking at my dinner, trying to read my book, finally distracting myself with TV. Mostly, I continued a contentious inner dialogue:

Me: She's an adult. She can do whatever she wants. It's not your place to stop her.

Other me: But if she's an adult, why isn't she acting like one? What she is doing is thoughtless, impulsive and could have lasting effects on her marriage. And, yes, she is still married, even if she prefers to ignore that fact. Am I being a good friend if I let her carry out this ill-advised escapade? Should I condone adultery?

Me: "Adultery" what an archaic word. It's so moralistic. Maybe a little fling will be good for Amy. Maybe it's just what she needs to get a new perspective on her relationship with Phil. He doesn't need to know about it. I certainly would never tell him.

Other me: But a relationship based on secrets is not a relationship built on a strong foundation. I know that from experience.

I argued with myself like that throughout the evening. My normal bedtime was around 10:30 pm. But I found myself waiting up for Amy to return. Around 11 pm, Amy walked in the door. She stopped and looked at me. I must have had a scowl on my face.

"Why the look, Mom? I'm home before curfew," Amy said, giggling guiltily.

She had clearly been drinking. But in her inebriated state, she broke the tension between us. She spoke the unspoken. I had to laugh.

"How was Andrea?"

"Kind of fun. Kind of a jerk."

"Sit down and tell me."

Amy sprawled across the couch dramatically.

"He took me to this Italian place in North Beach. Apparently, his brother-in-law's niece is married to the guy who owns it. Or something like that. I couldn't keep it straight."

"Was it good?"

"Yes. Basic Italian. Very authentic."

"And Andrea?"

"He regaled me with stories about Milan, his family … his export business. It sounds more boring than it was. He's a good storyteller. But it was tiresome after a while. He never asked about me."

"Maybe he was just being polite … discreet."

"Or maybe he didn't want to find out too much, like how I was married with two grown kids."

"You didn't tell him?"

"What would be the point of that?"

"And him … is he married?"

"I have no idea. We weren't there to share the mundane aspects of our lives."

"What were you there for?"

"Seduction."

"Did he? Did he try to seduce you?"

"With his words." Amy let out a laugh, then looked at me slyly. "You want to know if his words had the intended effect."

"Did they?"

Amy sighed. "No. Sadly, we never did anything."

"Are you going to see him again?"

"I doubt it. He's going back to Italy on Tuesday. He invited me to look him up the next time I'm in Milano," Amy said, dismissing the notion with a laugh. Yet a little wistful smile lingered on her face.

"Why did you do it?"

"I don't know … for fun? Just to see what it would feel like to have someone try to seduce me."

"And what did it feel like?"

"It felt … a little dangerous … a little silly … like a game … a game where winning was losing. As it turned out, no one won."

"You got nothing out of it?"

"An unfulfilling experience."

"You know I felt betrayed."

"That's ridiculous!"

"You promised me you wouldn't see him."

"I did not. I didn't promise anything."

"You said you'd be a good girl."

"I was a good girl … I say now with some regret. I kept hearing your disapproving little voice in my head. You can be very judgmental."

"I didn't stop you."

"You couldn't have."

"I wouldn't have, even if I could. That voice was your own guilt talking."

"Yes, maybe … and I'm trying hard to get rid of that guilt. Can't we all just enjoy ourselves for once? What really is stopping us? How are we hurting anyone? Wouldn't we all be happier and make each other happier if we just relaxed and enjoyed ourselves? It shouldn't have to be so damn complicated."

Amy's little rant was intended to rationalize her actions, but there was something about her plea for greater enjoyment that resonated with me. Later in bed that night, I pondered whether I was on the side of morality, or if I was just being a "bourgeoise," as Amy would put it. There's an old philosophical question: *If a tree falls in the forest, and no one is there to hear it, is there a sound? Here's my version: If someone acts against society's moral dictates, but no one is hurt by it; is it immoral?*

If Amy had slept with Andrea without ever telling Phil, was there some harm in the act? It would be a betrayal, but only in some ideal, platonic sense. Or would it? Can a human act be abstracted like that, without repercussions, psychological or otherwise? Something would have changed if Amy had acted on her impulse—in her and between her and Phil—even if a word of it was never spoken.

Despite Amy's desire to "enjoy" without complications, we humans are complicated. The force fields that bind us are delicate and subject to disturbance. Amy had broken my trust when she snuck off with Andrea. It was a short-lived betrayal, and we patched things up. But I learned that she was capable of secrecy. I could not undo that knowledge. That constituted a small disturbance in the force field that bound us together. Would it have a ripple effect that would magnify over time?

For several days after the Andrea incident, there was tension in the air. I had no residual hard feelings. As far as I was concerned, we were back to being the best of friends. But, then, I had won in a sense. "Won" is not the right word. I had imposed my sense of right and wrong. It was my "little voice" that had prevented Amy from following through to the logical conclusion of the "seduction." I sensed that Amy resented me.

She was acting slightly annoyed for no particular reason. Once we both arrived at the bathroom simultaneously. Amy let out a sigh of frustration and made a dramatic show of inviting me to go first. Later that night, when we were getting ready for bed, I insisted that Amy use the bathroom before me. When it was my turn, I noticed that Amy had pushed my lipstick collection to the corner of the shelf to make room for her things. It was petty, unimportant, but it angered me. I decided to let it slide. In raising Tasha, I learned that it was often better to let things slide. Confrontation would have played into her hands. Time was on my side.

The problem was that Amy's chafing at my moral control spilled over to Danielle. One day, when Amy went to the utility room to wash her clothes, she found Danielle's wet clothes still in the washing machine. She flew into a mini-rage.

"What the hell! Danielle!" she yelled.

Danielle, who was working on her jewelry in the room next door, trotted over to Amy.

"What's wrong?"

"You can't just leave your shit in there. Are you actually dealing with your clothes or not?"

"Yes, I'm washing my clothes. Sorry. I'll put it in the dryer. Then you can use the washer."

Danielle knelt down to remove her clothes from the washer.

"Never mind. Whatever. I'll just come back later."

Amy picked up her dirty clothes bag and started to leave.

Then she turned back.

"You know what, Danielle?"

Danielle looked up at Amy, expectantly.

"Never mind ... it's just ... I mean, are you happy? Are you happy with your life?"

"I don't know ... kind of ... "

"I mean, you're living like a nun ... eating squirrel food, and ... do you see people? Are you sleeping with anyone?"

"Not at the moment." Danielle stood up and faced Amy. "Are you?"

"Ha! No ... but, I'm not thirty years old. And I have a husband who would be happy to fuck me any time I let him."

Danielle looked away. "Good for you."

"Sorry ... this isn't a contest. I was just ... I was truly just wondering if you were happy. If there was something I could do to help."

"I don't need any help. I'm happy making my jewelry. I'm happy eating my squirrel food. I just want to do my thing … and get along."

"Okay … then don't leave your shit in the washer."

"I didn't mean to …"

"I'm joking! It's me. I'm kind of a little on edge these days. Just ignore me."

"That's hard to do."

"Yes, I guess it is," Amy said with a laugh. "It's better to not be ignored. Don't let yourself be ignored. That's my piece of advice."

"Okay, thanks for the advice. I need to get back to my work."

"Show me what you're working on."

Danielle led Amy into her jewelry studio. She picked up an unfinished, bronze-colored necklace.

"This is a commission. The woman wanted something Egyptian, something Cleopatra might wear. It's not my normal style at all. You think it's too much?"

"Not for the right woman. I'd wear that … with the right dress … to the right event."

"Yeah, I could see you wearing it."

"So could you. You could wear it. It's all in your attitude."

"I don't want to have that attitude. I don't want to be Cleopatra. I'd feel like I was in a Halloween costume."

"Everything is a costume, my dear. Every time we get dressed in the morning, we're putting on a costume. Might as well make the most of it."

Danielle smiled at Amy's apercu. The two of them had connected. And Amy was determined to make the most of it.

17

Seduction

"I'm not making Italian. I hate Italian food!" Amy declared.

"How can you say that? You just went out to an Italian place."

"That wasn't my choice. Anyway, it's not that I hate it. It's just that it's such a ridiculous trend. There have to be twenty Italian restaurants for every French restaurant. And French cuisine is richer, more varied, more sensual ... more sexy. It doesn't make any sense."

"I think it might be because Italian food is less expensive, and there was that whole Mediterranean diet thing. Supposed to be good for you."

"Pfew!" Amy replied. "Pleasure is good for you. You want to live a long time? Eat what you enjoy. That's the secret to longevity."

"There's probably some truth to that," I admitted.

"Pasta!" Amy exclaimed with disgust and a hint of victory, as if she had just plunged her épée into the heart of her enemy.

"Okay, so it's going to be French. But you're not planning to make like a steak frites or something, are you?"

"Why not?"

"You can't do that to a vegan. It's too ... carnivore-ish. And she just agreed to this deal, this meal exchange, because she doesn't want to alienate you."

Amy sighed. "Okay, fine ... we'll ease her into sensual eating."

Amy threw herself into her plan of gustatory seduction. She spent hours shopping and preparing. I tried to help, but Amy shooed me away. When the time came, Danielle was summoned from her workshop into the living room where a flute of Crémant was waiting for her. (Crémant, Burgundy's answer to Champagne, is cheaper and just as good as Champagne, at least to my untrained palette.) Then Amy brought out a tray of cheese gougères—little savory, puff pastries made with a mixture of French cheeses. I noticed that scrawny, little Danielle ate three of them, and didn't refuse when Amy refilled her glass.

The wine loosened Danielle's tongue. She started telling us about an older man, one of her jewelry clients, who wanted to take her out to a fancy French restaurant. To weasel out of the invitation, she told him that she was a strict vegan. Undaunted, he told her that he would find a vegan restaurant and get back to her. Then he put his arm around her and forced a kiss on her mouth.

"Blech!" Danielle interjected. She held up her third, half-eaten gougère. "But if I could've eaten these things, I might've gone with him," she added with a tipsy laugh.

"Would you have slept with him?" Amy asked.

"Ew! Of course not. I don't know, though. Maybe now ... since Austin ... I miss it." She let out a devilish little wink of a laugh.

"Good!" Amy exclaimed. "Good for you! Appetite, any kind of appetite, is a sign of health!" Amy raised her glass. "To appetite!"

We all clinked our glasses. Danielle laughed and spilled some of her wine. "Uh oh," she said and laughed again.

Amy quickly refilled her glass, while I used my napkin to wipe up the spill.

"All good," I said, stupidly, as if anyone else cared. I finished my second glass of Crémant and felt a buzz that was making me giddy. Danielle was finishing her third glass. Her eyes were slightly unfocused. And she had accidentally dislodged a strand of hair while gesticulating to emphasize a point. It now stood out at a forty-five-degree angle from her head. Had I been sober, I would have mentioned it to her. Instead, I simply stared at it, amused. She's a messy drunk, I thought.

Meanwhile, without us even noticing, Amy was filling our glasses from a bottle of white Bordeaux. She was the only one who seemed to be handling her alcohol well. After she had gotten us well marinated in alcohol, Amy brought out the main dish, sole meuniere, with a side of green beans smothered in butter. The sole had been sautéed in butter. Amy proclaimed that butter was the secret to French cuisine. They had plenty of cows and plenty of butter. It was inevitable that the French would discover that everything tastes better soaked in butter.

"Wow!" we exclaimed, when we saw the perfectly browned fish filets.

"Stop! It's nothing."

It was not nothing. I had never seen Danielle eat with such gusto. It was if she had been starving herself. And maybe she was starved, starved of pleasure and starved of affection. As the wine diminished, so did our inhibitions. Amy started by confessing that she used sex as a kind of weapon with Phil. Her level of participation in sex acts was in direct proportion to how nice or generous he had been. And she would withhold sex altogether if he was bad.

"You make it sound like a dog training technique," I said.

"Well, yes, and that's entirely appropriate."

"You mean, you think men are dogs?" Danielle prompted, drunkenly.

"Not all of them," I said, somehow feeling defensive about my dear Lawrence.

"Oh, come on! I can't be the only woman who does that. Lexi, tell me you never used sex to train your husband."

"Not consciously. But if I went to bed resentful, I would use the classic too-exhausted excuse."

"Same thing. Dog training. What about you, Danielle?"

"I never did that. Honestly. We enjoyed … we enjoyed each other too much … we did, anyway, until he met that … " Danielle's voice trailed off.

"Oh, dear. You must miss it," Amy said, sympathetically. She got up, put her arm around Danielle, and gave her a kiss on the mouth. "Don't worry, sweetheart. We'll find you a replacement."

Danielle didn't seem to mind this aggressive display of affection. In fact, she seemed quite moved. I wondered what Danielle would think in the morning when she was sober. I wondered what I would think.

I know Amy's insistence on pleasure was offered out of generosity. But she had coerced a vegan to break her vows. And she had tempted me, a modest drinker, into inebriation. It felt as if we had been initiated into some kind of Dionysian cult. Mind you, I had enjoyed the experience. But was Amy's campaign of indulgence leading us toward anything good? Was it a path to happiness? Or was it all just a simulacrum of happiness? I wondered what a Zen master would say? I had certainly heard stories about drunken monks.

The next day, I looked up the question of drinking and monks. Apparently, Lao-Tzu, the author of the Tao-Te-Ching, had this to say on the subject: *One should not take any alcoholic drinks, unless he has to take some to cure his illness, to regale the guests with a feast, or to conduct religious ceremonies.* Certainly, Amy was regaling her guests, and she was attempting to cure Danielle's illness, and, in some way, she may have seen it as a kind of religious initiation. Lao-Tzu was not doctrinaire. He understood the complexity of the human soul. He must have understood that denial can be as poisonous as overindulgence.

When I thought about our drunken meal together, it made me smile. I understood that indulgence was not a path to happiness. But what was abstinence, or even moderation, without a bit of indulgence? One defines the other. One makes the other possible. This is the paradox we live with.

I also noticed a change in the relationship between Amy and Danielle. Amy's crusade to seduce Danielle into the world of sensuality may have been misdirected, but it was a form of attention, a display of affection. And Danielle craved both attention and affection. Despite the repelling force of their convictions, Danielle was drawn into Amy's orbit.

18

Judgment

"Is Danielle there?" Tasha asked.

"No."

"Good. Then I'll be over in a few."

Tasha was coming over to pick up a large package she had had delivered to the house. Receiving packages at her apartment building in a marginal (although recently gentrifying) area of Oakland was risky. So, she kept her childhood home as her mailing address. The package deliveries were our connection, a tenuous chord that attached our lives.

The package turned out to be household supplies—paper towels, toilet paper, dish soap, laundry detergent—things one would ordinarily buy in a store. Tasha assured me, however, that ordering these items online was much cheaper.

In normal times, I cherished these moments when Tasha would stop by to pick up packages. It gave us a chance to visit and catch up. Today, however, there was tension in the air.

Tasha opened the box to confirm the contents and brusquely said, "Okay, bye, Mom."

"Wait a minute. Sit down."

"I've got things to do. My house is a mess, and I only have time on weekends."

"You can spare a few minutes."

Tasha sighed and sat down on the couch. "Is Amy here?"

"Not at the moment."

"What's the deal? Is she planning to stay long?"

"I don't know. She seems reluctant to come to terms with Phil. I think she's punishing him."

"For what?"

"He said something mean. And he's not been a good playmate."

"Playmate? Seriously? What does that mean?"

"Well, Amy retired and she wants to have fun, but Phil refused to retire with her. And, anyway, they don't enjoy the same things. I think maybe Amy is realizing how incompatible they are. When they were both busy with their work and kids and everything, it wasn't that big a deal. Now she seems to be questioning their whole relationship. It's been hard for her."

"Hmm … haven't they been married for like a zillion years? Isn't it a little late to be questioning whether she married an asshole?"

"But he's not an asshole … well, maybe just a little bit. But he's been a good husband, a good father. So that's the thing. That's what makes it hard."

Tasha shrugged, unconvinced. I think she hadn't yet come to understand that having a lasting relationship inevitably means compromise. It means accepting that your partner will never be perfect, will never live up to all your expectations. It was the same with friends. Tasha simply dropped friends when they disappointed her. She would "unfriend" them. I wondered if my divorce had anything to do with her attitude. I had, after all, "unfriended" my ex-husband, Tasha's father.

In the past, I would counsel Tasha not to drop friends, but instead just demote them, place them a couple of notches down on the friend list. Other than Greg, that's what I have done in my life. And, sad to say, many of my friends have been demoted. But they are still friends.

I was about to restate my thoughts about relationships, but Tasha had already moved on to another topic, which in her mind was more pressing.

"This situation you're in, with Danielle freeloading and taking over half the house and Amy staying here for who knows how long … don't you think that's a little crazy? I mean, who else are you going to let stay in your house? Are you, like, planning to run a homeless shelter?"

"No. Amy is my best friend and I'm helping her out, giving her support. It's a tough time for her. And Danielle … that's just a question of kindness. She was desperate, and she needed help … and, remember, she was a friend of yours. And you suggested it."

"I never suggested that she move in with you. You let her set up her fucking workshop here!"

"Yes, so she can make enough money to move out."

"Why is that your problem?"

"It's not my problem. But she was here in my house, and she needed help. So, I helped. Being kind is supposed to be a good thing."

I was thinking about the Zen monk who adopted the child after being falsely accused of being the father. He had accepted what fate, or Karma, had brought him. But I didn't think I could explain that to Tasha, not in the short time we had. And I was fairly certain that Tasha's heightened sense of justice would have rejected the spirit of the story. After all, the child wasn't his. Why would he have to accept responsibility for it? That would be unfair. And Tasha was all about fairness.

"So how's all this kindness working out for you?"

"Fine. I'm actually enjoying it. I've become Amy's new playmate. And Danielle ... she's been a good guest. She's accommodating. And she's a nice person. She's a little shy, but I'm getting to know her."

"If you think she's shy, you don't know her. She can be a bossy bitch."

This revelation, rather than making me dislike Danielle (which I think was Tasha's aim) simply intrigued me.

"Why do you say that?"

"Well ... she took over the house, didn't she!"

"Because I let her."

"And ... and she wanted me to, like, use my contacts to help sell her jewelry."

"She was desperate. She needed money. Why wouldn't you help?"

"Okay ... whatever. She's obviously manipulated you with her helpless little girl act."

"She offered to pay rent. But I told her to save her money so she could find a place of her own."

"Why don't I move in and save money?"

"Because we both know that you'd be unhappy living here. We have ... different habits."

"Doesn't Danielle have different habits?"

"Yes, she's a vegan. But otherwise she's very quiet and careful not to disrupt my routines. Besides, you act like she's planning to live here permanently. She's not. She's going to move on."

"You hope."

"I think we'll both know when it's time."

"You're like enjoying this whole thing, aren't you?"

"It hasn't been too unpleasant yet, although there's definitely a clash of personalities between Amy and Danielle."

"Yes, Amy's actually a nice person." Tasha picked up the laundry detergent from her box and studied it. "Is this what I ordered?" Then she put it back in the box and turned to me. "What's it like living with just women?"

"You mean, without men? In some ways it's much easier. The demands are ... smaller. There's a certain tacit understanding about what our needs are. So that reduces the tension ... not that there's no tension. There's always going to be some tension when you're living with someone. But it's not like there's any competition between us, Amy and me. We're too old for that. I don't know, you can't really make any generalizations. Every person, every woman, is different."

"Hmm. Maybe that's the way to go. Just live with women."

"Maybe. But men have a way of haunting you."

"Haunting you? How?"

"Well, memories in my case ... and in Danielle's case too. And for Amy, there's this living presence lurking in the background that eventually has to be dealt with."

"Yes, lurking men. That's a problem." Tasha laughed a little. "You know that Dad separated from Melissa?"

"No, I didn't know that. We don't talk much ... your father and I."

"Yeah, I think they're getting divorced. Then he'll be free to lurk."

"He can lurk wherever he wants, as long as it's not around here. Do you see him much?"

"No, but ... I don't know ... recently he's starting to call. He wanted to have lunch. I think he's lonely."

I suddenly felt a strange emotion, pity for Greg. He had been a bachelor for a number of years after our divorce. Then he married Melissa. I thought he might make it work this second time, just as I had with Lawrence. Now he was alone again at the age of sixty-five. That, I suppose, is why I felt sympathy. I knew what it was like to be old and alone. But I had my women. Who did Greg have? I brushed away the thought. He was just another man haunting my memories. Whatever loneliness he was feeling was undoubtedly his fault. I didn't want to assume any responsibility for his situation, nor feel any empathy. Yet I did. As shredded as our relationship was, there was some bond, however tenuous, that kept him from vanishing entirely from my life. He was lurking still, in ways I didn't completely understand.

19

Confusion

My talk with Tasha left me confused. What exactly was I doing living with these two women? I was enjoying their company. And I was certainly eating better. But how long could that last? The situation was so tenuous. Amy still had to resolve the Phil question. And Danielle had her life to live, love to find. She couldn't hide out at my place forever. Then there was a pinch of guilt thrown into the stew of emotion. Should I have invited Tasha to live with me? Did she mention that in a pique of jealousy? Or was she serious? What exactly did I want?

I tried to convince myself to accept the confusion. After all, only the dull live without doubt. That was the whole concept behind the Dunning-Kruger syndrome, the idea behind Austin's band name, Stupid Genius. Intelligent persons would never describe themselves as a genius. They are too aware of what they don't know. And confusion is a normal state for anyone who thinks and feels. That line of reasoning, at any rate, was how I consoled myself. On the other hand, at my age, hadn't I earned the right to a bit of certainty? Apparently not. What I had earned was the ability to accept a lack of certainty. And that ability proved important because my confusion was about to grow.

One evening after dinner, Danielle asked if she could talk to me. The tentative way she approached me indicated that this was not going to be a casual conversation. We went into the living room where all important discussions took place.

"So ... I was wondering if it would be possible for me to have someone stay with me for a few days."

I had considered the possibility that Danielle, being a healthy, young woman, might want to have someone sleep with her at the house. And I was prepared to agree to that arrangement. But asking if someone could stay in the house for an extended period of time was not something I had ever considered.

"And who is this 'someone'?"

"A friend … from college. He's here visiting … kind of looking for work. He used to live here, and he's thinking of moving back."

This was sounding frighteningly familiar. Moving back here … looking for work … that was Danielle's situation. And she ended up living with me. Was Tasha right? Was I inadvertently starting a homeless shelter for unhappy millennials?

"How well do you know this young man?"

"Really well. We used to be … well, he was my boyfriend for a while. He's really nice."

On the one hand, I wanted to support Danielle. If this was an opportunity for her to find love, to establish a healthy relationship, I wanted to give her that chance. But who was this guy? Should I permit him to stay in my house, to invade my little queendom? What were his circumstances? Was he so broke he couldn't afford to rent a room of his own? And, more importantly, was he taking advantage of Danielle? I didn't want her heart to be broken again.

"Okay, I'm going to be blunt with you. And I want you to be honest. Is this guy here just to freeload and take advantage of you? Or is this possibly the start of a real relationship?"

"I think … it might be the start of a relationship."

"You 'think?' Has he indicated an interest in restarting a relationship with you?"

"Yes. He told me he missed me, and he's been thinking about me."

"And you? Are you interested in him?"

I realized at this point that I was starting to act like an overbearing mother interrogating her daughter, instead of a landlord questioning her adult tenant. But I didn't care. Someone had to take care of Danielle. And, despite her chronological age, she was still essentially a young adult.

"Yes, I guess. I mean, he's very nice, but … I don't know. At the time, I thought he was kind of boring. But he was always so kind to me. And he cried when I left and went to New York."

I was beginning to like this hapless, sensitive man. At least, he didn't seem like the type of man who would run off with a pole dancer.

"Does he have a job?"

"Yes, he's a journalist, sort of. That's what he wants to do, anyway. Right now, he works as a writer for a non-profit. They do economic analysis. But they're progressive."

"Is he vegan?"

"Not yet."

I had to smile at her response. Clearly, Danielle had the intention to give this relationship a try. And who was I to prevent that?

"Yes, of course, he can stay for a few days. But, I'm warning you, this cannot be a permanent situation. Three days, and that's it. Out he goes!"

After finally making a decision, my stomach churned with indecision. New questions popped into my head. If this guy has a job, why isn't he renting his own room, a place where he and Danielle could meet and make love in private? I didn't even know his name. What was I getting myself into? I prided myself on being thoughtful, on weighing all sides of a question before deciding, but in reality I often just acquiesced to people's demands. I liked to think I was just being kind, but I was also being cowardly. I didn't want to risk appearing unkind.

Amy walked in the door. Her sweater was hanging off one shoulder, and she was clutching her purse to her chest, as if to ward off a flying object aimed at her heart.

"You okay?"

"Fine," she replied in a tense way that wasn't very convincing.

"Well, I have a little news. Kind of good news, and not so good news," I announced.

Amy just stared at me impatiently. Normally, she would lean into a conversation starter like that one.

"So … the good news," I said. "Danielle has a potential suitor, a young man she used to date in college."

"And? The not so good news?"

"He's going to be staying with her, here, for a few days."

"Okay," Amy said, seemingly unconcerned with the news I had just delivered. "I need to go rest a little."

She got up and headed toward the bedroom. I decided not to disturb her.

That evening it was my turn to cook. We had worked out a schedule where Danielle would make a vegan meal for all of us once a week. Amy would cook a French-influenced meal (with no red meat) once a week. And I would cook a meal that was primarily vegan, but had an animal protein for those who wanted it. (How typical of me to be the compromiser.) The rest of the week, we were free to make our own arrangements.

After several weeks of this plan, neither Amy nor Danielle succeeded in converting the other to their dietary regime, or more aptly, their dietary philosophy. Pleasure versus ethics. Joie de vivre versus the mindful life. It wasn't that simple, of course. Amy would undoubtedly argue that pleasure with artfulness and in moderation was mindful. That was the epicurean creed. Danielle, on the other hand, would argue that her vegan regime was full of pleasure, all the more enhanced by the fact that it was guiltless. That was why I had such a hard time deciding between them. I wanted both.

That night in bed, just before we went to sleep, Amy suddenly let out a stifled sob. Her face was turned away from me, so I couldn't read her emotions. I rolled over toward her and placed my hand on her shoulder.

"What's going on? Talk to me."

Amy rolled back toward me, wiping away a tear. "Nothing, really. It's not even worth talking about."

"Of course it's worth talking about."

Amy rolled on her back and stared up at the ceiling for a moment. She took a deep breath, as if she were preparing to do something daring.

"I met with Phil today. He asked me to meet him. He was very insistent."

"So? What'd he say?"

"Not much. He told me how great things were going for him at work … and how he was enjoying being able to watch a football game uninterrupted. He thought he was being funny, I guess. Then he told me I was being childish, 'throwing a tantrum' were the words he used."

"So, no apologies? Nothing about how much he misses you?"

"No, he just blamed me."

"What did you say? How did you handle it?"

"I told him he hurt me, and I was starting to see our relationship in a different light. How we never really understood each other, not deeply. I told him I wasn't sure we could ever live together again."

"How did he react to that?"

"He said, ok, if that's how you feel and got up and left." Amy turned back toward me with tears in her eyes. "I didn't want to say those things. He just made me so angry! He can be such a stubborn ass! Now I think I've blown it."

"No, you haven't blown it." I pulled Amy toward me and hugged her close. "Yes, he's being stubborn. It might take a little while. He'll come around, but you'll need to help him. You have to give him an opening."

"An opening?"

"Yes, one of you has to be willing to show some vulnerability, be willing to say I love you."

"But I don't know if I do."

"Of course not, not right now. You're too angry."

Amy pulled me close again and kissed me on the mouth. "I love you."

She started caressing my body tenderly. "I love you too," I said and started to pull away. Amy held onto to me and gave me another kiss on the mouth, longer than the first. This time I pushed myself away.

"It's easy to love me. We haven't been married for forty years."

I don't know why I said that, maybe to pull Amy away from her momentary impulse, to force her to put the situation in perspective.

"I've known you almost as long as I've known Phil," she said.

"Yes, men seem to always get in the way. But we so desperately let them."

My statement left Amy quiet for the moment. Perhaps she was puzzled. I implied a level of desperation on her part that she had not been willing to admit. And I implied that that desperation was somehow willed.

I rolled back to my side of the bed and said, "Let's sleep now and talk in the morning."

I was stalling for time. I knew that morning would only bring our state of confusion into greater focus, not resolve it.

20

Re-evaluation

WHEN I WOKE UP the next morning, I had a perplexing phrase on my lips: *Nature abhors a vacuum.* The words seemed to have arisen from a dream, although I had no memory of that dream. Yet the phrase seemed somehow important.

I got up quietly and left Amy still asleep next to me. Even with earplugs, I heard her snoring especially loud during the night. At one point, she woke me up with a gasping sound. I was half asleep, but I believe she got up and then came back to bed. This morning, I didn't want to disturb her.

I sat down alone in the kitchen with my coffee and toast. What was happening? Not long ago I was a widow attempting to navigate a new life. I was coming to terms with being alone. And I think I was succeeding. It was a process, but I was making friends with myself. And that self was encouraging me to be brave, to enjoy what I could in life, to find peace, and to seek a new meaning in my solitude. Now, that solitude had been invaded.

When Amy kissed me the night before and told me she loved me, what exactly were her intentions? Was she just expressing tenderness toward a close friend? Or did she have something else in mind? Was she actually thinking of staying with me permanently? As what? A lodger? A partner? A lover?

Suddenly it struck me. *Nature abhors a vacuum.* I was in the process of filling my vacuum. Amy was replacing my husband. Danielle was replacing my daughter. And her new boyfriend ... was he replacing my son? Was I trying to recreate the family I lost?

On the one hand, all the pieces fit together, but the whole notion seemed absurd. I was just being kind. I was being generous. And fate had thrown me into this situation. Or had it? Had I somehow invited this to happen? Had I been the unconscious puppet master drawing this ersatz family together? I was beginning to doubt my own motivations.

Late that afternoon, when I was leaving my tutoring assignment, I got a call. It was Phil. My first reaction was fear. What does he want? What can I say to him without betraying Amy? I didn't want to get in the middle of their marital issues. It wasn't my place.

With my heart racing, I answered the phone. Phil's voice was unusually gentle. He asked how I was, how the kids were. And he asked if I would be willing to talk with him, privately, without telling Amy. Against my better judgment, I said yes. It was something in the way he asked. I had never heard Phil sound so vulnerable. For the first time, I sensed how much he must have suffered from this separation.

I sat waiting for Phil at the café where Amy and I met frequently, the one with the Eastern European pastries. It was a stupid choice. Phil had asked where I wanted to meet. I was flustered, and I offered the first place that came to mind. Or maybe I was just craving a slice of their poppy-seed walnut cake. Either way, it felt like a kind of betrayal. Not only was I meeting Amy's husband secretly, but I was doing it in one of our favorite spots.

Thoughts raced through my mind. What could I say to Phil without meddling? Without breaking Amy's trust? Was there anything I could do or say that would actually make things better? I didn't even know what Amy really wanted. Did she want to reconcile? Or was their relationship truly over? If I encouraged Phil, would I just be prolonging the agony of their breakup?

Phil walked up to my table, a little out of breath.

"So sorry I'm late. I had a hard time getting away from work."

He stood next to me, waiting for me to greet him.

"That's okay," I said, getting up.

Phil reached out to embrace me. I let him. It was how we had greeted each other for years, but it was awkward this time.

When he sat down, Phil pulled his phone out of his pocket and put it on the table next to him where he could keep an eye on it. His mind was still half on the job, despite his despair, despite the urgent need for advice. It irked me. And it made me even more sympathetic to Amy's point of view.

"Thanks for meeting with me. I know this must be a little weird for you. I know it is for me."

"Well, yes, it's weird. I'm not sure how I can help, but I'd like to."

"Here's the thing. I tried to talk to Amy, but ... I just couldn't get a clear reading on what she was thinking. I guess we got a little angry at each other, so that didn't help. I was wondering if maybe you had a little insight into what's going on in her head."

"Honestly? No, no I don't. I do know that she's angry at you. You hurt her somehow, something to do with blaming her for not taking care of her mother."

"Yes, I'm sorry I said that."

"Did you tell her you were sorry?"

"Well, yes ... I think I made that clear."

I doubted the words "I'm sorry" ever crossed Phil's lips, but I wasn't there to badger him. So, I let it slide.

"Well, it never hurts to say it again."

"Right, but the thing is ... it's grown into something beyond that ... like she's angry about other things. She said she's rethinking the relationship. I mean, what the hell? What brought that on? That's what I'm trying to figure out."

"I'm afraid I can't help you with that. Only Amy can tell you what she's thinking, what she's feeling. But I can tell you what I would do if I were in your shoes."

"Yeah? What's that?"

"I would woo her."

"Woo her?" Phil laughed a little, as if that notion had never occurred to him. "You mean like ask her out on a date? Bring her flowers and chocolate?"

"I suppose that wouldn't hurt. But I had something a little deeper in mind. I would start by telling her how much you miss her. Tell her how much you love her. Tell her you want her to speak from the heart, and you will listen, really listen. Tell her you're willing to change, to do whatever it takes to save your marriage. Let yourself be vulnerable, Phil. Let yourself be wrong, for once, and admit it!"

I found myself raising my voice, letting my anger slip out. I was doing what I didn't want to do. I was badgering Phil. He sat there a little stunned by my tirade.

Finally, he took a breath and said, "Look, I get what you're saying. But this thing is a two-way street. I can get down on my knee and beg, but she's got to meet me halfway. Right? You know what I mean?"

"If you want to have any chance of this succeeding, you need to do it with a full heart, without expecting anything in return. Just be honest and kind and understanding … and see what happens."

"Sure, I understand what you're saying. You make your best pitch and then … you never know."

"It's not a pitch. You can't practice it."

"No, of course not. I didn't mean that." Phil glanced down at his phone. Then he rubbed his forehead, as if he had a headache. I couldn't tell if he was just annoyed by having to go through this whole wooing thing, or if he was trying to truly absorb what I said. Finally, he looked up and said, "Hey, can I get you anything? A refill on that coffee?"

"Yes, I'd love a refill, and, if you don't mind, I had my eye on that poppy seed cake."

"You got it."

Phil popped up and headed toward the counter with a new bounce to his step. I got the distinct impression that he was satisfied with my answer. He had come looking for a sales strategy, and I supplied it. He just had to act humble, listen, and be nice. This would be a piece of cake, so to speak.

21

Manipulation

SINCE I SUSPECTED THAT I might be a secret puppet master, manipulating the people around me, I decided to embrace it. I would make my hitherto unrealized skill work for me. I would be a master manipulator.

It was Tasha's upcoming birthday that gave me the idea. Normally, I would take Tasha out to dinner to celebrate. I would invite my son, Brandon, and whomever Tasha was dating at the time. Brandon was out of town, however, and Tasha wasn't seeing anyone. Contrary to all common sense, I decided that we would hold her birthday celebration at home. And Danielle would be included. I was going to maneuver Tasha and Danielle into a reconciliation. And I was going to somehow demonstrate that I wasn't crazy, after all, to have invited these women into my house.

There was only one problem. Danielle's prospective boyfriend was supposed to arrive that very day. His presence would completely change the dynamic and, undoubtedly, disrupt the reconciliation between Tasha and Danielle. Applying my newly developed skills as a master manipulator, I decided to get Danielle excited about the event before I broached the subject of leaving her boyfriend out of it. I had some leverage in the matter. I knew that Danielle was anxious to renew her friendship with Tasha.

At dinner that night, I broached the subject of holding a birthday celebration for Tasha. Both Amy and Danielle embraced the idea. Amy immediately volunteered to plan the dinner. But I asked Danielle to take the lead.

"I think this will be an opportunity for you and Tasha to make amends."

"I totally get it. I'll work up a menu and share it with you guys. Then you can add, you know, whatever you want. I know Tasha's not a vegan."

It was settled, except for the boyfriend question. Later that evening, I approached Danielle.

"So, you know, Tasha's birthday is on the eleventh, and that's the day that your friend is arriving."

"Oh … well, that won't be a problem. Will it? I mean, he could just join us … or … "

"Danielle, if you want to make this special for Tasha, I don't think it would be a good idea for … for … "

"Seth."

" … Seth to be there."

"Maybe he could just hang out in the bedroom?"

"That would be weird, don't you think?"

"Yeah … kind of … "

"Could you ask him to find accommodations just for that one night? He has enough money for a cheap room, doesn't he?"

"Yeah, probably." Danielle slumped a little, her lips working as if she were trying to find the words to protest. But the words remained unformed, beaten into submission. There was a war going on in her head—fear of disappointing Seth against the desire to reconcile with Tasha.

"Look, I know it's hard for you. You don't want to disappoint him. But what kind of a relationship would this be if you couldn't ask him for a simple favor? Just one night. You can look at it as a kind of test. Does he really want to see you or not? Or is he just thinking of this as a free room … with possible benefits. You'll know by how he reacts."

Danielle bit her lip for a moment, undoubtedly pondering the cruelty of her fate, and perhaps the hard truth of what I was saying.

"Okay. I'll ask him."

What an excellent manipulator I was! If only I had known earlier in my life that I had this skill. How useful it would have been. My exchange with Danielle also taught me something about manipulation. Sometimes the most effective approach is the tell the truth in its most honest and brutal form.

Once the plot was hatched, I enticed Tasha to come to the house by telling her to "stop by."

"I have a little birthday surprise for you."

"Can't you just bring it with you?"

"No, it's not that kind of surprise."

"What kind of surprise is it?"

"If I told you, it wouldn't be a surprise."

"Mom, you're being weird. What are we talking about? Did you hire a male stripper or something?"

"How did you guess?"

"You're not going to tell me, are you?"

"No."

"Okay, fine, I'll stop by."

When the special day arrived, Tasha walked in the door and was greeted by a homemade happy birthday banner illuminated by string lights. The lights created a warm, golden glow in the room. The house was filled with the smell of our carefully prepared vegan French fusion dinner.

Amy and Danielle stepped out of the shadows and yelled, "Happy Birthday!" Tasha was genuinely surprised. Amy ran over to Tasha and gave her a big hug. Then Danielle reached out to her.

Tasha accepted her hug less enthusiastically.

"Wow! So this is the surprise. No male strippers. I'm disappointed."

"You'll get over it when you see the dinner that Danielle made … Danielle and Amy," I said, correcting myself.

The meal began with a note of tension.

"So how's the jewelry biz going?" Tasha asked Danielle, with a hint of malice.

"Good. I added a couple of new customers, boutiques in San Francisco. It's great, except I have to work, like, ten or twelve hours a day."

"Oh, so you're making good money now," Tasha commented pointedly.

"I'm doing ok, starting to save a little money."

"Right. I guess it helps that you're not paying rent."

I stepped in. "Yes, we're trying to get her to the point where she can move into her own place, a place with room for her jewelry studio, which, with first and last month rent, deposit, etcetera is not cheap, as you know."

Tasha stared at me for a moment. It was difficult to read her expression. I assume she was thinking "traitor," but perhaps I was exaggerating her response. Tasha moved on graciously to commenting about how delicious the vegan fritters were, a special dish Danielle had made with deep-fried chickpeas, carrots, and zucchinis.

A couple of bottles of wine later, Danielle started regaling us with stories about Austin. Austin claimed that he was a vegan. But one day Danielle came home early and found him gobbling down a steak and a beer. Blood from the steak was pooling, disgustingly, in his plate. His only excuse was, "My doctor said I needed more B12!"

Then there was the time, she was awakened in the middle of the night by the sound of drums. She got up to find the members of Stupid Genius, drunk and stoned, getting ready to rehearse. Danielle told them to stop. "You can't make noise at, like, 1:00 in the morning on a weekday. We're going to get kicked out!" Austin replied, "It's not a weekday. Tomorrow is Friday, and we have a gig." They all laughed drunkenly and proceeded to rehearse. The neighbors banged on the door, but they wouldn't stop. Eventually the police came. Several of the Stupid Geniuses swallowed their joints. Despite the fact that the whole room smelled like marijuana, the policeman let them off with a warning.

We all decided that they had earned their name Stupid Genius, especially the stupid part. Then Danielle told Tasha that the reason they broke up was that Austin started screwing a pole dancer who wanted to be a singer in his band.

"Oh my god! What a fucking asshole! You are so lucky to be rid of that scumbag."

We all agreed with Tasha's assessment. And, just as I had plotted, Tasha started warming up to Danielle. She began to see her as a comrade, a fellow wounded soldier in the battle of the dating wars. Then Danielle sealed their renewed friendship by bringing out a present for Tasha. It was a pair of onyx drop earrings with little diamond chips embedded in them. I knew immediately that they would look great on Tasha. They were bold, yet elegant. Perfect.

"Wow! These are amazing! I love them." With that, Tasha gave Danielle a warm kiss on the cheek and a big hug. "Thank you so much!" My victory was almost complete.

Later, at 1:30 or 2 in the morning, Amy and Danielle excused themselves and left to go to bed. I was woozy with sleep. But Tasha was in a heightened state. I couldn't abandon her. So I sat with her in the living room as she launched into an analytical discourse on the evening.

"That was so much fun! I mean, my first reaction was, 'Oh, shit! I have to spend my birthday with that bitch, Danielle.' And Amy, she's nice, but … we're not really friends or anything. But, you know, people talk about 'sisterhood.' It was kind of like that. We're all women without men. All women who have been fucked over by men. Fuck men! We don't need them. We really don't. They don't know how to have sex, anyway. I can tell you from experience that women are much better at it. Men are always in a hurry. What's the deal with men, anyway? Something got screwed up in the plan."

"What plan?"

"Evolution or whatever. Men are not made right for sex. I mean, okay, they've got a dick. But the rest of it is … like … something was left out."

Tasha was still buzzed from the wine and in a manic state beyond sleepiness. I nodded and smiled. But as Tasha continued her discourse, I thought about Lawrence, how I missed him, how tender he could be, what a good friend he was. This was not the time, however, to contradict Tasha. After all, my scheme was working. She was very close to endorsing my "crazy" situation of living in a small community of women. Then she said it.

"We should all just live with other women."

"That's not a bad idea," I said, my skill as a manipulator fully validated.

22

Courtship

SETH WAS USING HIS fork to move around the tofu pieces in Danielle's Thai noodle dish. He was, apparently, in search of the remaining noodles. Danielle watched with a slight frown on her lips.

It was our first dinner with Seth, and this was one of several awkward moments of silence.

"So, Seth … Danielle said you work for a non-profit that does economic research. What are you working on these days?" I asked.

"I'm working on a piece called 'Why the Trickle Down Economy Isn't Working.' It's basically about how the recent tax cuts are only helping the wealthy."

I could see Amy and Danielle already losing interest. Economics was not something they understood, nor something they cared to understand. I persisted, however. At least it was a topic of discussion Seth could engage in.

"So why isn't it working?"

"Well, it's complicated, but basically, businesses were already making record profits before the tax cuts, so they had no incentive to reinvest in their businesses, to do things that would significantly increase wages or employment. Instead, they just pocketed most of the money they saved, more or less."

"The rich screwing the poor. That's the leitmotif of world history. What makes you think you can change that?" Amy inquired.

She seemed determined to test Seth's mettle, which, in her mind, was much more interesting than economics.

"Honestly, we probably won't. On a good day, maybe a thousand people read one of our articles. We can only hope that some of those people have some influence, but … " Seth shrugged.

I liked Seth. Yes, he was disrupting our little circle of women. And he changed the nature of our conversations. We moved from intimate feelings to abstract ideas. But this was to be expected. Seth was a stranger. I had a feeling that, over time, he would willingly share more intimate aspects of his life.

Seth had a genial, boyish face. And after the dinner, he jumped up to help clear the table. He seemed honest, self-effacing, and open. On the other hand, I wasn't feeling any spark between him and Danielle. Or I should say, Danielle was not reciprocating whatever spark Seth projected. I suspect it had to do with more than just his dislike of tofu.

Nevertheless, Seth's stay with us passed uneventfully. When I asked Danielle how it went, she simply answered, "It was nice." I knew I was being a busy-body, but I wanted more.

"How nice? Are you going to meet again?"

"Probably. He still wants to move back here. But it's not easy to find a job. And it's insanely expensive to live here."

"You two could share the rent."

Danielle looked at me with a slightly shocked expression. I realized I was jumping way ahead of any plans she might be considering. And given her precarious position in the household, she might have taken my comment to mean I was anxious to get rid of her.

"We're not, like, planning to live together or anything," she said.

"No, of course, you two are just getting reacquainted. He seemed like a really nice guy, though."

"He is, but … "

I knew what the "but" meant. Nice is never quite enough. Being too solicitous in bed, for instance, can ruin the romance. And nice can come across as passive, not a particularly attractive quality in a man (or a woman, for that matter). I wanted desperately to give Danielle advice. I wanted to tell her that nice is precious in a relationship. It's what makes a relationship last. I wanted to tell her that nice men get better in bed over time. I wanted to tell her not to let go of this relationship so easily, to give it a chance. Instead, I said, "Well, you'll see how it goes."

One night after Seth had left, Amy walked in the door carrying a bouquet of brightly colored, mixed flowers.

"Here," she said, handing me the bouquet. "Do whatever you want with them."

The flowers were a vestige of a dinner with Phil. I was hoping, for Amy's sake, that Phil would listen to my advice and woo her with sincere apologies and confessions of deep love. The disdainful way that Amy handed me the flowers was not a good sign.

"What do you expect me to do with these?" I asked.

"Whatever, it's a cheap bouquet, and I hate those colors."

"Okay, so Phil doesn't know your taste in flowers. He's not the first man who doesn't notice things we think are important. But, other than that, how did it go?"

Amy sat down on the couch and let out an ambiguous sigh. "Well, he apologized. He said he didn't mean to hurt my feelings."

"Did he admit that he was wrong?"

"Not exactly. It was more like he felt he was misunderstood. Then he wanted me to tell him what he had done that caused me to question our whole relationship. He seemed kind of bewildered, like he hadn't done any soul searching on his own. He was waiting for me to explain everything."

"Did you?"

"You see? That's the problem ... my needing to explain."

"But did you at least try?"

Another sigh. "I told him that his having to ask was part of the problem. Then he got angry and started accusing me. He was saying things like, here I am trying hard to patch things up and I'm not meeting him halfway. That sort of thing."

"Do you think that's true to some extent?"

"No ... maybe a little. Maybe I wanted something more from him. Or maybe I'm confused ... if I even want to try to patch things up. I don't know."

"Did he say anything like 'I miss you' or 'I love you?'"

"Let's see ... yes, I think he did say that he missed me."

"But you weren't convinced?"

"No, it's not that. I do think he misses me. I miss him. But just saying you miss someone ... that's not enough, is it? I felt this underlying anger, like I was putting him through this ordeal, that this whole thing was my fault, that I could easily just forget the whole thing and go back to the way things were. That's what he really wanted. The dinner was just a ploy to convince me."

"Why call it a ploy? Maybe he's bad at this sort of thing, but that's not a reason to doubt his sincerity."

"'Bad at this sort of thing' pretty much sums up our whole marriage. That's the real problem."

Amy looked distraught. Her words were dismissive, almost cavalier. But her eyes were watery and vulnerable. She was disappointed and angry. I suspected, however, that her anger was only a thin gauze holding back other feelings—deep, subterranean feelings that had accumulated, unarticulated, for years. Anger was easier to handle than confronting those feelings.

I sat down next to Amy and gave her a hug. "I'm not taking sides, Amy. I love being with you. And I know Phil is a far from a perfect husband … but he's a decent man, a good man. If I were in your shoes, I wouldn't throw that away. I would accept the imperfection. I would open myself to the love he's offering, even if it's offered in an awkward way."

Amy sobbed and the tears burst forth.

23

Betrayal

THE NIGHT AFTER AMY's dinner with Phil, she was unusually quiet. Our habit was to chat and then read in bed together before going to sleep. This night Amy didn't pick up her book. She lay on her back with her eyes open.

"What's going on?" I asked.

She rolled over toward me and put her hand on my hip. "What would happen if I decided not to go back to Phil?"

"I don't know. That would be up to you."

"Would you want me to stay here ... with you?"

"As long as you wanted."

"But what do you want?"

What did I want? How rarely anyone asked me that question. I wasn't used to thinking deeply about what I wanted. I had taken as my role model the Zen monk who accepted the child he was given. In the same way, I had accepted Amy and Danielle into my life. Or so I told myself. But I also had a suspicion that I somehow encouraged this situation. Perhaps it wasn't my fate. Perhaps it was what I wanted. After all, I could have said no to Danielle. I could have insisted that Amy leave after a few days. So, what did I want?

I had to admit that I was lonely before the company of these women filled my life. But there was something about that loneliness that was forcing me to examine myself. It was teaching me more about who I was, what my deepest desires were. You could say that, for the first time in my life, I was learning what I wanted. Not in some superficial way, but in a way that could lead to new meaning in my life. And, given that my time on earth was limited, that seemed vitally important. Creating this new "family" had interrupted that journey.

"What I want is for you is to be happy," I replied, sounding to myself like the mother I was, talking to her daughter. But that was my habit. That was my training.

"What would make you happy?" Amy persisted.

I had to assume that Amy was asking me if I was ready to commit to a long term relationship with her. She was asking if I was ready to accept her as my partner, perhaps to accept her as my lover. Over time, she had become more physical with me. She would regularly kiss me goodnight on the lips. I didn't stop her, although it always felt uncomfortable to me. I didn't stop her because I loved our intimacy. I liked having her body close to mine. I liked feeling her hugs and caresses. But I couldn't quite get myself to accept the idea of going further. I had never been physically attracted to women.

Young people today feel free to experiment with same-sex relationships. But I was not young. And it would not be an experiment. It would be a commitment. I was not ready to have a sexual relationship with Amy. And I couldn't overcome the feeling that Amy was not truly free to give herself to me. Or, more accurately, I was not free to receive her.

"I know what you're asking," I said, after an uncomfortable pause. "You want to know if I'm happy living with you … if I would want you to stay with me permanently, to have a relationship, maybe even a sensual one."

"So? What's your answer?"

"Yes … and no."

"Ugh!"

"I'm not being evasive. I love you. I love having you here. I could see us living together for … for a long time. I worry about old age, what it would be like to be old and alone. You would be the best companion I could ever wish for. And I would be your loyal companion. It's all a very attractive proposition, but … "

"Why does there always have to be a 'but' with you?"

"The 'but' is that you happen to have a husband, a husband who is devoted to you, who loves you in his own, sometimes oafish, way. I can't get in the middle of that."

"You wouldn't be getting in the middle of it if it didn't exist."

"But it does. And, I'm sorry, but I'm not going to be the evil woman who breaks up a marriage of some forty-odd-years. There was an evil woman who broke up my marriage, my first marriage. Remember? I'm not going to be that woman."

"Yes, she broke up your bad marriage, and you married someone who really loved you. Are we forgetting that inconvenient fact?"

"Our situation is different. Phil never cheated on you. And he really does love you."

"Does he love me? Or does he just love having a wife? I'm sure he misses that. Wives take care of things. Wives take care of their husbands. Wives are convenient for business parties."

"It's more than that, and you know it."

"I know it? How do I know it? How do you know it?"

"I talked to Phil."

"When?"

"Not long ago. Last week."

"And you didn't tell me?"

"He made me promise to keep it confidential. I thought maybe I could help."

"Help with what? What did you tell him?"

"I only told him to be honest with you, to really listen to you. That's it. I promise."

"So you were giving him advice ... advice on how to approach me?" Amy was clearly upset.

"Yes, I guess, sort of ... if telling him to be honest and to listen is telling him how to approach you. I'm sorry. It was probably a mistake. I thought I was helping you."

"Did you tell him to give me those shitty flowers?"

"No, of course not."

"I'm going to sleep."

With that, Amy rolled over and pulled the covers over her shoulder. I turned off the light and stayed awake, anguished by the thought that I had somehow betrayed my best friend. As they say, "No good deed goes unpunished."

24

Decision

WHEN I WOKE UP the next morning, groggy from having had only a few hours of anxious sleep, Amy's side of the bed was empty. I had a moment of panic. Had she left the house? Was she so angry with me that she had abandoned me without a word? I listened. No sound from the bathroom. No sound from the kitchen. I sprang up from the bed and opened the closet. Her clothes were still there.

I could smell coffee. Without bothering to put on my bathrobe, I hobbled toward the kitchen. (My back was always stiff in the morning.) I walked into the kitchen. It was empty. Could she have left the house early this morning without telling me?

I continued my search into the living room. There she was, sitting calmly, fully dressed and sipping a cup of coffee. She was reading something on her phone. I was afraid to confront her. Normally, I would have rehearsed what I was going to say to her. I would have argued that I hadn't actually given Phil any specific advice about how to act or what to do. I had simply told him to be open, to listen and to be willing to admit his mistakes. I was being a true friend. I wasn't betraying her. But instead of calmly laying out my defense, I found myself standing before her in my pajamas, hair unkempt, unprepared.

"Hi," I said, undoubtedly looking like a mad woman. "Hi," Amy replied calmly, perhaps too calmly. "So ... are you still mad at me?"

"Why would I be mad at you?"

"Because ... "

I stopped myself. Amy was clever. She could be more than clever. She could be wily. Why would I give her a reason to be mad at me? Let her supply that reason.

"No reason," I replied. "You're up early. And I didn't hear you."

"I was trying to be quiet so I wouldn't wake you."

"Oh," I said. "Thanks."

I was very aware of the asymmetrical situation I was in. Amy was sitting down, dressed and composed. I was looking ragged and decidedly un-composed. I sat down on the couch and tried to pat my hair into place. I noticed that the top button of my pajama was undone. I quickly buttoned it. When I looked up, I thought I detected a slight smirk on Amy's lips.

"I'm going to start seeing Phil again," she announced.

"What do you mean 'seeing' him?"

"We're going to meet regularly for a while ... on neutral territory. I guess you could say we're going to be dating."

"Okay, good," I said, with as positive a tone as I could muster.

I thought to myself, So this is your revenge. Why did that thought enter my mind? After all, I had been the one who had advised Amy to give Phil a chance. I was the one who had rebuffed her proposal to live together. So why did I feel my heart breaking? Because I loved Amy. Because I was comforted and entertained by her company. Because I would miss her touch, her kisses, and caresses. Because I was afraid of being alone again.

I struggled to contain this unwelcome, untamed feeling. I wanted to be like the Zen monk, accepting with complete equanimity anything that life threw my way. I wanted to be brave. I wanted to embrace being alone as a path to self-discovery. I wanted to be free to

explore what I wanted. That's what I told myself. But my heart was telling me what I really wanted.

I began to chastise myself. Why had I stood so stubbornly on my high moral scruples? After all, whether Amy left Phil or not was her decision to make. I hadn't been an evil woman. I hadn't seduced her. This might be my last chance to have a deep relationship, and I was throwing it away for some principle that now seemed so unimportant.

"I'll miss you," I said, wiping away a tear.

Amy came to me and hugged me.

"Maybe it won't work out. You know what an asshole Phil is."

We both laughed and held onto each other.

25

Abandonment

AMY WAS HAVING DINNER with Phil, and I was dining alone with Danielle. It was quiet without Amy, and the crunching sound as we bit into our vegan tacos seemed loud and unsettling.

Danielle had a habit of holding her thoughts in. But once you got her talking, she was surprisingly willing to open up.

"How is your business doing?" I prompted.

"Good! I'm having a hard time keeping up with the orders. I think I might need to hire someone to help."

"Wow! That's amazing. Congratulations."

"Thanks."

"So … if you're thinking of expanding, does that mean you might be looking for more space?"

"No, not if I can help it. I like it here … with you. But I can afford to pay rent now. I'd like to."

"Keep your money, Danielle. You'll need it. You know that I love having you here. You're a darling person. But at some point, don't you think you need to spread your wings a little … start your own life?"

"Sure. I just don't know what that life would be. I don't want to be alone just to be alone. Do you know what I mean?"

I knew very well what she meant. I had discovered how little I wanted to be alone. But it felt selfish to cling to this young woman, holding her back from life, just to assuage my loneliness.

"What about Seth? How's that going?"

"He wants to come back for another visit."

"And you? What do you want?"

"I don't know. Seth is … it's complicated. I know Seth seems like a nice guy, and he is. But he's kind of damaged. I mean, his mother died when he was sixteen. He's never been that close to his father. And he was an alcoholic when I knew him in his early twenties."

"And now?"

"He's been sober for seven years."

"Is he serious about your relationship?"

"Yes. He wants us to live together."

"How do you feel about that?"

"I'm not sure. I mean, I love him, but … it's more like a good friend kind of love."

The corners of Danielle's lips curled slightly into a smile. "He's sweet."

"Sorry if I'm offering unwanted advice, but … sweet men are hard to find."

"I know," she said, her eyebrows furrowing. I couldn't tell if she was annoyed by my advice or if she was reliving bad memories.

"I like Seth," I continued, undaunted. "I can't tell you what to do, but I would give him a chance. I know you're feeling kind of lukewarm, but you'd be surprised at how many lukewarm romances turn into enduring, loving relationships. My husband was my best friend. That's why our relationship lasted."

"What was he like, your husband?"

"He was older. On the surface, he wasn't particularly exciting. He was in the insurance business. But he was fun to be with. And he was kind. And he was generous. And, in a lot of ways, he was quite adventurous."

"Like how?"

"He was interested in trying new things."

Danielle laughed. "You're not going to tell me the details, are you?"

"No, I'm old-fashioned that way. But you'll discover your own details."

"Right."

"Give Seth a chance." I put my hand on hers to emphasize the point.

"Would you let him stay here again?" she asked.

"Of course, any time. Well, as long as it's just for a short visit."

The next morning, I decided to go for a hike. It was a cool, bright day. Fall in Berkeley is a bit like late summer in other parts of the country. Contrary to popular belief, the trees do display the oranges and yellow in autumn. But the temperature hovers around 65° F. And there are usually more sunny days than not. It wasn't just the lovely fall day, however, that motivated my desire to go for a hike. Amy, with my blessing, was in the process of reconciling with Phil. Undoubtedly, that reconciliation would mean that she would eventually move back in with him. And here I was, encouraging my one remaining companion, Danielle, to leave and start a life with Seth. Apparently, I was intent on dismantling this "family" I had created.

I say "created" because I had the distinct impression that I was manipulating this whole situation. But I had no idea what my motivations were. It was as if this "I" who was doing the manipulating was beyond the control or understanding of the "I" who was me. I realize that sounds clinically insane. But that's how I felt. And that's why I needed to go on a hike. I wanted to bring these two "I's" back into harmony.

I remembered the first time I hiked in the woods alone. It was mid-summer, not long after Lawrence died. I felt a need to confront my solitude. At the time, I was anxious about the idea of hiking alone in the woods. There had been wildcat sightings in the park. And there had been a murder a few years back. I knew from experience that there were areas in the park with no cell phone reception. I imagined myself tripping and breaking a leg, unable to call for help.

Of course, the probability of any of these events actually happening was extremely small. My son would have told me that I had more chance of seriously injuring myself in the shower than of suffering injury while hiking in the park. But thoughts like these have a way of surfacing despite our attempts to think them away.

I did my best to brush aside my fears. But there was something else bothering me. It wasn't fear. It felt more like sadness. Being alone in the woods felt … lonely. I had become accustomed to being alone since Lawrence's passing. But my days were filled with my daily routine, buying food, preparing meals, cleaning, paying bills, watching TV, checking social media posts from my friends and associates, doing my daily crossword puzzle, working on the occasional writing assignment … and other extracurricular activities like yoga, French classes, and tutoring. This was different. Hiking was something one did with a companion.

I took a deep breath and told myself that this was my life now. I would be alone at times when I had never been alone before. I would need to make friends with myself. And the only way to do that was to spend time alone. I faced this prospect with some trepidation.

What if I wasn't a great companion? What if this self of mine didn't have much of a sense of humor? What if it couldn't help me laugh off my exaggerated worries and fears, like a good friend would? What if my self was a harsh critic? What if it was just plain boring? I had no choice; I would simply have to put this self to the test.

I started up the trail. The hills were still a golden yellow. The winter rains hadn't yet arrived to transform them into a lush green. Most of the wildflowers had disappeared, but there were surprising little bursts of purple and yellow from hardy, thistle-like plants. The fields that had been covered in the spring with white Queen Anne's lace, had gone to seed and curled into flowers made of tiny pink pods. Further along the trail, I was surprised by a sprinkling of small, delicate lavender-colored flowers that somehow survived the heat of the summer. I soon passed through the shade of a small redwood grove. I stopped, looked up at the trees, and breathed in the air.

The redwood trees were models of forbearance. These relatively small trees (some only a hundred feet high) could possibly have been a hundred to two hundred years old. Yet they stood as tall and healthy as teenagers. I put my hand on a tree near the trail and asked it to lend me its strength, endurance, and equanimity. The Ohlone people, who roamed these hills before the Spanish missionaries enslaved and destroyed them, believed that every living thing had a spirit. I didn't have the same belief. But I figured it certainly couldn't hurt to ask the tree spirit to help me. If nothing else, it acted as a kind of prayer to myself. It was a way to encourage myself to be as brave and resilient as the trees.

The spell of self-communion was suddenly broken when I heard the sound of men coming down the trail. My old fears awoke. Who were these people? Friend or foe? I was alone. I was a woman. I was old. What would happen? I stood frozen for a moment. I even contemplated racing back to the car. Instead, I stood up tall and marched ahead. It wasn't that I had overcome my fear. It was certainly still there. But I had made a decision to walk side-by-side with my fear and see what would happen. As it turned out, the assumed malefactors turned out to be a happy group of three twenty-somethings—two bearded men and a young woman. They looked like graduate students. I smiled and said hello. They returned my smile and said hello. And that was that. The dragon had become a puppy dog.

As I walked along the trail, my pounding heart slowed down. I looked out over the hills and thought about the concept of being alone. On some level, we are always alone, trapped as we are inside this shell we call a body and this perception we call a mind. On another level, we are never alone. As the Ohlones might have felt, we are all connected, not just with other people, but with all things.

Understanding this intellectually and actually feeling it deeply are two different things. As humans, we are constructed to perceive of ourselves as separate beings. We need this distinction in order to survive. A few very wise people have been able to pierce the illusion of separateness. They live in two worlds. One that accepts the idea that we are individuals, and another that understands that the individual we've constructed is nothing more than a reflection in a mirror, a pixel that, mixed with trillions of other pixels, makes the universe. That is why a Zen master never feels lonely. She knows that loneliness is built on an illusion of separateness.

I, on the other hand, still suffered under the illusion of separateness. I was capable of loneliness. Yet this little outing made me feel better. I had established a closer bond with this new friend I was trying to make, my self. It had been a good companion, encouraging me to be like the trees—brave, enduring, calm. I had a feeling that this new relationship with myself was going to work out after all.

That first hike I took alone, months ago, had helped me reconcile myself to my solitude. Then, somehow, I managed to fill the vacuum of my solitude, and put aside the internal work I had started. Perhaps I wasn't truly ready to confront that solitude. Now, I sensed that I would soon be alone again. Amy was on the path to reuniting with Phil. Danielle had a suitor and was making money again with her jewelry. I had been a gravitational force holding them close. Now other forces were exerting their pull.

It was time for me to nurture my inevitable solitude. I wanted to recapture that brave spirit which had allowed me to see my loneliness as a stepping stone to greater self-understanding, a stepping stone to greater inner peace.

"Where are you going?" Amy asked, as I slipped on my jacket.

"I'm going out for a hike, up in Tilden Park."

"Really? Alone?"

"Yes, alone."

"Maybe I should go with you."

"You don't have to."

"But I want to. I need more exercise, anyway," she said, grabbing a ring of belly fat to emphasize the point.

I so desperately wanted Amy to come with me. I craved her company all the more because I felt it would soon be lost. But life forces us to deal with loss. And this hike was meant to fortify me for that loss. This was a journey I would have to take alone. I would reacquaint myself with the redwood trees. I would shake hands again with myself and say, *Hello, me. Can we be friends again?* And I would do this while acting normal, as if I were a sane person out for an afternoon hike.

26

Proposition

THE CARDBOARD BOX I handed to Seth was hand-labelled "Blocks &
Dapping." I had no idea what Danielle used these tools for, but the
box was curiously light. Even though Danielle had inhabited a large
portion of the house, her presence, too, had been light. It was if she
landed in the house like a butterfly and simply spread open her wings.
Now she was fluttering away. I was terribly sad to see her go.

Seth had found a job writing customer emails and social media
posts for a large software company. He was making more money,
enough (when combined with Danielle's income) to rent a two-
bedroom apartment in a pleasant area of Oakland. I wondered how
much my encouragement had to do with Danielle's decision to move
in with Seth. He was, no doubt, a compromise in her mind. But it's
hard to resist a sweet man who unabashedly declares his love for you,
no matter your reservations.

I worried about their future together. Seth was not the man of
Danielle's dreams. That meant that every day he would need to win her
heart, bit by bit. That could prove exhausting over time. And I knew
all too well how soul-deadening his new job would be. Without any
particular interest in technology, he would have to feign enthusiasm
for the latest "breakthrough" advancement—probably something
about conquering the challenges of big data, the unimaginably large
flow of untamed information that could provide business insights
and a competitive advantage if only one had the latest version of his
company's software. Yet their very existence as a couple depended on
the income from that draining job. Would there be a breaking point?
Seth, after all, was an alcoholic.

These were troubling thoughts. But I managed to push them aside. I was happy for this young couple. They would be generous with each other. They would be good friends. They would find a way to survive together, just as I had in my marriage with Lawrence.

Amy and Phil, on the other hand, were a different story, or at least they appeared to be. Lately, Amy had been coming back from her "dates" with Phil in good humor, always with some funny little anecdote to relate. They had been to a traditional French restaurant, and Phil had ordered escargot, making the mistake of pronouncing the "t" at the end. When Amy corrected him, he had joked, "That 't' escar got me." Amy had found that quite clever. And, in her opinion, it exhibited a new humility on Phil's part. She was reading a lot into a corny little pun. But it clearly indicated a new attitude on her part.

One evening she came home from a Phil date and announced that we needed to have a serious talk. These serious talks always took place in the living room. It was a more formal setting than the kitchen or the bedroom, a suitable place for a summit meeting of two equally powerful, adult actors. We sat across from each other, and I waited for her to announce that she was moving back in with Phil. I was only partly right in my assumption.

"Did you have a nice time?" I asked.

"Yes, Phil was ... well, he's been ... not just nice, but I think he's changed. He seems much more open to the idea that his view of reality is not the only view possible. He's listening more and seems actually interested in learning about this whole new unexplored world."

"What world is that?"

"The world outside the one that he has constructed in his own mind. The world where everything is settled and orderly. Priorities are set. Rules established."

That made me smile. I imagined a somewhat battered Phil, desperate to renew their relationship. I imagined Amy, headstrong as she was, laying down new rules of engagement. Of course, rules are just rules. They don't necessarily imply a true change of heart.

"So ... are you two discussing what the new rules will be?"

"Yes, you could say that."

"And have you come to any conclusions?"

"Well, that's an ongoing discussion, but we've made one big decision."

Amy paused and smiled at me. I couldn't read the smile. There was something condescending about it. Or was it just for dramatic effect?

Finally, Amy continued, "Phil and I would like you to come and live with us."

"Are you kidding?"

"No. I'm serious. We talked it through. He understands how attached I am to you. He knows how important you are to my happiness. And he wants me to be happy."

"I'm ... I'm shocked. What are we talking about? A ménage à trois?"

"No! Of course not! Although he might enjoy that," she said, only half joking.

"We would continue as we are now," she continued. "You would be my close companion. You would be part of the family. We've got that lovely bedroom downstairs that looks out onto the garden."

"I'm sorry. I'm having a little bit of a hard time processing this. Are you sure you wouldn't rather just get a dog?"

"Oh ... I'm sorry. Did I somehow insult you? I really didn't mean to. It's just ... I love what we have here. And, as difficult as it is to admit, I love Phil. Why should I have to give up one for the other?"

"Yes, that would be very nice ... for you."

"Not for you?"

"Well, you're suddenly confronting me with this proposition, something you discussed, apparently in depth, with Phil. But you and I have never discussed it."

"We're discussing it now, aren't we?"

"Is this what you call 'discussing it?' It feels more like a proclamation."

"I didn't mean it that way. I realize it would be a big change. We can talk it through. Take some time. Think about it."

I followed Amy's advice. I took some time. My first reaction, of course, was that the whole proposition was insane. Amy just wanted to have her cake and eat it too, without considering the consequences and without considering me. I had a life of my own. I had let her into my life, into my house, as a favor. Now she was assuming some kind of ownership over me. She assumed that she could set the rules for me just as she had set them for poor, beaten-down Phil.

After the "proposition," Amy and I continued to live together, following our usual routines. She didn't press me for an answer. She was too clever for that. And, after several days, her strategy was beginning to work. I missed Danielle's presence. I had been a mother figure to her. And now she had left the nest. Once again, I was just a woman without anyone relying on me. I served no other purpose than to exist. As those feelings overtook me, I thought of Lawrence and how his presence was what saved me after Tasha and Brandon left the house.

Could my relationship with Amy replace Lawrence in my life? In some ways, it already had. But when I imagined living with Amy and Phil, the picture was fraught with problems. I could easily become the enemy, the countervailing power who would always tip the scales in favor of Amy. That would breed resentment. Amy had used her separation to beat Phil into submission. But over time his dominant nature would take over. If he saw me as the enemy, it would quickly get unpleasant. And Amy might even start to blame me for the dissension that would cause between Phil and her. Rather than being needed and appreciated, I would be the object of resentment.

There were also practical issues. What would I do with the house? Rent it? Then I would be completely reliant on them for shelter. What if I became ill? Would they willingly care for me?

Wasn't that exactly the same issue that caused their separation in the first place? Phil hadn't wanted to take in Amy's declining mother.

My mind easily went to dark places. I forced myself to consider the positive aspects of this new living relationship. Couldn't we all get along? Couldn't we enjoy each other's company? Couldn't we all help each other and be kind and understanding? Couldn't we all suddenly become perfect saintly human beings? How likely was that?

Several days after the proposition, Amy and I were about to go to sleep. I turned to Amy.

"I can't do it."

"You can't …?"

"Move in with you and Phil."

"But … we never really talked about it. You didn't give me a chance to … to …"

"Pitch the idea?"

"If you want to put it that way."

"You don't need to, Amy. You're my dear friend. And you always will be. But I thought it through, and it's not a good idea for either of us."

"Well ... you'll need to explain that, because ... I thought it through too. And I think it would be a good idea for both of us."

"This was a painful decision. I didn't make it lightly. But I've made up my mind."

"You don't even want to discuss it? Why are you being so closed-minded? I know it wouldn't be a conventional situation. But at our age, what do we care about convention?"

"I don't. I don't care about convention."

"Then why?"

"I'm sorry, but it's a personal decision. Maybe I'll figure out how to explain it to you at some point. But I can't ... not right now."

What was I to tell her? That she had temporarily beaten Phil into submission? That Phil would revert to his domineering self? That I would inevitably be blamed for the growing tension in their relationship? She would have denied it all. Rightly or wrongly, I decided to close off the discussion.

"That seems unfair," Amy protested.

"Yes, it's unfair. I'm so sorry to disappoint you. No matter what happens, let's please stay friends, very close friends, forever."

I could hear Amy let out a sort of frustrated snort.

"You're making me choose."

"Yes, I guess I am, in a way. But only about our living arrangement, not our friendship."

"I'm going to keep working on you."

"Yes, I always assumed you would."

With that, I sealed my fate. I would, once again, be a lonely widow.

27

Solitude

AMY MADE A COMPELLING case. She pointed out all the things we would miss if we no longer lived together: Holding hands when one of us was feeling sad. Sharing dinner. Laughing about odd encounters we had during the day. Spontaneously sharing thoughts and feelings whenever they visited us. Criticizing shows we watched together on TV. Reading in bed together. Goodnight hugs and kisses. The warmth and closeness of a body next to yours. Wait! Was she saying that we would continue to sleep together?

"Why not?" she answered.

"Because Phil would not look kindly on it."

"Oh, Phil. He wouldn't care. I mean, we wouldn't sleep together every night, just sometimes."

"My dear, you're hallucinating," I said, assuming the jokingly condescending attitude that Amy often used with me. "No man would allow that."

"Do you hear what you're saying? 'Allow.' Phil doesn't get to 'allow' for the simple reason that he doesn't have the authority to prevent it."

"But he does have the authority to make your life miserable, as do all spouses."

"It's not like we'd be having sex. Why do you think he'd mind?"

Why would Phil mind? How absurd of her to ask that. She was delusional. I had been holding back my true thoughts. But I was finally compelled to set her straight.

"My dear, you've beaten Phil into submission. So far, you've leveraged his loneliness and his affection for you into a form of surrender. But how far do you really think you can push it? You're being naïve."

"And you're being conventional, ma chère bourgeoise."

"Fine. Call me conventional. But what's important is not how conventional I am. It's how conventional Phil is."

Amy had conjured up a fantasy of our life together, the three of us. And she admitted that it was a bit unrealistic. She conceded that there would be "kinks" to work out. But she had faith that we—as open-minded, mature adults—would work it out. And eventually it would become apparent to all that it was a "win-win-win."

I was not convinced. And it wasn't just my conventional reflex. I didn't have the same faith as Amy that we would "work out the kinks." And who would suffer the most if the kinks didn't work out? Moi, ma cherie.

On the day Amy moved out, my heart was aching. Phil had taken time off work to help with the move. He greeted me with a smile and a big hug. I felt like I was sinking. My legs felt weak. I could see that Amy's eyes were red and ready to drip tears that she valiantly held back. Neither of us spoke much. We were afraid of what might come out of our mouths.

With Phil's help, Amy's several boxes and suitcases were quickly packed into their car. Before they drove off, Phil gave me a big hug and whispered "thanks" into my ear. Apparently, he thought I had been his ally all along, that I somehow convinced Amy to return to her rightful place as his wife. There was some truth to that belief. I had convinced Amy to give Phil a chance. But, in the moment, I felt more guilty than virtuous. I succeeded in undoing our cozy little world. I had broken a bond. I resented his "thanks."

"As soon as we get Amy settled back in, we'll have you over for dinner!" Phil declared, just before he slipped into the driver's seat and carried my Amy away. Phil's invitation felt ominous to me. I remembered our somewhat awkward dinners in the past, when Amy and I would slip into the kitchen to quickly have a "real" talk. Was I in a time warp? Had our time together slipped into a vortex, returning us to the exact moment before Amy left Phil? I think that, in Phil's mind, that was exactly what had happened. Amy was returning, and we would all just forget this unfortunate interlude.

I desperately hoped that Amy would not let that happen. I knew it would never be the same for me. We had developed a bond that could not—should not—be broken. I resolved to spend as much time with

Amy as I could, despite the fact that we would no longer go to bed and wake up together. We would no longer share our deepest thoughts and feelings throughout the day. We would no longer hold hands whenever we needed a friend's touch.

28

Resolve

AMY'S DEPARTURE LEFT ME empty. And that emptiness left my mind vulnerable to unwanted thoughts. In my grief, I began to think about my age and my eventual demise. This was not my customary mood. Most days, I forgot how old I was. We spend most of our lives not being old. It takes some getting used to. There are sneaky little reminders, of course. My back was stiff when I got up from bed. And I had started taking a short nap mid-afternoon. But otherwise, I felt pretty good. There wasn't much to remind me that I was sixty-three, the beginning of old age. I could even fool myself when I looked in the mirror. I would focus just on my hair, for instance, and avoid scrutinizing the creases around my eyes. And I relied on my growing presbyopia to blur out the details.

But death is sneaky. It has a way of reminding you of its presence. I had recently received an email from an old high school friend. She told me that Jacqui, a high school acquaintance of ours, had died of a heart attack. I remembered Jacqui as an all-American girl. She was pretty and smart, in a non-bookish way. She was involved in student government and wrote for the school newspaper. Inside or outside the classroom, Jacqui was always the center of attention. She was vivacious in the truest sense of the word. She was alive. I never even tried to befriend her. She was out of my league. Now I had the news that she had died from an illness we associate with growing old. The aliveness that glowed from her had faded.

This, more than the aches and pains, wrinkles, or my loneliness made me feel old. I knew this was coming. As we age, people in our lives, contemporaries, start dying. When I was in my twenties, the idea of someone dying in their mid-sixties would not have given me pause. People in their sixties, after all, were old. Now, I find it shocking. My first thought on hearing about Jacqui's death at the age of sixty-four was how sad it was that her life had been cut short.

I had seen old age and death. First there was my father who ostensibly died of liver failure. But the real cause was old age and probably his life-long cigarette addiction. I had gone down to Los Angeles to visit him in the hospital. We didn't really say goodbye because I thought he would recover. Then I got a call the next week from my uncle saying he had died. We were not close. And it was, in some way, a clean, clinical death. I was not there to witness the grim details. He just vanished from one day to the next.

When my mother died, it was different. I watched her diminish over a period of a year. She grew small, and she would sit still for hours wrapped head-to-toe in blankets watching black and white movies from the forties. According to the doctor, the blood vessels in her brain were clogged, which explained her memory loss and moderate dementia. My sister and I, along with the kids, watched her fade slowly. So when she finally died, it wasn't anything sudden or shocking. We had already lost the woman we knew and loved.

The most painful death, of course, was my husband's. When Lawrence got sick, I had to care for this man who for years had cared for me. It was not a burden. I loved him, and I owed him so much. But it pained me to see him humiliated by infirmity. I would have to lift him from his wheelchair onto the toilet seat and stand by to help him get up. I knew he was beyond shame at this point, and he appreciated my nonjudgmental help. Still, it hurt deeply.

So, I had seen death. I knew what was coming. At night, when I was the most vulnerable, vivid thoughts of death swooped in to fill the hole left by Amy's departure. I resolved to fill my mind with something else.

When I was younger, I was filled with a desire to write, to express my innermost thoughts in a way that could never be conveyed in the desultory, self-centered, short-hand of normal conversation. And I had tried. There were the short stories that were rejected. There was an unfinished novel I tackled later in my twenties.

That novel was a poetic, interior journey written in a kind of Joycean stream-of-consciousness. When I showed it to my former English Literature professor, she called it "lovely." Then she proceeded to explain why it would never be published.

Despite my failures, an ember of desire to write continued to burn in my heart. The demands of life had pushed it deep, beyond my everyday consciousness. I had made practical choices, earning a living for example. So, I ended up spending my creative energy meeting the demands of the marketplace. Any time I tried to push the edge of creativity in my work, it was invariably rejected.

Meanwhile, the urge to finally tell a story that was my own, to finally transmit my deepest thoughts and feelings without fear of corporate censure, grew inside of me. Now I had the time and space to write. I had no excuse. I would write a novel. I knew from experience as a professional writer that it was important to establish a routine, a time and a place, and stick to it.

After breakfast the next morning, I sat down to confront the blank screen on my computer. What in the world was I going to write about? I've had my ups and downs in life, as has everyone. But my life was essentially banal. I was a white, educated, middle-class, heterosexual woman. My parents died, but not tragically. They simply weakened from old age. My children were alive and thriving. I was hoping to have grandchildren before I died, but so were millions of other women my age. The one dramatic event in my life was the painful divorce I experienced. But that was only dramatic to me. According to the most recent statistics, roughly forty percent of first marriages end in divorce in the United States.

So what, then, was to be the topic of my novel? I considered the old dictum: "Write what you know." It seemed like good, common-sense advice. I decided to reconsider the topic of my divorce. There was, after all, the sordid element of a heartless temptress. I didn't find Vicki to be a particularly interesting character in real life. She was a young, self-centered idiot, who probably had no idea of the kind of havoc she was wreaking with her little fling. On the other hand, she had given me a gift. She saved me from a life with Greg and had given me Lawrence.

Almost seventy percent of second marriages end in divorce, but mine had endured. Maybe it was because Lawrence was so much older. He had learned to value love.

I could have told a heartfelt story detailing my betrayal and divorce. But I had been burned in the past trying to tell a simple, heartfelt tale. And my divorce was not exactly the stuff of a best seller. Who would be interested in something that happened daily to millions of women around the world?

Perhaps I could start with the Vicki affair and make the whole thing more sordid. There could be an attempted murder. Let's say they conspired to murder me! Greg was an accountant, after all. He knew that he would take a financial hit if we divorced. The tax implications of filing as a single person were disadvantageous. Was that enough motivation to kill me? Hardly. I had to think this through. I had to think like a criminal.

Here is the plot synopsis I eventually developed:

CRAIG, a mild-mannered accountant, happily married with two young children, meets an aspiring actress, VANESSA. He is bewitched by her. Vanessa represents everything that is missing from his life— adventure, freedom from his duties as a husband and father, and exciting sex. The actress is an accomplished dominatrix, who fulfills a sexual fantasy that Craig had never confessed to his wife. He is more than attracted to this temptress. He is addicted. That addiction clouds his judgment and leads him down a dark path.

Vanessa convinces him to murder his wife. There is more than freedom from his marriage at stake. Craig's wife is soon to inherent a considerable sum of money. Her dying father has confessed to her that he has hoarded millions of dollars and kept it secret from the family. She, his only child, will inherit the money. According to a pre-nuptial agreement, the wife would maintain control of all inherited money until her death. If Craig divorced her, he would see none of the money.

On the other hand, if his wife were to die a natural death, Craig would inherit the money.

With the help of Vanessa's cunning advice, Craig plans to make his wife's death appear to be of natural causes. He will slip her a poison used by Russian agents that induces a heart attack.

There is, of course, one problem with this plan. Craig makes the mistake of trusting Vanessa. And her motives are hardly driven by love. Vanessa desperately needs money to move to Los Angeles and finance her attempt at stardom. The last thing she needs is a nerdy, accountant husband trailing alongside her on the red carpet.

After Craig kills his wife and marries Vanessa, Vanessa intends to murder Craig using the very same poison he used on his wife. She will tie him up while playing out a bondage fantasy, then make him drink the poison "wine." The police will arrive to find an overweight, forty-five-year-old man, naked and bound, and assume his weakened heart could not take the excitement. And Vanessa will then be free to use the wife's inheritance to launch her career.

Of course, there was an element of revenge in my little plot. The idea of Greg (a.k.a. Craig) naked, bound and beaten greatly appealed to me. However, I quickly realized that the plot had holes. If the Craig character murders his wife, then he'll be saddled with the care of his two children, which is exactly what he was trying to escape. Should he and his wife have no children? But without the children, the murder would lose its poignancy.

After spending several days trying to work out the sordid plot details, I came to several realizations. (A) I was bad at writing murder mysteries. I simply couldn't think like a criminal. (B) On re-reading the plot outline, I realized that the whole thing sounded idiotic. It was definitely not something I, myself, would read. And (C) there was nothing about the novel I was intending to write that would in any way contribute to art or literature. I would not be participating in the great "continuum" of culture. I would be doing what I had already been doing, participating in the commerce of the marketplace.

It was a painful decision, but I put the novel aside. For a few days, I thought that I had found my path, my meaning and purpose on earth. I chased away my morbid thoughts. Now I had to admit that I failed. The unfinished manuscript would sit on my hard drive, joining the thousands of other unfinished novels that lie unread on hard drives throughout the world. I was joining a noble club of those who, at least, had attempted to make some small contribution to our human story.

But that thought provided little consolation. The path I was convinced I discovered was disappearing into a fog of confusion.

29

Reappearance

THE CALL FROM GREG sent a surge of anxiety through me. We rarely spoke. There was no need to. The kids were grown and independent. I hadn't relied on his financial help for decades. We kept a cold, but cordial, distance between us. So when his name appeared on my phone, I immediately assumed something bad had happened.

"Hi, Lexi. It's Greg. Remember me? The asshole who let you down?"

This didn't sound as if he were about to announce a tragedy. In fact, it didn't sound like Greg at all. Where did this humor come from? This disarming self-awareness?

"Greg … hmm … let's see … are you the Greg who has a daughter named Tasha? And a son named Brandon?"

"Good guess! Yes, I'm that guy. How are you?"

Greg hadn't expressed any interest in how I was for decades. We had had brief discussions, mostly concerning decisions about the kids. Then there would be years when we wouldn't talk at all. Occasionally, I would get little bits of news from Tasha. I supposed she, in turn, would relay bits of information about me to Greg on occasion. He probably knew that I was living alone again. Was the timing of this call a coincidence?

"I'm … fine. I'm doing fine. And you?"

"Well … good, I guess. Did Tash tell you that Melissa and I separated?"

"Yes, she did mention that."

"Yeah, it's actually been about six or seven months now that I've been living alone."

"How has that been?"

"Hard. It was an adjustment. I'm used to … being with someone. Like you, I guess. It must've been hard when Lawrence passed."

"It was."

"Yeah … how are you doing now?"

"I'm … doing okay."

Something in me wanted me to say *I'm doing great!* just to spite him. But, instead, an evil spirit of truth overtook me, and my tentative tone revealed that things weren't all that great.

"Listen, I know this sounds a little crazy, but … I thought maybe we could get together … y'know, have a coffee or something."

"What exactly did you have in mind?"

"Nothing … just a chance to talk, to catch up. I've had some time to think … and I regret that we haven't been more in touch over the years. I've always respected you."

Respected me? What an odd thing to say. Why say it now? And what exactly did he respect? That I put together a satisfying life after his betrayal? That I did a good job raising his children?

That … what? I was about to articulate these questions, when he continued in a softer tone:

"And maybe … I never really apologized fully for what I did."

What was going on here? My first thought was: *A little late for that!* But there was something in the tone of his voice that convinced me of his sincerity. And, if he truly wanted to apologize (even if it was too little, too late), how could I refuse him that chance? It would be ungenerous of me to prevent it. And I was curious. Had Greg actually changed? What was this reopening of our relationship all about? I agreed to meet.

After the phone call with Greg, I called Tasha. The phrase, "*The asshole who let you down*" sounded like a direct quote from her. I wondered whether she may have instigated Greg's call.

We started our call in the usual fashion. Tasha had a new boyfriend, and I had to tease out personal information about him.

He's a couple of years younger than me. He's a programmer at a startup company. They make mindfulness applications. No, I've never tried them. It's, like, meditation, and stuff like that. He says he's monogamous. No, I don't know if he's serious. But if he's not, I'm going to dump his ass. No, he hasn't invited me to meet his family. No, he's not on particularly good terms with his family. No, I don't know why. And, anyway, it would be up to him to tell you, not me. Yes, he appreciates my humor. Of course, he's nice. I wouldn't date him if he wasn't.

The topic shifted to her job. After a few of the usual complaints about her non-profit employer, where everyone is "slacking and protecting their territory," I finally broached the topic of Greg.

"So, did you know that your father called me?"

"Really?"

"Yes, guess what he wanted."

"I don't know … sympathy?"

"Maybe something like that. He wanted to get together for a coffee."

"Oh! So? Did you say yes?"

"I did. He said he wanted to apologize."

"Wow! Really?"

"Was that something you had suggested to him?"

"I may have mentioned something like that to him at some point. But I never thought he'd actually do it."

"He referred to himself as 'the asshole who let me down.' Is that something you might have said to him?"

"Probably."

"So, what do you think about all this?"

"I think it's nice that he's reaching out. You two have needed to have this conversation for a long time."

"So, it's all about mending fences? He doesn't have anything else in mind?"

"Like what?"

"That's what I'm asking you. You said he was lonely."

"Yeah, but … I mean, the breakup with Melissa shook him up, but I don't think he has any ulterior motive. But who knows?"

"He said he had done some thinking."

"That'd be a switch."

"Do you feel like he's changed in some fundamental way?"

"Maybe. I think he's feeling kind of vulnerable. But has he really changed? I don't know. I guess you'll find out."

After the call with Tasha, I was left to ponder the situation. Tasha had clarified some things, like her role in instigating Greg's call. But many things were left unexplained. Namely, Greg's motivation. Was it just about a long-overdue apology? Did he want sympathy, as Tasha had suggested? Why come to me? How lonely would a man have to be to come to his long-estranged, ex-wife for sympathy? Or was he hoping for something more? The last thing I needed in my life was to be some kind of consolation for a heartbroken old man. Of course, I was a heartbroken old woman. A perfect match.

30

Gray

I opened the closet door and looked through my clothes. *Pathetic.* I hadn't bought a new article of clothing since Lawrence died. And I barely took care of the clothes I did have. What was my incentive? I wasn't seeing anyone. And I felt no need to impress Amy or Danielle with my sartorial splendor. But now I was about to see someone— Greg. And it annoyed me that I cared how I looked.

There was, of course, a certain perverse desire to present myself in the best possible light, a way of saying, *See! This is what you missed all these years.* But it was too late for that. That kind of thinking might have made sense twenty years ago. Now I was a doughy, gray-haired retiree. A thought struck me: *He hasn't seen me with gray hair! What will he think?*

I remembered my decision to let me hair go gray. It was perhaps six months after Lawrence died. At the time, I thought of it as a practical decision. My income was shrinking. And I was shocked when I looked at my credit card bill. As I read through the list of charges, I quickly found the culprit—my timing belt repair. I had an old car, which was perfectly fine with me. I actually had a certain affinity with my car. It was old and dented, and it had lost its luster. That was a pretty fair description of me.

My car and I were old friends who had aged together. But, old as it was, I could rely on it to take me from point A to point B. Good enough. I certainly didn't need anything shiny, new, or powerful to bolster my self-image.

However, just as I had accumulated various non-fatal maladies— hypothyroidism, back pain in the morning, occasional hip pain—so my car was going to need additional care as it aged. And that was going to be expensive. This fact forced me to re-examine my budget.

I hadn't been offered a writing job in over a month. And I was relying more and more on the savings that Lawrence and I had accumulated. I was never good at accumulating money. It never seemed like an important priority. My parents were the same way. They were never motivated by acquiring material possessions. So maybe it was genetic.

I had a younger sister, however, who apparently inherited a different set of genes. Darlene had moved to Las Vegas with her family about twenty years ago. She and her husband were flipping houses as a way to accumulate wealth. They started in Marin County when houses there were relatively affordable. It has since become the fifth richest county in the United States. They made a small fortune buying and selling several houses there, each one bigger and more luxurious than the last. When it became harder to turn a profit, they moved to a new boomtown, Las Vegas.

The idea of moving to a desert city that was a geographical and moral wasteland was beyond my comprehension. But Darlene's goal in life was always to become rich. And Las Vegas offered an opportunity. I don't know what drove her ambition. Was she compensating for something she missed in her childhood? Did she not feel loved? It was hard for me to understand because, although our parents had divorced when I was six, I always felt secure in the knowledge that both my mother and father loved me. Darlene was three when my parents divorced. Maybe it scarred her more than me.

After Lawrence died, Darlene suggested that I come to visit them in Las Vegas. She was too tied up with "work" to come to the Bay Area to visit me. By work, I supposed she meant some real estate deal she was cooking up.

The last thing I wanted to do was to go to Las Vegas. I hated casinos, all the noise ... all the sad shedding of hard-earned dollars by people who could hardly afford it ... the corny shows that passed for entertainment ... the pathetic facade of 1950's style sexiness ... the greed painted over with bright lights and free drinks. So, I politely declined her invitation. I told her I had too many details to deal with after Lawrence's passing.

We were both relieved that the obligation to visit was dispensed with. I didn't dislike Darlene. She and I had a congenial relationship. But I simply couldn't relate to the life she had chosen. In some ways, I got along better with her husband, Jack. He was a boozy, good 'ol boy with no ambition of his own. He was always welcoming when we met, and he would greet me with a hug that lasted a little too long. Then, after a few cocktails, he would invite me out to see the pool they were building or the new landscaping they had commissioned.

During these little excursions, he would drop little, teary-eyed confessions. He once told me that he hadn't wanted to move to Las Vegas. It took him too far from his extended family in San Francisco. He also confessed that he was worried about their two sons, who followed Darlene into the real estate business. He thought that they had become too hard, too driven by money. I kept these little confessions to myself. It was not my place to relay them to Darlene. It wouldn't have made any difference in any case. I once intimated to her that perhaps Jack wasn't happy. And she brushed off my comment saying, "Jack can say silly things when he's had a few too many."

During our conversation, Darlene asked how I was getting along. I told her that I was doing ok. Compassion was not one of Darlene's strengths. So, it seemed fruitless to discuss my deepest feelings with her.

Then she asked, "You're doing ok financially, right?" She followed this quickly with, "I'd like to help, but I've got all my cash tied up right now. We just closed on a house." I understood her concern. It was not about me. She wanted to pre-empt any possibility that I would ask her for money. I considered myself extremely fortunate that I didn't need to ask her for financial help. It would have been ugly.

That brought me back to my current budget worries. Was there any monthly expense I could eliminate? I thought about the expensive café mochas I ordered when I would occasionally go to a café. Would I have to eliminate this one little pleasure when I had so few in my current life? That seemed wrong, an act of self-punishment bordering on the masochistic.

What else? I tried to create a list of expenses worthy of elimination. My cable subscription? That would mean giving up certain shows

I watched religiously. It would mean giving up the few hours of distraction that acted as an emotional opioid in my life. I had already admitted to myself that television acted as a drug, but I rationalized my addiction as being more healthy than having an actual drug addiction. And I honestly feared that in my current state of grief I might fall into a real drug addiction. I'm not talking about heroin or meth. What I feared was prescription drugs like anti-anxiety meds or what we used to call tranquilizers.

Through what I consider to be an act of courageous self-awareness, I reduced my list to the one item that caused the greatest emotional turmoil—my monthly hairdresser appointment. Should I let my hair go gray? The very thought scared me. It wouldn't be a simple act, a practical budget decision. It was a kind of declaration, a declaration to the world that I was old, that I was no longer an active participant in life.

I knew that gray would be a further step into invisibility. I had already noticed that young people tended to ignore me. The days when men would turn their heads to get a second look were long gone. But there were other hints that my age reduced my social gravity. Sometimes it would be a simple act, like a young person brushing by me on the sidewalk or a sales clerk passing me by to help a younger customer. At other times, it was more apparent. When I complained to my doctor about my hip pain, she shrugged and said, "We're all getting older." I suppose if the pain had been constant or if I were truly disabled, she would have paid more attention. But it still felt a bit like a demotion on the scale of human importance. I was old. My pain was only worth a shrug.

So, letting my hair go gray felt less like a healthy acceptance, than a kind of giving up. It wasn't anything physical. I would still be generally healthy. My mind would continue to function. I wasn't acquiescing to death. But I would somehow be smaller, diminished. That, at least, is how I felt.

Very few women in my social circle had stopped dying their hair. Like me, they were holding on to a version of themselves that had long passed. I considered how odd this was. These were the women of Berkeley. They ate organic food. They were concerned about the environment. They had grown up in an era when "natural" was almost a spiritual concept. Yet they regularly had poisonous chemicals poured onto their scalps.

I tried to remember when my mother finally let her hair go gray. It might have been just before she turned eighty. My mother, Lillian, was quite pretty. When she was young, people compared her to the actress Ava Gardner. Unlike me, she always had men vying for her attention. The men who courted her most ardently, the ones with promises of undying love and financial stability, won out. And she ended up in three unfortunate marriages.

My mother had lived on her own from the age of seventeen. As a fun-loving, pretty, independent young woman, I can only imagine the wild times she had. But by the age of twenty-six she was ready to settle down. She wanted stability. It came in the form of my father.

My father was a handsome man, an engineer. What attracted my mother to him turned out to be the thing that eventually repelled her. He wasn't just stable, he was virtually immobile. He would spend weekends lying on the couch chain-smoking. My mother would urge him to get up, do things, go places. She once suggested that they go to the nearby mountains to breathe the fresh air and see the trees.

According to my mother, he replied, "Once you've seen one tree, you've seen them all." After my father died, I learned from his brother, my uncle, that my father was very likely clinically depressed. But he lived in an age when it was shameful to go to a psychiatrist.

And anti-depressants hadn't been invented yet. How different my parents' marriage might have been had they married today.

When I was six, my parents divorced. I rarely saw my father after that. My mother kept searching for that thing she had missed with my father—passion. But she still yearned for the financial security she had sought with my father. It was the most unscrupulous, dishonest men who offered her what she craved. They were con men who knew how to read a woman's inner desires. They would court her, profess their love, cede to her every whim, and exaggerate their financial situation. It was only later that she would learn about their lies, their debts, and their character flaws.

In her seventies, my mother finally gave up on men. It was probably her happiest period. Having been courted by men all her life, however, she retained a good dose of vanity. That's why it took her so long to let her hair go gray. When she did, her hair turned out to be an attractive gray, with a hint of the lustrous dark hair that crowned her head as a young beauty. Now, with her short-cropped hair and her admirable bone structure, she still looked stunning.

This gave me hope; although, sadly, I had not inherited the movie star looks of my mother. In fact, I neither looked like my mother nor my father. Unlike my parents, I was tall, and I had a somewhat prominent nose. I sometimes teased my mother that I was the offspring of her affair with the milkman. She would laugh, but she never outright denied it.

I missed my mother greatly. In my deepest period of grief, I desperately wanted her to be alive and to comfort me. Now I missed her good humor, her self-sufficient spirit, her joy in small things and her love. I never imagined my mother struggling to get out of bed, or asking herself brooding existential questions. I must've gotten that from my father (assuming my father wasn't actually the milkman). I couldn't be with my mother now, but I could draw from her strength.

Yet I still struggled with the decision to let my hair go gray. I understood the self-delusion of pretending to be young and vital when you are clearly not. I knew that, at my age, I was all but invisible to men, with or without gray hair. Wasn't I just trying to fight an unwinnable battle against time and entropy? Shouldn't I just let go?

But wasn't life a kind of battle no matter one's age? Life is renewal. According to the experts, every ten years we have a completely new set of cells. We have, in essence, regenerated an entirely new body! Life is regeneration. Life is the opposite of entropy, the "gradual decline into disorder" that is pervasive throughout the universe. Entropy would eventually win, but I was still alive. And life calls us to defy the law of entropy.

As usual, I found myself magnifying the importance of this decision. Was I really going to turn it into some kind of profound, philosophical choice? It had started out as a practical decision. I needed to eliminate a monthly expense. I told myself it was a simple decision. Yet the decision did not come easily. I found myself silently asking my mother to lend me her strength and common sense. I didn't believe that my mother was literally watching over me, but calling upon her memory, nevertheless, comforted me.

The next time I saw my hairdresser, I revealed my plan to go gray. I expected her to object. After all, lowering my monthly expense meant lowering her monthly income. Instead, she was understanding and warm. She gave me a hug and told me that most of her clients who had made the decision were very happy with the result. Then she explained her plan. She would lighten my hair gradually until it was almost blonde. Then I could allow my gray roots to grow in gracefully.

For a moment, I got quite excited about being a blonde. Then I reminded myself that that was not the point. In my thirties, going blonde would have been a fun experiment. Now it was just a means to an end. I reassured myself that I would continue to battle entropy, but I would not rely on the color of my hair to lead the charge.

31

Reappraisal

NOW THAT I WAS contemplating my meeting with Greg, I was confronted with my bold determination to carry on as a gray-haired older woman. It annoyed me that I was worrying about my gray hair. Why was I even having these thoughts? *Who cares what I look like? He's older than I am. And he was always a little flabby. He was practically bald by the time he was forty. In a game of competitive appearance, I will surely win. Win what, though? Would my reward be a little taste of revenge?* All of these thoughts were idiotic.

I decided to wear my go-to outfit—the same one I wore when Amy and I went out together—stretchy gray slacks with a black turtleneck sweater. Greg didn't deserve better than that. The weather was turning winterish. The skies were gray with clouds, and it was threatening to rain. The temperature was 52° F, which is cold for Northern California. We had agreed to meet at a local café. I made sure to be a few minutes late.

I walked in and scanned the room. I didn't see him. *How insulting to be late. What a way to start an apology.* Then an old man waved at me from across the room. It was Greg. When I reached his table, he stood up and greeted me with a handshake.

"Hi, Lexi. Long time, no see."

"Yes, it been a while," I said, taking a seat.

"You're looking … good," he said.

I could tell that he was a little shocked to see me as an older woman with gray hair, just as I was shocked to see how he had aged. Saying I looked "good" felt a bit forced. I couldn't get myself to return his compliment. So, I simply thanked him. It wasn't that Greg looked bad. He wasn't unhealthy looking. He had cut his remaining hair down to a little gray fuzz. And he had a close-cropped, almost white beard, carefully trimmed. That was something new. It reminded me of Lawrence's beard, the memory of which caused me a moment of pain.

So, Greg was well-groomed for the occasion. But he had gained considerable weight, which is probably why I didn't recognize him. The weight gave his face a kind of Santa Claus look, especially when he squinted his eyes into a smile. He was wearing a pale yellow, pull-over sweater. I noticed a small moth hole under his left breast.

The yellow sweater was not something I would have recommended, but it was the hole that elicited my sympathy. Most wives (or partners) would've spotted the hole and had him change sweaters. Only a lonely old man would venture out into the world with a hole like that, right in front where anyone would spot it.

"So ... how are things? You still working?" he asked.

"Barely. I guess I'm too old. These technology companies ... they assume that anyone over fifty is over the hill, out of the loop. In my case, that's probably true. I've lost whatever interest I had, which was never very much to begin with."

"So how do you fill your time?"

"Mostly just doing what I want. I volunteer as a writing tutor. I do some yoga. I see friends. I go out to the occasional exhibit. I've been learning French, but in a pretty haphazard way. I certainly couldn't carry on an actual conversation with a Frenchman."

"How about with a French *woman*?" he said, with a smile.

"That would be even harder, I imagine."

Greg looked a little puzzled by my response.

"They would be less kind," I explained.

"Oh," he said. "Really?"

"No, not really. I don't know why I said that."

Greg laughed a little nose laugh. I felt stupid. I was tense, and I have a tendency to speak without thinking when I'm tense. My stupid remark, however, had served to ease the tension between us.

Hoping to move past my faux pas, I continued, "Anyway, those are some of the things that fill my time. But I'm seriously thinking of doing some of my own writing ... a novel or something. I just haven't made the leap."

"You should. You should give it a try."

"Thanks. I will, but … what about you? How are you filling your time?"

"I'm working … a little less, but I still have my old faithful clients. I honestly wouldn't know what to do with my time if I didn't work. I never had any hobbies. Of course, you knew that."

"Retirement is nice. Doing whatever you want, whenever you want to do it, is something you can easily get used to. I recommend it."

Greg smiled his Santa Claus smile. "I guess I'll have to try it … one of these days. But I think I'd miss my clients … the contact."

"But you'd have more time for your friends."

A wistful, little smile crossed Greg's face. "Yeah …" was all he could manage. How sad. The hole was expanding before my eyes. It not only included a place where a wife should have been, but a place where friends should have been. I didn't want to pity him, but I did.

"So … ," he said, with forced determination. "I did want to apologize."

I could see that this was a painful moment for him. I waited, with what I hoped was a sympathetic expression on my face.

"I wanted to let you know that what I did … I know it was a long time ago, a lifetime ago, but it has haunted me. I hated myself for what I did to you, to the kids."

He struggled to get the words out.

"So, yeah … I want to apologize. I want you to know that I recognize that … that … that I blew it, big time. And I regret it. I've always regretted it."

He had said all this looking down at his clasped hands. Now he looked up.

"I'm not asking you to forgive me. I just wanted to, y'know, apologize. And I appreciate your giving me the opportunity to do that."

What does one say in a situation like this? Before our meeting, I was prepared to thank him for his apology and then move on. But I wasn't prepared for the depth of his apology. I wasn't prepared for how painful it was for him and for me.

"I do forgive you," I said, knowing that I might regret those words later, after the emotion of the moment subsided.

"Thank you," he said. "Oh! Here … " He reached down next to his chair and placed a white box tied with a red ribbon on the table. "For you."

"You shouldn't have done that. You didn't need to."

"Well, I wanted to. And we're getting near the holidays and everything. Open it."

I lifted open the box. It was an assortment of chocolate truffles.

"It's stupid. I know," he said. "But I couldn't think of anything else. We, uh … we don't really know each other that well anymore."

"Like how I've been trying to lose weight, for instance?" I said with a little, ironic laugh.

Greg blushed a little and his smile drooped.

"Just kidding," I said. "Sorry. It's not stupid. It's perfect."

Our conversation turned to the kids. Apparently, Tasha discussed her job in depth with Greg. He seemed to understand the nuances of the power relationships within the organization much better than I did. On the other hand, he had no idea that Tasha was dating someone.

When I announced this information, he said, "Really? I knew Brandon was seeing someone, but not Tash."

This was news to me. My son was seeing someone?

"Yeah, they met on some kind of tech chat room or something."

That jogged my memory. "The young woman from Houston?"

"Yeah, that's right. I think she's going to move up here."

"Oh … okay."

I was trying to hide my consternation that Greg knew more about my son's romantic life than I did. But that was Brandon. Had he told me about it, I would have pried him for details and even gotten a little emotional. On the other hand, I could imagine Brandon announcing the relationship to Greg in the most matter-of-fact terms. It would go something like this:

She'll be moving in with me on February 7, three days before she starts her new job.
Good. So, she'll have a few days to unpack and settle in.
Right. That's the idea.

I was a little jealous of Greg. But I was happy that he and Brandon could talk robot-speak to each other. I don't mean to say that in a pejorative way. It's just that my son, Brandon, is different, perhaps more like his father. When Brandon was nineteen, he was attending college and studying computer science. At the end of the semester, I was dismayed to learn that he had failed all of his classes.

Instead of studying, he was developing a smartphone app with a friend. The app became quite popular, and he was immediately hired by a giant tech company. The company, apparently, had no interest in whether Brandon had a well-rounded education. He had demonstrated his programming skills, and that was good enough. Soon Brandon was making twice the money that I was making as a copy writer.

It shouldn't have surprised me. Throughout his schooling, Brandon had a habit of pursuing whatever interested him, and disregarding anything that didn't. He would get A's in his science and math classes, apparently without studying. When it came to English or Social Studies, however, Lawrence and I would have to force him to do the minimum required to pass. I remember once closing the door to his room and telling him not to come out until he had completed his English essay. Lawrence and I took turns guarding the door. After an hour, I checked in on him. He had been working on a design for a solar-powered aircraft that combined a lighter-than-air element with an aerodynamic fuselage, powered by electric propellers. The design won him an award at the district science fair. He got a "D" in English that year.

More recently, at a family gathering, we were discussing whether a computer could ever have a human-like mind. Brandon asserted that there was no significant difference between a human mind and a computer mind. Already, computers were easily passing the Turing test. To pass the Turing test, a computer would need to be able to communicate with a human in a way that was indistinguishable from a human being. As proof, Brandon pointed to a computer that had recently won a debate against a champion human debater. To top it off, the computer used human-like speech to make its points. I argued that computers might be able to "think," but they could never have feelings or soul. Brandon calmly replied that emotions could easily be programmed into a computer. It was up to us, the creators, to make computers as human-like as we wished. He dismissed "soul" as too vague a concept to even argue. When I objected to this easy dismissal, he made a brilliant, if painful, argument.

"When someone is brain-damaged, and they can't even remember who you are, much less who they are … do they still have a soul? What exactly is a soul disconnected from the brain?"

I was not a religious person. So I had no ready theological answer to his hypothetical question. It just felt wrong to assume that a computer could have real feelings, that a computer could love, for instance. It might simulate love, but it couldn't truly feel love. For Brandon, this was not a provable thesis.

That is not to imply that my son had no feelings. He was concerned about me. He just demonstrated that concern in his own peculiar way. He and Tasha had discussed my situation after Lawrence died. Brandon inherently understood the discomfort that might be caused by a brain that was not fully engaged. He agreed with Tasha that I needed "to do something." The concepts of loneliness and grief were a little more difficult for him to comprehend.

I was naturally concerned about my children and how they were handling the loss of their stepfather. Brandon had fond memories of Lawrence as a father figure who was more present in his life than his biological father. By the time Brandon was a young man, however, Lawrence had become more like a grandfather than a father. How else would a twenty-year-old relate to a man in his seventies? And when a grandfather dies, it's sad, but not devastating for a young man.

Tasha, on the other hand, had cried with me. It broke her heart because Lawrence had been kind and generous with her. When she was a child, she called Lawrence "Dad." She had no problem with the idea that she had two dads, one she lived with and one she visited regularly. But when Tasha was in high school, she started calling Lawrence "Larry." She did so affectionately. And Lawrence accepted it.

Although Tasha felt the loss of Lawrence more than Brandon, during the previous ten years or so of her life she and Lawrence hadn't had a close relationship. As with Brandon, Lawrence was more like a grandfather to her. His loss created a void in her emotional life, but it didn't change her day-to-day life, as it had mine.

So, Tasha soon directed her concern to my well-being. Brandon, for his part, suggested that I learn how to design web sites. He thought it would re-engage my brain and, perhaps, give me some added income. And he offered to pay for the classes. From Bandon's perspective, it was a logical solution to my situation. But logic could not repair my battered soul, the soul that Brandon wasn't convinced actually existed.

As these memories flashed through my mind, Greg and I spent perhaps ten or twenty seconds in silence. I didn't notice the time pass, consumed as I was with my memories. When I returned to present consciousness, Greg spared me any sense of awkwardness. He seemed to be patiently studying me, as if trying to peer into my mind.

"What were you thinking about?" he asked.

"Our children."

"What about them?"

"About how different they are. Brandon is more like you, I think. And Tasha more like me ... even though they're both very much individuals."

"Turns out that, despite everything, they came out okay. We didn't do a horrible job raising them, after all."

"We?" I asked.

"Mostly you."

"Let's not forget Lawrence."

"No ... I certainly would never forget Lawrence. I appreciated what he did for the kids. Was he a good husband?"

"Yes, he was."

"Good. I'm glad you found him. I didn't want you to be unhappy, if you can believe that."

I nodded. I was trying to hold back a sob that was threatening to disrupt my composure. We were dipping into a pool of painful, tender memories.

Greg continued, "I tried to be a good husband, too, in my second marriage. I was given a second chance, and I didn't want to blow it."

It was odd for Greg to be telling me this. What was I supposed to feel? Happiness that he had a second chance after destroying our marriage? Sadness for him because, ultimately, it didn't work out? He was talking to me as if I were a sympathetic friend, not the object of his betrayal. Greg was studying my face again. He must have read my ambiguity.

"Sorry … you don't want to hear about that. That's not why … . I didn't come here to talk about my problems."

"It's okay. I mean, we might as well be honest with each other. There's no point in … I don't know … pretending we both haven't had entirely different, separate lives."

"Yes, we both did the best we could under the circumstances."

I didn't like the implication of that statement, as if our experiences were equivalent … as if we had both experienced the same pain from the rupture of our relationship … as if no one was to blame.

"You know I regretted our divorce. I never wanted it."

"Are you implying that it was my fault?"

"No, not at all. I take all the blame. That's why I wanted to apologize."

Greg was being infuriatingly disarming. Despite myself, I smiled at him.

"Yes, I appreciate the effort," I said.

What an idiotic response. But, at the time, it was the best I could do. And, apparently, it was good enough for Greg.

We exchanged a few more sentences, carefully avoiding any raw emotions. We literally talked about the unseasonably cold weather. Finally, I excused myself, using a non-existent call I had to make as my excuse.

Greg stood up and said, "We shouldn't wait this long to meet again."

"No, there's no reason not to stay in touch."

Greg reached out his hand to shake. I gave him a quick little hug instead. It was sprinkling outside. Greg had an umbrella and offered to walk me to my car. I declined his offer. I wanted some time alone to digest what had just transpired. As I walked back to my car, ducking under the awnings of the restaurants and gift stores that lined the street, I felt something wet on my cheek. It was undoubtedly a drop of rain, but for a moment I wondered if it was a tear.

I tried out some arguments to counter the strange tenderness that I was feeling toward Greg.

People don't change. Greg was on best behavior. His so-called apology was motivated by loneliness. It was self-serving. And who was he to think that with a simple verbal apology he could erase all these years of betrayal and neglect? Chocolates! What a cliché! I let him apologize. I did my duty. Now it's over. I'm not required to see him again. No regrets.

Except I knew that I would have regrets if I didn't see him again. Maybe he had changed. Pain and loss can do that to people. And time. As we age, it's harder for us to ignore our regrets. There are fewer distractions. And the clock is ticking. Greg must have felt that. It was brave of him to apologize. I'm not sure I could have summoned the courage to do that. Why shouldn't two lonely old people find solace in each other's company, two old people with a shared history, no matter how painful?

As I slipped into my car, my sweater smelling like a wet dog, I resolved to sleep on it and then talk to Amy. She would have something to say about whether men were truly capable of changing.

32

Questioning

AMY SIPPED HER TEA and looked away, seemingly deep in thought. I had asked her to stop by to discuss the Greg situation. I knew she would be more than willing to share her opinion on that subject. But I had posed a more difficult question. How had Phil changed since they reconciled?

"It's hard to say," was her disappointing response.

"Well, are you two getting along?"

"Getting along," she repeated with a little ironic laugh. "Yes, we're getting along. But we were getting along before our ... our separation. So that's not really the question, is it? You're asking me whether there's some qualitative difference in our relationship."

"Yes, that's what I'm asking."

"Nothing that you could point to ... on the surface, anyway. We've slipped into our old routines. Phil is a little more attentive, when he's around, which is not very much. He's still working long hours, ostensibly to prepare the way for his successor, even though that successor is only a concept at this point."

"A concept?"

"No actual person has been selected. I don't think that will ever happen if it's left up to Phil."

"So, no talk of retirement, then?"

"No. We're each leading our lives, just like before."

"You said he was more attentive."

"Yes, he'll make some pronouncement, then catch himself and ask if it's okay with me."

"Does he mean it?"

"He thinks he does. I haven't tested his conviction. I guess you could say that we've both been careful not to test the situation. We're afraid. It's a little uncomfortable."

"That's why it's hard to say."

"Say what?"

"Whether Phil has changed. You haven't put him to the test."

"Right."

"What would that test look like?"

"Well, if you moved in with us, that would be a test," Amy said, laughing to let me know that she wasn't entirely serious, although she was.

"So, I would be the guinea pig?"

"Or the catalyst, the alchemy that releases the magic."

"I don't have those powers. You're going to have to conjure up your own magic."

"Magic … like the magic we had when we first fell in love?"

Amy looked away, as if peering into that magical past. Then she let out a little bitter laugh and continued:

"But we were young. We were attracted to the things we lacked. I leaned on Phil's aggressive ambition then. Now I have no use for it."

"You have no use for it, after you've already reaped the benefits of it."

"What benefits?"

"The house, the car, the kid's college education … you couldn't have had any of those things without Phil's ambition."

Amy pursed her lips and looked at me as if she were a teacher about to scold a pupil.

"You know very well what I meant. Yes, I've enjoyed the material rewards of being married to a successful man, but I'm talking about now. It does me no good now. Not even the house, the car, the furniture. I could happily live in a tent."

"I would have a hard time imagining you in a tent … at least not for any extended length of time."

"Whatever … I don't know why you're suddenly being so argumentative. What were we even talking about? I forgot."

"The magic of first love."

"Right. Magic. Did you ever have any magic with Greg?"

"Magic?" Now it was my turn to dismiss my memories with a bitter laugh.

I continued, "No, no magic. Greg was a sweet man, a little shy, but very stable. Steady. My mother liked him a lot. In that respect, he was kind of like my father. But I think my mother hoped he wouldn't come with the downside of my father's steadiness—the inertia, the lack of joy, the depression. That was the thing that finally broke my mother. But, on the other hand, unlike Greg, my father wasn't a bad man. He didn't lie or cheat or anything. It seems, in retrospect, that my parents could have worked it out. But maybe not. In any case, Greg seemed like a comfortable couch. I thought I could rely on him. How ironic. Right?"

Amy gave me a sympathetic smile and a roll of the eyes.

"Have you ever wondered whether Phil ever cheated on you?" I continued.

"If he has, and he's had plenty of opportunities … all the business trips he's taken … I wouldn't want to know about it."

"So that's never been an issue."

"I've never made it one."

"Do we have that amount of control? Can we make or not make an issue?"

"I guess … sometimes. You choose your battles. Nobody's perfect. But I suppose, like with your mother, there's a breaking point."

Yes, I knew about breaking points. With Greg, that breaking point had been sudden and painful. But now I was contemplating somehow patching up that break. And I needed to have Amy's advice.

"So … getting back to Greg … "

"All you said was that he was nice. He apologized. And he gave you a box of chocolates. By the way, where are those chocolates?"

I had provided cookies with our tea, but apparently Amy had her mind set on tasting the chocolates. Was it simply a bit of gluttony? Or was it a form of divination? You never could tell with Amy. I went to get the chocolates and offered her the box. She picked one out and tasted it.

"Okay. Not cheap. These are good."

"You want another?"

"No! No, please. Take them away."

I took them away, returned and waited for Amy to speak, as if I were sitting at the foot of an oracle to whom I had just made an offering."

"Well, he spent some money on those chocolates."

"That's it? That's all you have to say?"

"I'm still trying to figure this out. Obviously, he touched you somehow. But if it was just pity for a pitiful man, then I think you need to let go of that. He made his bed a long time ago."

"And decided to sleep in a different one."

"Ha," Amy said, without smiling. "But that was a long time ago. You asked me if I think people can change. My answer is no, people don't change, not basically. Phil is still Phil. Has he learned a few things? I hope so. Are those important, profound things? I can only hope so. You simply don't know enough about Greg to tell if he's learned anything important in life. But don't expect him to be a different person."

"So, you think I should see him again … in order to find out if he's changed … or not changed but learned some important things?"

Amy shrugged. "I'm not sure why you would do that."

"For a lot of reasons. He's the father of my children. And … "

I was struggling to come up with a reason that made any sense. Amy watched me with a slightly amused expression on her face.

" … I had a sense that he *had* changed," I explained. "His apology was … sincere. There's no other way to describe it. And why would he go through the pain of apologizing if he hadn't done some serious soul-searching? He had nothing to gain."

"You said it yourself. He's lonely. A lot of men check out their old lovers when they find themselves single."

"But I'm not an 'old lover.' I'm a woman who was married to him, a woman who divorced him for cheating on me."

"That doesn't prevent him from snooping around. He probably figures it was a long time ago. And he knows you're single now … maybe a little lonely yourself. No harm in testing the waters."

Amy's cynical answer was undoubtedly meant to discourage me. I suppose she had my best interests at heart. She didn't want me to get my hopes up that somehow Greg had transformed himself and that I could have some kind of real relationship with him. But her comment only made me more determined to see Greg again, if only to find out what his true motives were and whether he had truly changed.

Could people change? Were men, in particular, capable of changing? Amy's answer to that question was ambiguous at best. She hoped that Phil had learned a few things. What he had learned, apparently, was that he couldn't just take Amy for granted. She had a breaking point. He had to at least consider her wishes, even if he was unlikely to act upon them. And he was hardly making any concessions. After all, he was spending more time at work, not less. He had made no plans for retirement. As far as I could tell, he was making a show of being considerate, all the while seeing what he could get away with. It was calculated, strategic, like a con man manipulating his mark.

But Amy was no mark. She understood what was happening. She had simply resigned herself to the situation ... for now. If the need arose, however, she could change the power balance simply by leaving. She had done it once, and now she could do it again. That was what was different in their relationship. Phil hadn't changed, but he understood for the first time that there could be serious consequences if he behaved badly.

I told myself that Greg wasn't Phil. You can't generalize to a whole subset of humanity based on one particular case. Lawrence, for instance, had been a good man. He was kind and considerate, and it came naturally to him. He wanted the people around him to be happy. I reminded myself, however, that just as I couldn't overly generalize from the example of Phil, I couldn't overly generalize from the example of Lawrence. Greg remained a mystery, a mystery I wanted to solve.

I waited several weeks before contacting Greg. I told him that I had some questions to ask him. That was true, of course. And, by couching my invitation in those terms, I was also hoping that it would send a neutral message: I would like to see you again, but not because I'm interested in restarting a relationship.

I suggested we meet again at a café. Greg suggested that we have lunch. I agreed. I knew it meant that I would be stuck with him longer than I had anticipated. But it would have been awkward to refuse his invitation.

We met at an Italian café—his suggestion. It was a moderately expensive place with excellent pizza and a cozy neo-rustic interior. The conversation was awkward at first. It's hard to make small-talk with someone with whom you have little in common—no common friends, no common experiences other than sharing DNA in your progeny. It made me realize how truly we had become strangers.

Desperate to make conversation, I asked Greg about his holiday plans. That was a mistake.

"I don't really have any special plans. I was hoping to get together with the kids, but Brandon is traveling and Tash has other plans, I guess. Katie and her husband asked me to stop by, but ... I guess you never met Katie, did you?"

Katie was the stepdaughter that Greg had inherited when he married Melissa.

"No, I never met her. Did you two have a good relationship?"

"I tried. I thought of her as my daughter. But being a stepdad is tough, especially with a teen. It was kind of a tightrope walk. She used to try to use me when she got into an argument with Mel."

"Use you?"

"Yeah, try to get me to take her side. Sometimes I actually agreed with her, but that was an impossible position for me. The stress ... phew! But now we're on good terms, I hope."

So Greg had no holiday plans, except a possible visit with his stepdaughter. He had lived with Katie throughout her childhood, so it made sense that he would have a closer relationship with her than with his biological daughter. Nevertheless, I was miffed at Tasha for spurning Greg's invitation. He was going to spend the holidays alone. I could tell myself that it was his fault, he had caused his own loneliness. But I felt bad for him.

"So ... tell me something," I said. "When we met, you wanted to apologize. I'm curious why you decided to do that? Why now?"

"Well, I guess it was the breakup with Melissa. That hit me in the gut, y'know? I wasn't expecting it. So, it kind of forced me to reevaluate. I mean, what am I doing wrong here? Why haven't I been able to maintain a serious relationship? Those kinds of questions. And I did some thinking. I kind of reviewed my life. And I just felt like the apology ... it was the right thing to do. It was like a step."

"A step to what?"

"I don't know ... a better me?"

"So, you just came up with this idea on your own?"

"Yes ... well, not exactly. I've been seeing a therapist. I mean, I came up with the idea, and she agreed ... thought it might be good for me."

"Was it good for you?"

"Yes, I think it was. Here we are, having lunch together."

"Yes, here we are. Was that your goal to reestablish a relationship with me?"

"I wasn't necessarily expecting that. But I'm glad that we can sit here and talk to each other."

I took a bite of my pizza. So far, I was satisfied with his answers. But there was something else I wanted to know, something that was perhaps even more important to me than the reasons for his apology.

"Do you mind if I ask you a personal question?"

"Go ahead."

"Okay. What happened with Melissa? Are you okay talking about that?"

"Yeah, it's complicated. I mean, I'm not sure I can actually answer that question. I don't know myself. We can't really know what people are thinking. I guess she got tired of me. Something like that. Katie was grown and married. And, y'know, Mel is younger than me. She's fifty-six. Pretty attractive still. Maybe she thought this was her time, her last chance to live it up or find herself or something. None of that makes sense to me. I thought we had something pretty good. What was the point of ... of throwing that all away?"

Greg's eyes started to redden with potential tears. For the first time, I felt how deeply hurt he was by Melissa's decision to leave him. Had that hurt been deeper than the hurt he felt at the time of our divorce? At that time, he was still relatively young. He still had the second half of his life to lead. Now the second act was over. Was there to be a third act? Was I to be part of that third act? Was Greg to be part of my own third act?

"You spent time with your therapist trying to figure out what you did wrong. Right? What did you come up with?"

"Nothing, really. I was a good husband ... I think. I'm not very exciting to live with. Maybe I didn't spend enough time showing my appreciation, telling her I loved her ... and showing it."

"Serious grounds for divorce," I said, wryly.

Greg didn't smile. I felt compelled to explain.

"I mean, being more appreciative ... telling her you loved her more often ... that seems like something that the two of you could've worked out."

"Yeah, that's what my therapist said. But Mel ... she didn't give me a chance. It was like her mind was made up, no matter what I said or did."

This sounded vaguely like Phil's complaint. He thought that Amy had closed off discussion. He had acted as if the two of them were equally at fault. All they needed to do was negotiate as two equal adults, and they could resolve this childish dispute. It was an attitude that was doomed to failure. I wondered if Greg was also missing something. I wondered if he had never really looked deeply enough inside himself to understand his hand in the dissolution of his marriage.

"If you were ever in another relationship," I asked, "what would you do differently, now that you've thought about it?"

"Oh, man! Everything. I'd do everything different. For starters, I'd never take the person for granted."

That was exactly what Phil was supposed to have learned. Was Greg, like Phil, just realizing that bad behavior has consequences? Or was this a declaration of a sincere insight? I wanted to believe that it was the latter. Perhaps I was just feeling charitable.

"You're not that old, for a man," I said. "I think you'll find someone who'll appreciate the new you."

"Thanks. That means a lot to me."

Greg was being so perfectly humble and so perfectly sincere in his answers that I couldn't help wondering if it was an act. His answers almost sounded scripted, as if someone had handed him words that would make him sound like a truly chastened, truly changed man. Who could have written that script? Greg had been seeing a therapist. Was he simply imitating a changed man, one that his therapist approved of? If he was just acting the part, however, he was doing a hell of a job. For all his faults, I doubted that Greg had it in his heart to dissemble to that extent. He was not a good actor. Even when he was hiding his affair with Vickie he was terrible at it.

I looked at Greg sitting across from me. His eyes were relaxed and his lips formed a kind of Buddha smile, the smile of someone who had confronted a difficult truth, and rather than struggle against it, had simply accepted it. I wanted that smile on my lips.

"Well, I think we should find some time to get together during the holidays," I suggested.

"That would be wonderful."

What had I just done? I had invited Greg to renew our relationship. I had made it official. It was an impulse that I knew I might regret. How odd that, at this point in my life, I found myself acting before thinking. One would have thought that age would make one more circumspect. Apparently, my age was having the opposite effect. Perhaps I was just more willing to rely on instinct. Or perhaps I was getting myself into trouble.

33

Mind Reading

I COULDN'T GET THE idea out of my head. What would happen if Greg and Phil talked to each other? I thought that they would have some profound lessons to share. Or perhaps they would simply commiserate over the vagaries of female relationships. Or, more likely, they would talk about sports or business. What was I thinking? How likely was it that Greg and Phil would discuss their innermost thoughts? It might take years for them to feel comfortable enough to share their feelings, to be vulnerable with each other.

Nevertheless, I was determined to thrust them together. I committed to inviting Greg over for the holidays. And it made sense to invite Amy and Phil to join us. I certainly couldn't have Greg over alone. That would have been incredibly awkward. And it would have sent the wrong message.

When I mentioned the idea to Amy, her reaction was typical.

"So, you impulsively invited Greg to dinner, and you want us to … what? Protect you?"

"No! Of course not. But I couldn't exactly have him over alone. That would be just … weird."

"And having him over for dinner isn't weird?"

"Okay, can we get past the fact that I invited him, and move on to … to planning it?"

"Oh, now you want to implicate me in this folly?"

"Yes, exactly, I want to drag you into the dark, mad hell of my life."

"Okay, now it's starting to sound interesting."

Without my asking, Amy started to help me plan the menu. She agreed to bring the *pièce de résistance*, as she put it. With the plan settled, I decided to try out my other folly on Amy.

"Don't you think it would be interesting to see Phil and Greg together?"

"Uh … I can think of more interesting pairings."

"I think we should leave them alone together at some point. The only thing is, I would love to hear what they say to each other."

"Nothing of interest, I can assure you, my dear."

"But what if I prime Greg … tell him to dig for insights from someone who has had to … to readjust his thinking when it came to relationships?"

"Are you setting this up to amuse yourself? Or do I detect some missionary zeal here?"

"I have no idea what you're talking about."

"Do you think you can fix Greg? Help him become a reborn … whatever … kind, thoughtful, loving man?"

"I don't need to. Greg is already working on himself. He's seeing a therapist. It's just that he said that he's trying to figure out why he hasn't been able to have a lasting relationship. And I thought, there's nothing like talking to someone who has done some reevaluating, someone who could share some personal experiences."

"My dear, you're giving them both too much credit. But, sure, if you insist, we can leave them alone. As for listening in, barring wiretapping them, that might be a little difficult."

I decided against wiretapping, although I have to admit that I considered it. I had another plan. Amy would prep Phil, tell him that Greg was struggling and needed advice. I, in turn, would prep Greg, telling him that Phil had struggled with some of the same relationship issues as he had. And I would encourage Greg to ask Phil's advice. What we didn't tell Phil and Greg was that we were planning to interrogate each of them afterward, resorting to torture if necessary to extract the truth.

The dinner was pleasant enough. Because of Greg's unique position as father of my progeny, we were able to share stories about our children. The discussion turned eventually to the state of the economy, which Phil and Greg both agreed was more precarious than it appeared.

When the men started throwing around macro-economic statistics, Amy and I took our leave, ostensibly to discuss my pathetic wardrobe situation. In reality, that was the last thing about which I would have asked Amy to advise me. Our tastes were quite different. Amy preferred colorful clothing. And when her outfit wasn't colorful enough, she would liven it up with a patterned scarf, a habit she probably picked up in France. I preferred blacks, grays, and subdued earth tones. If I wore a scarf, it would also be black or gray ... or white if I was feeling particularly gregarious. And, in any case, I had no intention of buying new clothes. I felt, given the state of the environment, it was a moral imperative to reduce our consumption ... the diminishing effect on our GNP be damned.

Thanks to Amy, the men had been supplied with a *digestif* (snifters of cognac) to lubricate the conversation. Hiding behind the bedroom door, we could hear them talking. Much to our chagrin, however, we couldn't hear what they were saying. Only Phil's occasional boisterous laugh would pierce through to our hiding place. We recommitted to our plan B—interrogation after the fact.

The next day, Amy and I shared the information that we had been able to extract respectively from Phil and Greg. Here is the conversation, as best as I can reconstruct it, using inference and novelistic license to fill in the missing parts:

> GREG: *So, I don't know if Lexi told you, but I'm getting divorced. It came as a surprise to me ... kind of a punch in the gut. I'm still trying to figure out what happened. Wondering if there was something different I could've done.*
> PHIL: *Yeah, I hear you. Amy and I ... we've had our ups and downs. You think everything is going along fine, and then suddenly your wife announces that it's not. Then you've got to deal with that.*
> GREG: *So how did you deal with it?*
> PHIL: *Well, I tried apologizing, groveled a little, y'know. But that doesn't work. It's not enough.*
> GREG: *What's enough?*
> PHIL: *Well, as best as I can understand it, they want you to kind of ... read their mind. You have to figure out on your own what they're thinking ... and what you did wrong. Then you have to make amends.*
> GREG: *How did you make amends?*

PHIL: I … I'm not exactly sure. Persistence, I think … that's important. Just keep trying. Be nice. Try to be understanding. And be patient. I think that's the hardest part … patience.
GREG: Mel, my wife … I don't think she's even open to me making amends. And I don't even know what that would entail. It's not like I did anything wrong.
PHIL: No, exactly! That's the thing. You don't need to have done anything wrong. But you've got to admit to it anyway. That's where the mind-reading part comes in.

Amy laughed when I showed her the reconstructed dialogue.

"You've nailed it! You really do have some writing ability."

Coming from Amy, that was high praise. I decided to store away that compliment for the next time I got up the courage to try my hand at writing a novel.

For now, having considered the conversation that took place, we decided the experiment was a failure. The men appeared to have learned very little from their experiences. They were self-justifying and emotionally deaf. But they were not entirely wrong.

"Do we expect men too much of our men? Do we expect them to read our minds?" I asked Amy.

"Yes, of course we do. But reading our minds is just asking them to pay attention, to see our side of the story. That's just so hard for them they have to call it mind reading."

"But if we know it's hard for them, don't you think we need to help them? They have good intentions."

"Help them? They're not children. We're asking them to change. If we help them, tell them what to think and do, they'll never change. They'll never get better."

Amy was right on one level. These were grown men, not children. It was not our job to mold them into caring adults. But I couldn't help thinking that, in some areas at least, they could use a little molding. Some men simply lack the emotional understanding, for whatever reason, to "mind read." That's undoubtedly true of some women, as well. Up to what point do you accept the deficiencies of understanding in your companion and try to help them? And at what point are those deficiencies so repugnant that they become grounds for separation? I felt sorry for Melissa. I fear she may have reached that point too soon. I knew the loneliness that was likely to follow.

34

Intention

I SAT STARING AT my breakfast—toast, butter, jam, coffee—the same breakfast I served myself every day. It was not a punishment to eat the same thing every day. I liked this breakfast. That's why I ate it regularly. I took care of myself. I was eating a relatively healthy, if uninspired, diet. I bathed regularly. I brushed my teeth and flossed. I cleaned my clothes and brushed my hair. I always had something to do during the day—yoga, tutoring, French class, talking to Amy, talking to my daughter, paying bills, light housework, shopping for food. This was my life. I didn't mind it.

There were advantages to living alone. I was on my own schedule. I had gotten up late. It was almost 9 o'clock when I finished eating my breakfast. I wore an old bathrobe. When I discovered some toast crumbs in my lap, I brushed them onto the floor and told myself that I would sweep the kitchen later that day ... or maybe the next day. That was a kind of freedom.

So what was this feeling of grief gnawing at me? Was "grief" the right word? I suppose it was, if grief is the feeling of missing someone, or something, that is no longer there. I wasn't sure who or what I was missing. I just knew I was missing it. I reminded myself that this was not at all a Zen-like attitude. Why was I making myself miserable over something that was not there? Something I had no control over?

I blamed my encounter with Greg. His presence in my life brought up so many emotions. There was the pain of his betrayal, of course. And his reappearance had rekindled memories of Lawrence and our life together. On the other hand, there was the tantalizing prospect of a man entering my life, a decent man, a man I had loved when I was young, a man who regretted his youthful error and was trying to make amends. I had the power to forgive him. I could simply reach out and re-establish a relationship, a relationship based on hard-earned wisdom. It would be easy. Could I love him again? That seemed unlikely. But I could see us being friends again, being companions.

I caught myself, once again, feeling kindly toward Greg. Was my moment of breakfast "grief" making me irrational? I decided I needed a dose of cynicism. Amy, of course, would provide that. But I already knew her attitude toward Greg, which boiled down to this: Not worth it. I decided instead to call Tasha. After all, she knew her father much better than I.

"Why'd you invite him for dinner?" she asked.

"I guess I felt sorry for him."

"Okay. But that's not really your job. You don't owe him anything."

"It's not about owing. It's about … forgiving. He apologized for what he did."

"Well, that's easy."

"I don't think it was easy. And he didn't ask for anything in return. He didn't ask for forgiveness."

"Why are we even talking about him?"

"I wanted to get your thoughts … about how he's changed."

"Changed? I don't know if he's changed. I know that he was surprised when Melissa asked for a divorce. I know that he's feeling lonely. But has he changed? I don't know."

"I guess I can tell you this, since he told me. He's seeing a therapist."

"Okay, that's something. That's a surprise."

"Was he a good father to you?"

"What kind of question is that? Of course not. A good father wouldn't have fucked up your marriage."

"But since then, has he been good to you?"

"He's helped me out sometimes, given me some money when I needed it, given me some business advice. But we never really talked that much. When we were young, me and Brandon, we had our weekends together. He was nice to us. He'd take us places, but we never really got close. Melissa was nice to us, though. She'd have us over for dinner sometimes. I always got the feeling that she was the one who instigated it, not Dad."

"What about recently? Has Greg reached out to you?"

"Kind of … he wanted to get together over the holidays, but I didn't really want to. It would be kind of awkward … and, anyway, I had other plans."

"Don't you think it would've been kind to meet with him?"

"What's the deal, Mom? Why are you all of sudden taking his side? Why are you so interested? You're not, like, planning to date him or anything are you?"

"No, I wouldn't call it dating. But I was considering, maybe, seeing him a little more frequently."

"Oh, my god! That is just weird! Are you that desperate?"

"I'm not desperate. And I don't know what you're thinking, but this would just be on a friendly basis."

"Mom, if you're lonely and want to date someone, I'm pretty sure you could find someone better suited to you. Why don't you try one of those senior dating sites?"

Was Tasha right? Was I settling for a relationship with Greg without even attempting something better? I felt an obligation to try.

I stared at the question. On one side of the screen was an abstract design with spontaneous splashes of color. On the other side was a monochromatic, geometric design that was lovely in its simplicity and depth of perspective. I was required to choose one as part of my personality test, the test that would match me with prospective "silver" singles.

The prompt advised the test subjects to choose quickly without thinking too much. I was stuck. I was thinking. I appreciate abstract paintings. And I like color when it's handled with beauty and lucidity. I can sink into a Rothko or a Pollock. This particular abstract design, however, seemed banal and glib. I was drawn more to the austere, geometric design, but only because it was the stronger of the two designs. That left me in a quandary. I didn't want my potential suitors to be misled. I didn't want them to think that I was as cold and austere as the monochrome design, or that I was incapable of being spontaneous and life-affirming.

This impasse made me question the whole concept of online dating. Did I even want to "date" someone? My life was good. It was uncomplicated. I was free to come and go as I pleased. I had friends. I had my children. I had interests. Why did I need to complicate my life by dating? And where was this dating supposed to lead? I had convinced myself that I didn't want to get involved in another serious relationship at my age. It would be destined to failure and disappointment. Habits would be petrified. There would be no years of emotional debt accrued, nothing that would serve to support the years of selfless service required if one or both of us became sick or decrepit in old age.

After reaffirming my opposition to late-life dating, I immediately began to question myself. Was I just chickening out? What did I have to lose? Maybe there was a lovely man waiting for me, a widower like me, who could be a kind and interesting companion, someone who could laugh with me about the assaults of old age, someone who would motivate me to comb my hair before coming to breakfast, to buy a new blouse, to make better meals. Why not give it a try?

This indecision was my fundamental flaw. I was cursed with a reflective mind. And when you see all sides of a question, the world looks like a maze. It's hard to choose a path. I wondered if the whole Zen attitude I affected was just an elaborate device I constructed to avoid decisive action. Yet Zen Buddhism wasn't about being passive. It was about accepting what couldn't be changed. My solitary existence could be changed. I could choose to date.

I selected the geometric design and finished the questionnaire. I was curious to see the results, but I told myself to lower my expectations. I was a sixty-three-year-old woman with gray hair. I was no beauty. Some might call me attractive, but only after getting to know me. Online dating didn't allow for that "getting to know" period. I thought of Gordon, my eighty-ish, pot-smoking, would-be seducer. That put things in perspective.

Ironically, later that day, Greg called and asked me if I wanted to see a revival of "Top Girls," a Caryl Churchill play, which I believe was a satire of Thatcher-like individualism. I had no idea that Greg was interested in plays, no less ones critical of unbridled capitalism. Or was it just a ruse? Did he just pick something he thought I would be interested in? And was he asking me out on a date? Or was he just looking for companionship? There was only one way to find out.

35

Validation

I LOOKED ACROSS THE table at Greg and wondered who this man was. Of course, he was my cheating, ex-husband and the father of my two children. But he was also a mystery, a stranger, someone I hadn't known intimately for decades, someone whom I didn't even know that well when we were married and living together.

I had suggested we go to a café after the play. I was eager to solve the mystery of the man in front of me, with his ruddy, Santa cheeks and eyes that looked back at me ingenuously.

"So ... tell me what you thought of the play."

I was hoping that Greg's answer would reveal many things. Was he actually interested in the play? Or had he just tried to please me? Was he attuned to the feminist themes of the play? Or, for him, was it just a story about ambitious women? Why had he even suggested a play? And, ultimately, where was this date headed?

"Wow! It was interesting," he said. "I read that it was written back in the eighties, when Thatcher was in power. It seemed like these women were somehow inspired by Thatcher's strength, or at least her ambition."

"Did you admire Thatcher?"

"I didn't admire or not admire her. I wasn't really political at the time."

"What about now, looking back, looking at the women in the play?"

"Well, they were not nice people, to say the least."

"Don't you think women have a right to be ambitious, just like men?"

"Of course. But there's ambition and ambition. I mean, there's a limit, right? I think that's what the writer, Churchill, was saying. You can take ambition too far, give up too much for it."

"You mean, like men do, frequently," I commented, more as a statement than a question.

"Yes, I guess some men do. But that's not a trait that anyone, women or men, should necessarily be imitating. Isn't that what she was saying? I mean, it turns out the main character is competing with her own mother! That's ... that's taking ambition pretty far over the line, don't you think?"

"Yes, that twist definitely drove home the point."

Apparently, Greg was paying attention. He was genuinely interested in understanding the author's intention.

"Do you go to plays frequently?" I asked.

"Not frequently. Mel used to like to go sometimes. I would go with her. She kind of had to drag me along at first. But I got into it. I think plays are a lot more thought-provoking than movies, at least these days. I'm not really interested in that comic book stuff."

"So, you didn't invite me just because you thought I would enjoy it?"

"Well ... I did think you would enjoy it. Didn't you?"

"Yes, of course. But I mean ... would you have gone anyway, if I wasn't available?"

"Yeah, probably. But you kind of want to have someone to talk to about it, not just go alone."

"Yes, having someone to talk to is important."

Greg smiled and took my hand, and then, looking a little sheepish, asked, "Is that okay?"

I nodded and left my hand in his.

"I hope we can do this again," he said.

Greg let go of my hand after a few awkward seconds. We talked some more about the play. This time I told him what I thought, namely that it was a critique of the kind of feminism that asks women to be just as individualistic and ruthless as men, to imitate their worst tendencies. Greg asserted that the only difference between men and women was that women, up until recently, lacked the same opportunities. Otherwise, they were just as good and just as bad as men.

"Look what happened when women finally got the vote … 1920, I think," he said. "Everybody thought we'd have a kinder, gentler country. But we didn't. We kept having wars and greed and … and corruption, just like before. Nothing changed."

"That's true. But maybe that had more to do with the fact that women still weren't in positions of power. They didn't control the money. And maybe there was something else going on … maybe they were still in the habit of acceding to men's will. Maybe there's still a process of unshackling of the mind taking place."

"Okay … okay … you might have something there. But you're still saying that women are somehow morally superior to men. I'm not sure I can buy that."

"All I'm saying is that it's a thesis that hasn't yet been disproven. You'd have to wait for women to truly be in a position as powerful as men are, to find out. And that hasn't happened yet. Do you know what percentage of women are CEO's of big companies?"

"No."

"About five percent."

"Okay, good point. I see you've thought about this. I admire that."

"You admire women who think?"

"Yes, as a matter of fact, I do," he said, smiling his Santa Klaus smile.

Greg drove me back in his well-maintained, well-traveled, Toyota sedan. I was happy he hadn't gone out and bought something clichéd, like a sports car or a luxury SUV. He was still a practical man, humble in that way. I'm not sure why I cared what kind of man he was. But I did.

He drove up to the curb in front of the house, set the brake and turned off the key. That made me anxious. I had flashbacks to awkward dates in my past, when all I wanted to do was open the car door and rush into the house. I wasn't sure that's what I wanted to do now. But I certainly didn't want Greg to try to kiss me.

"So … Lexi … I enjoyed this."

"So did I."

"You've been kind to me. And I didn't deserve it."

"Maybe you did. Maybe you're a better man now."

"I hope so. I'm trying. Do you … ? Would you consider … seeing me again?"

"Yes, of course. As long as you continue to behave yourself," I said with a little laugh. I wanted to lighten things up.

"Good," he said. "I'll behave then."

"Good night. And thank you for the play."

"You're welcome. It was my pleasure."

I stepped out of the car and headed for the door. Greg had made good on his promise to behave himself. When I stepped inside, I checked my phone. There were five responses to my online dating profile. I had no desire to look at them.

36

Expectations

"Tell me about your date with Greg."

Amy sat behind the wheel of her BMW. I enjoyed riding in her car with its comfortable, infinitely adjustable power seats, and the solid, understated luxury of its interior. I didn't think of myself as an envious person. But I secretly coveted Amy's car. I felt safe and pampered in it. And that was an especially desired feeling when the world outside felt as if it were heading toward chaos and destruction. Or perhaps I was projecting. Perhaps it was my life I felt was heading for chaos and destruction.

I once mentioned to Amy that I enjoyed riding in her car. She dismissed my comment by saying, "Oh, this old thing?"

It was "old," maybe seven or eight years old. But it still spoke of wealth and the comfort it can afford. Amy's dismissal of my comment represented a certain "laissez-allez" attitude common among the wealthy. Not wanting to appear too ostentatious, they show their disdain for material things by taking a neglectful, casual attitude toward their possessions. Yet they surround themselves with fine things.

Amy was driving us back from a lecture we had attended titled "Women in the Victorian Novel." One point the speaker made had stuck in my mind. She argued that, although women (Jane Eyre, for instance) were portrayed as individuals with a sense of agency, they were defined as heroines by their love and sacrifice, not by their derring-do. I wondered if I were more of a Victorian woman than a modern woman. Hadn't my life been about love and sacrifice? Was that a bad thing? Wouldn't the world be a better place if we all (men included) decided to make love and sacrifice a priority in their lives?

Of course, the "sacrifice" part can be taken too far. We don't want to go back to being simply child-bearing handmaids to men. My sacrifice had been to become a working mother, tending to my children and being a helpmate to my husband, all the while continuing to carry out my professional duties. Just like the Victorian heroines, I chose this path. I had no regrets, but I had no desire to relive the life I had led. It would be too exhausting. I was happy to continue to lend support to my children in any way I could. But the idea of taking on another man in my life was more problematic.

Amy had interrupted these thoughts with her question about my "date" with Greg.

"It wasn't really a date," I replied.

"What was it then? I mean, you went to a play and had a drink afterwards. Isn't that a date?"

"If you and I went to a play and had a drink afterwards, would it be a date?"

"You mean if there was no sex involved ... implied or otherwise."

"Yes, exactly."

"You're saying Greg is just a friend, with no ulterior motive in seeing you?"

"Yes, as far as I'm concerned."

"And as far as he's concerned?"

"I can't peer into his brain. He may have secret intentions, but all I can say is that he's been ... well, he's behaved as a friend would."

"I guess I'm just a little worried about you."

"There's nothing to worry about."

"Sure, but you're cultivating this relationship with some kind of hope of ... I don't know ... what exactly? You're getting your hopes up that this man, this unfaithful man who can't seem to maintain a relationship with a woman is going to become a friend ... a true friend. Or something more, perhaps?"

"I'm not looking for more. You're afraid I'll be disappointed. Maybe I will. But I can handle that. I'm just in a wait-and-see space. Whatever happens, happens. He's been pleasant to be with, so far. That's all I know."

Amy sniffed. "Okay, you're a grown woman, free to make your own mistakes."

Where did this unnecessary hostility come from? Was Amy jealous of Greg? How absurd. He would never replace Amy in my life. I wanted to reassure her. But I couldn't. I felt hurt by her lack of faith in my judgment.

So, I simply responded, "Is forgiveness ever a mistake?"

"Yes, if it comes back to bite you. How many women have forgiven their men for unforgivable treatment and then lived to regret it?"

"Seriously? Are you implying that Greg would deliberately hurt me in some way? Physically?"

"No, I'm just making a point. I mean, he did already hurt you psychologically. You can't dismiss that."

"He can never hurt me the same way again. He's not in a position to. And, anyway, that is hardly his intention."

"You admitted that you don't know his intentions."

"I know enough to know that he's trying to make amends for past mistakes."

"It's odd that you're defending him so vigorously."

"I'm not. I'm just stating the situation as I see it."

"Okay, I hope you get what you want out of the relationship."

Amy seemed to be backing down. But her response implied a certain dismissive attitude, as if she knew I wouldn't get what I wanted. The thing that Amy didn't understand was that I, myself, didn't know what I wanted from the relationship. I was just letting it happen.

The conversation with Amy disturbed me enough that I sought out a second opinion. That weekend, I invited Tasha to walk with me. We strolled along the Berkeley marina enjoying the expansive view of the bay, the San Francisco skyline, the Golden Gate Bridge and Mount Tamalpais to the north.

"So tell me how things are going," I said.

"Okay, Gary's being an ass, but that's nothing new."

"What's going on with him?"

"Oh, you know, the usual. He's acting like he's my boss, giving me shit to do that I don't have time for."

"Can't you just tell him that?"

"I did. I told him he's not my boss and he can't add to my workload.

Then he acts all hurt and accuses me of not being a team player. I think he's talking shit about me behind my back."

"Have you talked to your actual boss about it?"

Tasha scoffed. "Like she cares. She's just collecting her fat salary and doesn't want to make any waves. Gary's been there longer than I have."

"I guess you just have to stand up for yourself. That's something you're good at. I admire that."

"Yeah, I guess so."

"Anything good to report?"

"I'm dating someone."

"Really? Tell me about him."

"Her."

"Oh, tell me about her."

"Well, it's weird. It's the first time I've dated a femme ... which puts me more in the butch role, but not really."

"Is it working out?"

"Yeah, so far. But we've only seen each other a couple of times. So ..."

Of course, I wanted to pry further into Tasha's new relationship, but I knew from experience that she was signaling to me that the discussion was over. The relationship was too tenuous to discuss. I would need to wait for further details, if there were any forthcoming.

"What about you?" Tasha asked.

"What about me?"

"You never really told me what happened with Amy. I thought you two were kind of starting ... something."

"Something? You mean like something beyond friendship?"

"Yeah, I was kind of rooting for the two of you to hook up."

"No, we didn't. It was complicated."

"But you two were sleeping together."

"Yes, sleeping in the same bed. I mean, we were very close, intimate in a way. Amy was open to more, but I wasn't."

"Ugh. You should have let go for once and given it a try. Women are amazing in bed."

"I'm sure that's true. I'm just not ... I'm not looking for a sexual partner."

"Really? You don't want it? Or you're just not looking?"

"I don't know. You can never say never."

Tasha smirked, probably assuming that I was just repressing my true feelings. I wasn't. I was being honest with myself. Of course, I had a certain nostalgia for sex—the excitement, the sensation, the momentary forgetting, the release, the closeness. But I no longer sought that. I no longer needed it. I was looking for a different kind of intimacy.

I was content with the relationship I had had with Amy when we lived together, the tenderness, the warmth, the concern, the intellectual exchange. I wasn't sure if I could ever replace that. And that left a hole in my heart. But I accepted that pain, just as I had accepted the death of Lawrence. The older you get, the more pain you carry with you. It's just part of you. Your heart expands to accommodate the hurt.

It would be difficult to explain all this to Tasha. She was still looking for love in all its forms. Better to let her heart remain free to pursue her search, unfettered by my old woman musings on the state of my heart, riddled with holes but still pumping. It would be like offering someone a bouquet of flowers and, at the same time, reminding them that the petals will soon turn brown and drop. You could protest that there's a certain beauty to that very natural process, but it would certainly spoil the moment.

"I think you had an opportunity, and you let it go," Tasha said.

"Maybe. I miss Amy terribly. Sometimes I regret not fighting to keep her with me. But … I couldn't. There was too much baggage."

"You mean her husband?"

"Yes, Phil was part of the baggage. She needed to resolve that."

"You're too unselfish."

"If 'unselfish' is the worst criticism you can come up with, then I'm in pretty good shape."

"Don't worry. I'll come up with some other criticisms. Just give me a little time," Tasha said, laughing.

She put her arm around my shoulders and squeezed me close . We walked together for a time in silence, smelling the salty air, listening to the water lapping on the rocks of the breakwater, taking in the beauty of this vast body of water dotted by the white sails of small boats heading nowhere in particular.

"Why'd you invite me on this walk?" Tasha asked.

"To talk."

"About what?"

"I wanted your opinion."

"About?"

"Your father ... and me."

Tasha turned toward me, her curiosity peaked.

"You two aren't ... like, actually ... "

"No, we're not actually anything. Just getting reacquainted. The thing is ... Amy seems to think that, by letting him into my life, I'm headed for trouble."

"Trouble?"

"Well, disappointment. But you can't be disappointed if you don't have any expectations."

"And you want my opinion ... about what?"

"Well, what do you think about Greg ... and me, our budding friendship?"

"Is that what it is? Friendship?"

"That's what I want."

"I thought you said you didn't have any expectations."

"Other than that, just ... companionship ... as a possibility."

"And Amy has a problem with that?"

"No, I don't think so. But she thinks that maybe Greg has something else in mind. Or that I can't trust him."

"I don't have any problem with you and Dad patching things up. I think it's nice. It's kind of sweet. As far as the two of you actually having an affair or whatever ... that would just be fucking weird, though. But whatever ... You're a grown-ass woman. You can do what you want."

"I don't have any intention of having an affair, as you put it. That's the last thing on my mind."

"Then why are you asking my opinion? You already know what you think."

"I guess I was wondering if you thought I was missing something. Is my judgment clouded by wishful thinking?"

"I guess you'll find out."

"Am I wrong to trust your father? Am I wrong to think he's changed in some fundamental way?"

"No, I don't think so. Dad's not an inherently bad person. He means well. But he is what he is."

"I can't argue with that. He is what he is. I'm just not certain what he is."

"He's a sad, lonely old man … a situation he put himself in."

"I'm a sad, lonely old woman."

"You are not. You may be a little lonely, but you're definitely not sad."

I'm not sad. That's true, I thought. Tasha's off-hand comment lifted my spirits more than she knew. In fact, the whole conversation with her made me more confident. I was, after all, a "grown-ass" woman, rightfully relying on my own judgment. And if I were disappointed, I could handle that. My daughter, Sage (as she preferred to call herself) had offered sage advice and had, in her own way, given me confidence. It was a reversal of roles. One that I welcomed. I put my arm through Tasha's as we continued our walk. The conversation turned to Tasha's new girlfriend. I dug for more details, re-assuming my motherly role.

37

Physics

I HAD ONLY A passing interest in physics. But I found the theories of modern physics to be fascinating. They described a mysterious universe, with laws that didn't apply in the world I knew and understood. Yet those were the laws that, behind the scenes, governed the observable universe.

The familiar world of solid objects—the world of Newtonian physics, where objects appeared to behave according to principles like gravity, velocity, and inertia—was, in fact, an illusion. Instead, modern theoretical physics posited notions like parallel universes and twin particles that acted on each other in defiance of time and distance.

I didn't have the training or mathematical inclination to truly understand these reality-shattering theories. For me, however, they had a humbling effect. They were proof that we know very little about the nature of reality. This notion could be disorienting, but for me it was strangely comforting. It meant that any attempt to truly understand the world around me was essentially futile. I could only observe. And observing was what I was good at.

At this particular point in time, what I was observing around me was that the people who were close to me, the particles in my universe, were coupling. Amy was once again coupled with Phil.

Danielle was coupled with Seth. Tasha had a girlfriend she was seeing regularly. And even Brandon had found the electron to his proton.

I, however, was not coupled. Was I breaking some kind of cosmic law? What was this strange, uninvited force pulling me toward Greg? In any rational theory, we would have been particles that repelled each other. Or to put it another way, the atom of our family had been split, and the resulting energy had been released long ago. You don't put an atom back together again after an atomic explosion. But there it was, an unexplained attraction. This was an anomaly that could be the basis of a doctoral thesis.

I was repelled by the idea of online dating. It seemed unnatural, as if you were using a cyclotron to smash together particles that were never meant to meet. I had postponed looking at my online responses, but I needed to gain some perspective on Greg. So, I put aside my reservations and studied the five profiles of the men who pinged me.

I didn't trust the profiles. The minimum age was fifty-five. Yet the photos accompanying the profiles looked like men in their forties. Why would a man post an old picture of himself, when it would be immediately apparent on meeting that he was much older? Perhaps meeting in person was not the point. Perhaps the point was to fantasize. This hypothesis was supported by the glowing descriptions the men wrote about themselves. "Well-travelled." "Educated." "Stable income." "Sensual." "Seeking to share the adventure and pleasures of life."

Of course, one wants to present themselves in the best possible light. But how about a little honesty? No one mentioned dentures, bad backs, hip replacements, erectile dysfunction, cynicism about the fate of humanity, or fear of dying alone. No one, that is, except one brave individual. He proudly declared that he was eighty-three years old. Most of his teeth were missing. Arthritis prevented him from walking more than a few blocks. He was often in a crabby mood. He wasn't sure if he could get an erection, but was willing to try. Was this a joke? If not, he was the only one of the five prospective suitors who elicited anything other than contempt from me. Yet who in their right mind would want to date this guy?

I had lived a life. I had had two husbands. I had born two children. I had my share of enjoyable, even daring, sex. I didn't need to subject myself to the inevitable humiliation and disappointment of online dating. Not at my age. None of the "interested" men had even bothered to write a personal note. Was I supposed to reach out and sell myself to them? Was that what online dating meant when you were sixty-three years old with gray hair and an imperfect body? I didn't need that. I didn't want it.

My intention was to gain some perspective on Greg, and I had. He was looking better than ever. Greg had rotated back into my gravitational pull. It was as if he were a comet, a castoff from an earlier explosion. Yet forces were drawing his orbit ever closer to me. As astronomical phenomena go, it was unusual; but, with the right mathematical calculations, entirely predictable. It was the work of natural forces. It did not require a massive cyclotron to force us together.

Greg was right. I had been kind to him. It wasn't an effort on my part. He had been humble and honest. He had invited that kindness. I wanted his companionship. I wanted his friendship. The idea of rekindling a romance with him, however, repelled me. It was a physical reaction brought on by the trauma of our divorce. I was willing to let him be a man in my life. But would he be happy with that? Would he want more?

I looked once more at the picture of the honest, toothless, old man and laughed. I decided to let the mysterious forces of nature take their course.

38

Sustenance

I PLACED THE CARTON of split pea soup in my shopping cart. It was a good soup. They called it "homemade," meaning it was made on the premises in large vats by people who were paid to make it. It was not homemade, but it was close enough for me. I didn't have the patience or the will to make soup for myself.

I looked down at my cart. Bread. Butter. Marmalade. A freeze-dried Thai rice mix. Tofu. One large chicken breast. Mayonnaise. Black tea. A small container of half & half. I wasn't finished shopping yet. But I wondered if other shoppers could already discern that I was living alone.

I passed by a display of Swiss chocolate bars. They were exorbitantly priced. I bought two.

When I got home I texted Tasha.

Want to come over tonight? I bought two chocolate bars and I need you to eat one.
Can't. I'm with Julia tonight.
Bring her too.
She's taking me out.
Ok. Have a nice time.

I made myself a cup of tea and sat down in the living room. I wanted to eat one of the chocolate bars, but I had promised myself that I would wait at least two days before indulging. It was a form of self-discipline that I felt I needed. I was taking care of myself. There was no one else to do it for me.

I thought about reading the novel I had started. It was a contemporary novel about a recently-divorced, forty-year-old doctor. The first one hundred pages were devoted primarily to his sexual exploits, after his libido was unleashed by his divorce. It described a different world than the one I knew as a younger woman. The women the main character was dating were aggressively sexual. They texted him pictures of their breasts and buttocks. These were not young women. They were in their thirties and forties. I had a hard time imagining that this sexualized version of dating was the norm. But there it was in black and white. The author was a woman. And the reviews I had read never mentioned that the novel was unrealistic.

I wasn't in the mood for sexual exploits, so I decided to watch a few minutes of the "shit show" instead. The current story was about the international conference on climate change. Government representatives from around the world had failed to reach an agreement about how to combat the impending rise in temperature. I could feel my blood pressure rise at the short-sighted stupidity and greed of these so-called world leaders. I felt helpless. This combination of anger, frustration and helplessness was not healthy.

So, I switched off the TV and picked up the book. The book revealed that the main character, the doctor, was still having loveless sex with his divorced ex-wife. What a strange world we humans have created.

Late that evening, Tasha called me.

"Hey, Mom, what's up?"

"Nothing much. How are you?"

"I'm good. Just got back from dinner with Julia."

"It's still early."

"Yeah, we both have to work tomorrow. But … uh, I kind of felt bad that I couldn't come over. Are you okay?"

"Yes, of course, I'm fine."

"Did you eat both chocolate bars?"

"No, I was a good girl."

"Don't be too good."

"Okay. I'll follow your example."

"Yes, you should. Just the right amount of bad."

"You know … I've been meaning to ask you about something," I said.

"Go ahead."

"Have you ever thought about moving back in here, with me?"

"Mmm, not really. I mean, I've thought about it. I'd save a shitload of money, but … . Are you, like, serious?"

"I don't know. The way things turned out. I'm here alone in the house now."

"I don't know. Could you really handle it?"

"I'm not sure. Could you?"

"I'm not sure either. It would be kind of … weird. I don't know. There's the cat … and having people over … and you, like, go to bed at 9 o'clock or something."

"There would be an adjustment."

"Yeah, but who would have to adjust to who? It's your house. You'd want to make the rules. It would be like I was a teenager again."

"Oh, god, not that. It would have to be better than that."

"I don't know, Mom. I'd have to think about it. I may not even stick around here very long. It's so fucking expensive to live here. If I'm ever going to buy a house or anything, I'm going to have to move out of the area … out of the state."

"I don't want you to go."

"Are you going to buy me a house here?"

"I would if I could. And you and Brandon will get this house when … the time comes."

"Agh! Don't be so dramatic! I'll be old when that happens."

We left the question of Tasha moving back home undecided, but it was becoming clear that it was unlikely. I wasn't sure I wanted it to happen. My suggestion was an impulse brought on by split pea soup and one too many chocolate bars.

39

Gathering

January 23RD was an odd time to have a holiday party. But by the time I thought of it, it was too late to plan it any earlier. And my little network of friends and family had scattered geographically during the actual holidays. It turned out that nobody had plans for January 23rd.

The idea came to me while watching TV and eating my split pea soup. I was very aware of being alone and eating something to which I had attached a symbolic value. It was one of those moments when you lift your consciousness and look down at yourself. I saw a gray-haired woman, dressed in sweatpants and an old sweater, enjoying her soup in a large, empty room. She wasn't sad. Rather she had a wry smile on her lips, aware that she was playing out an ironic version of the lonely widow. It almost made her laugh out loud.

That's when it hit me. I was in control of my life. I had chosen the soup, the TV show, the being alone. This is what I wanted at that moment. But it was not my fate. I was connected to people, even if they weren't physically with me. I decided that I would have a gathering of those people, the people who spun in my orbit connected by various forms of love, blood, and obligation.

There would be nine guests, which was more than I could handle on my own. I intended to have the party catered, but Amy talked me into preparing most of the food at home. Her advice: "You buy the desserts, not the real food. It's never good. You have to make that yourself."

That was her verdict, and it was final. So, the two of us spent a good part of the day cooking together and talking. As usual, our conversation began by sharing our aches and pains. Amy had an inexplicable rash.

It didn't hurt or itch, but it was annoying and unsightly. I was getting mild headaches that I can only describe as brain fog. This led to a one-up contest to see who had the most physical ailments.

My opening gambit was my stiff back in the morning. Amy countered with a weird pain in her ankle that would disappear by noon. After several similar moves and counter-moves, I made what I thought would be my coup de grâce.

"I'm three fourths of an inch shorter than I was when I was in my twenties."

Amy scoffed, "Is that the best you can do? Everybody's shorter in their sixties."

Despite Amy's disdainful dismissal of my coup de grâce, I claimed victory. So did Amy.

Then Amy's curiosity got the better of her, and the conversation turned to Greg.

"Greg's coming. Right?"

"Yes."

"Does that mean something? Are you two … getting involved?"

"No, it's nothing like that. He's part of the family. I can't ignore that. And he's been nice to me. He is who he is, but he's not the same man I divorced."

"Sadder but wiser."

"Something like that."

"I wonder if he'll be happy just having a cordial relationship."

I had wondered the same thing. But I had pushed off the question. I didn't want to think about it.

"Well, he's not given any indication to the contrary."

Amy scoffed at that remark. "Men are men. They don't feel validated until they achieve some kind of conquest."

"What an old-fashioned, sexist notion."

"Doesn't mean it's not true."

The idea that Greg was secretly plotting to "conquer" me made me slightly queasy. I had imagined us being friends again, occasional companions. And that's where my imagination ended. I chose to ignore Amy's admonition. She was adamant in her opinions, but she wasn't always right.

I slipped the tray of chicken wings into the oven. For convenience, we had decided on finger food served on paper plates. We tried our best to accommodate the dietary restrictions of the guests—tofu for Danielle and a gluten-free cake for Tasha's new friend, Julia. Seth gave us permission to serve wine, although he would not drink it himself.

As Amy spread the sauce on the tofu squares, she said, apropos of nothing, "Men need us more than we need them. That's just the truth."

My immediate thought was, *That's certainly not true of all men.* But I had to admit that, from my experience, it was true. Phil could have let go of Amy when she left him. Instead, he fought to get her back. After two wrenching divorces, Greg could have concluded that women were just too much trouble. Instead, he went into therapy to understand why his relationships didn't last. What was this abiding need men had to have a woman by their side? What did we offer men that they needed so desperately, even when they were tempted to cheat on us? Was it a sense of completeness? Was it a connection to an emotional life which they valued on some unconscious level but can't attain themselves?

There were no definitive answers to these questions. I only knew that I didn't need a man to feel complete. I needed friends. I needed my family. But I didn't need a man. I could still desire a man. I could appreciate the special energy released by the friction of gender opposites. But having a man in my life no longer felt like a necessity.

After the guests served themselves from the buffet table, I spotted Brandon's girlfriend, Ashley, sitting alone. Brandon was elsewhere, engaged in a conversation with Phil and Greg. As I walked by them, I heard Brandon say, "Why would you want to do something that a machine could do better? We don't wash our clothes by hand anymore. It's not any different with A.I."

Phil laughed and said, "Then what are people supposed to do when machines are better at everything?"

I didn't stay to hear Brandon's answer. I assumed his answer would be: Work on making better machines. That, after all, was what he was doing.

Being retired was not much different than being replaced by machines. One is replaced. Whether it's by younger people or by machines, it makes little difference. My own answer to Brandon's question was not an answer at all: It was more like a question. Our job was to figure out what it meant to be truly human. I was still working on that.

I sat down next to Ashley. She had come to town for a job interview and was staying with Brandon for a few days. Before the party, I had only exchanged a few words with her, so this was an opportunity to get to know her better.

"So ... how has your stay been? Are you enjoying the Bay Area?"

"It's been nice."

"How did your job interview go?"

"It went well. I think they're going to offer me a job."

"Are you excited about that?"

"Excited? Well, it's a new company, but I'll be doing essentially the same work."

"What about the idea of moving here? Are you excited about that?"

"Yeah, it's nice here. I like the ocean being near, and there are a lot of good places to hike."

I couldn't decide whether Ashley was wary of revealing too much to me or if these terse, factual statements were her normal way of conversing. I decided that, if I was going to get her to reveal anything, I would need to take a bolder approach.

"So, do you and Brandon have plans for when you move here?"

"We're still talking about it."

"Will you be living together?"

"Uh ... I think so."

I was beginning to understand Brandon's attraction to Ashley. They could carry on an efficient communication without the distraction of emotion.

"Come with me. I'd like you to meet my friend, Amy," I said. I pulled Amy away from her discussion with Tasha and Julia. I wanted to introduce Amy to Ashley, partly to extricate myself from our perfunctory conversation and partly to be able to compare notes with Amy after the party. Amy smoothly assumed her role as substitute interrogator.

I slipped in to take Amy's place next to Tasha and Julia.

"So what are you two discussing?"

"Whether anyone should bring kids into a dying world," Tasha replied.

"Oh, I see, light party talk."

Julia laughed. "I want kids. Whatever ... we'll figure it out."

"You mean, *they'll* have to figure it out," Tasha said.

"Well, I figure if we can genetically modify plants to survive droughts or whatever ... why can't we genetically modify our kids to thrive in, y'know, whatever conditions there are in the future?"

"That's ridiculous. Jules is ridiculously optimistic. But that's what I love about her. Always a smile, no matter what calamity awaits us."

With that, Tasha gave Julia a kiss on the cheek.

"We need optimism because we need hope," I said.

"Without hope, we would just sit around and mope, like the frog in the pot."

"The pot?" Julia asked.

"The boiling pot."

Tasha put her arm around Julia. "See? She's so optimistic she doesn't even know we're frogs in a pot."

I was happy to see Tasha happy. And it appeared that cheerful Julia was helping her to be happy. So far, so good.

I moved over to check on Danielle and Seth, who were sitting quietly together, eating.

"How are you two doing?" I asked.

"We're good," Danielle replied.

"Are you mingling? Have you met Brandon and Ashley?"

"Yeah, we introduced ourselves."

"Good. I imagine that was a short conversation. Brandon tends to be ... uh, economical when it comes to conversation."

Seth, the writer, seemed to appreciate my description of Brandon's conversational style.

"You don't need to worry about us. This is our usual M.O. We kind of sit in our little corner and observe. Then when we get home, we get into this whole detailed analysis of all the people we saw."

I smiled. "You're basically observers, like me."

After Danielle moved in with Seth, she and I had kept in touch. I knew things were going well, both with her business and with Seth.

I was growing to appreciate Seth more and more. He had a depth of character that was a pleasant surprise. It came naturally to him, but it was undoubtedly due in part to his struggle with alcoholism. To overcome an addiction requires a deep self-examination. It builds character, and most importantly, compassion.

I always took my hosting duties seriously. It was important to me that my guests were enjoying themselves. In the kitchen, I opened another bottle of wine and walked back into the living room with the intention of filling empty wine glasses. I stopped to take in the scene. There they all were: my children, Tasha and Brandon; their significant others, Ashley and Julia; my unofficially adopted daughter, Danielle, and her kind partner, Seth; my best friend, Amy, and her husband, Phil; and Greg, the father of my children and, perhaps, new friend.

These individuals, with all of their imperfections, were my people. I had collected them with kindness. And I had caused them to scatter away out of kindness. This was a paradox that seemed natural to me. According to astrophysicists, in the beginning, the universe had shrunk into a tiny ball and had then exploded. Yet, after this scattering, gravity held the planets and the stars in a variety of strong or weak orbits. Eventually, one would assume, gravity would pull the universe back together again, only to explode once more when the mass became too dense. So, gravity both pushed the universe apart and held it together. Was kindness, then, my gravity?

It had pulled these people together and pushed them apart. Yet some mysterious, gravity-like force still bound us together. You could call it love, but that would not begin to describe the many subtle, sometimes perverse, forms it could assume, nor the inexplicable needs, desires, or collisions that lie behind it.

40

Conception

I SAT AT MY desk, staring at a blank screen. My intention was to begin to write … something, anything. What was the source of this urge? On my trip to France, I had been struck by how art infused the culture of that country. The French didn't see art as a study of past masterpieces. It was an ongoing process. That's why they had no problem constructing a glass pyramid over the entrance to the Louvre. They saw culture as a living thing that must be manifested by each generation. There was something about that concept of art as a continuum that pulled at me. I wanted to be part of that process, art as continuous renewal.

Danielle was the one who reminded me that animals have emotions. Birds and primates use tools. Many animals use a form of language to communicate. I think only humans create art.

Of course, there is no ultimate definition of art. Whatever we decide to call art is art. But art has some undeniable elements. It is an attempt to communicate a thought, a feeling, or an experience in a way that brings new understanding to the viewer, and often brings new understanding to the creator as well. It's a language, then, but its goal is not transactional in the usual sense. By "transactional," I mean having a clear goal in mind.

I once took an acting class. Whenever a student became vague in their performance, the instructor would yell, "What is your intention?" In acting, everything you say or do has an intention. Do you want to hurt that person? Do you want them to love you? Do you want them to go away? Do you want them to feel sorry for you?

Every moment has an intention. Every word has an intention. So it is in life. We are acting with intention, hoping for an outcome. Art is the exception. We give away our art freely. Of course, you might sell your art. You have to, to survive. But the impetus to create the art has no transaction in mind other than to reach out to your fellow humans and touch them in some way.

This, I decided, was the source of my inexplicable urge to write. Or maybe that urge wasn't so inexplicable. I spent my adult life writing to achieve other people's intentions. I worked in marketing. The goal of marketing is to sell something. Selling is the epitome of transactional communication. Any time I tried to be creative, adding a little bit of edgy humor for instance, it would be immediately quashed by the guardians of corporate branding.

I had thus spent my adult life suppressing my creative spirit. Now I was free to communicate my own thoughts, feelings, and experiences. I could write to connect without a transactional goal.

Perhaps my loneliness led me to it. But I was alone more than I was lonely. That gave me freedom and an empty space in my life to fill. There is a strange, startling quote from Proust:

The artist who gives up an hour of work for an hour of conversation with a friend knows that he is sacrificing a reality for something that does not exist.

Honestly, I'm not sure exactly what he meant by that. But there is something about the sense of it that resonates with me. The "work" is the "reality." I wanted to devote myself to that work.

I have had people say to me, "Why do you want to write? Writing is so hard." There is no answer to that question other than to say that you are compelled to do it. It is who you are. I had no special talents in life. But I could write a clear sentence and order my thoughts in a coherent manner. I was never ambitious in the usual sense. I was not meant to start a company or be a leader.

My natural inclination was to observe. And I enjoyed ruminating. With that combination of qualities, what was left to me but to write? I had no illusions that I could write a work of genius. But I was inspired by Proust, who took memories and discovered new insights in them about the people in his life, about himself, about the nature of humanity. Here is another quote from Proust that, perhaps, illuminates his quest:

Our vanity, our passions, our spirit of imitation, our abstract intelligence, our habits have long been at work, and it is the task of art to undo this work of theirs, making us travel back in the direction from which we have come to the depths where what has really existed lies unknown within us.

Proust is dead. Art must be renewed to live. I am no Proust. But if by recounting events from my simple, uneventful life, I can connect with you, dear reader ... if that connection nurtures you in some way, then I will be content.

I began this memoir with a question prompted by the death of my husband: Who am I? I was no longer a wife. I was no longer a mother raising her children. My workplace skills were no longer in demand. That has not changed. I will turn sixty-four next month. You could say my "productive" life is over. But my life is not over. I will continue to be a mother and a friend. And I will start to be a writer, a real writer.

Acknowledgements

First, I would like to thank publishers, Michael Mirolla and Connie Guzzo-McParland, at Guernica Editions for ushering my novel into the world. I'm so grateful to Guernica and all the other independent publishers who are dedicated to discovering worthwhile, yet otherwise ignored, voices and sharing them with the reading public.

I want to thank editor Kaiya Cade Smith Blackburn for her close reading of the novel, for having the good sense to leave the text basically intact, and for generously expressing her appreciation of the novel (which is not required of an editor).

I appreciate the thoughtful notes provided by beta readers like Rosalyn Art.

I owe a debt of gratitude to my daughter, Yarrow, for graciously allowing me to model a few parts of the character, Tasha, after them.

And, finally, I want to thank my wife, Pouké, for being the inspiration for *The Physics of Relationships*. I ask Pouké to read all my novels. I know I can rely on her to give me her unvarnished critique of my writing. Happily, she had no harsh words for *The Physics of Relationships*. I consider that a crowning achievement.

About the Author

Born in Los Angeles, **Chas Halpern** spent most of his life in the San Francisco Bay Area. Chas studied political science and French at the University of California, Berkeley. On a year abroad program in Paris, he met his future wife, the artist Pouké. Some years after their marriage, they adopted a multiracial baby daughter who now identifies as queer. Chas attributes his ability to create fully-realized female characters to his life spent surrounded by women he loves and respects. After a short stint teaching high school French, Chas established himself as a commercial writer and director, specializing in storytelling and humor. Eventually, he turned his skill at storytelling to writing novels. He explains: *"I enjoyed my life as a scriptwriter and director, but I always felt creatively constrained by having to meet my corporate clients' demands and by having to limit myself to storytelling that could be told in ninety seconds or less."* Chas now lives in Berkeley, California with his wife. He recently finished his seventh novel, *A Handful of Clouds*, the story of a divorced couple re-examining their relationship. When not writing, Chas can be found singing baritone opera arias around the house or playing pickup basketball at the local park.

Printed by Imprimerie Gauvin
Gatineau, Québec